CRACKDOWN

The plain Chevy carrying West and Baranck swung into the lot. At that moment they could see the doors closing on the Cavalier. Then there was a whump, and the interior of the car filled with a dark reddish haze.

"Dye marker blew," Baranck snapped into the microphone. "We're right in behind them. We're going to engage." He threw the mike to the car seat and shoved the car door open even as West slammed the vehicle into Park. Baranck felt the ground slap his feet, and now he was looking over his aimed shotgun barrel at the dark figure emerging quickly and awkwardly from the right door of the getaway car. He could see metal flashing in one hand.

West didn't think he had the time to go for the shotgun along the front seat. He threw the door open with his left hand as his right drew his S&W .45 automatic from its Bianchi holster. The weight of the bulletproof vest suddenly felt comforting.

He knew they had them. They were disoriented, blinded by the gas and smoke from the booby-trapped money bag. He heard Baranck yell, "Police! Drop your weapons!"

And then, incredibly, it happened.

The figure on his side, still wearing the ski mask, pointed at the sound of his partner's voice and triggered the pistol. West saw the muzzle flash of the gun, brilliant orange even in the bright afternoon sun, and was aware of how strange it seemed that he hadn't heard the shot.

D. A. HODGMAN
STAKEOUT SQUAD
LINE OF FIRE

A GOLD EAGLE BOOK FROM
W🦅RLDWIDE.

TORONTO • NEW YORK • LONDON
AMSTERDAM • PARIS • SYDNEY • HAMBURG
STOCKHOLM • ATHENS • TOKYO • MILAN
MADRID • WARSAW • BUDAPEST • AUCKLAND

First edition February 1995

ISBN 0-373-63410-2

LINE OF FIRE

Printed in U.S.A.

To Mark Seiden,
trial lawyer extraordinaire and former Metro-Dade cop,
whose brilliant and tireless efforts have won acquittals
for more than one Miami policeman wrongly accused of
manslaughter after shooting in the line of duty.

1

It was mid-February, perhaps seventy-five degrees Fahrenheit in Miami, not a cloud in the sky. The sort of day the snowbirds, the tourists from the north, came down for.

The three men in the ArmorDade truck could not appreciate the ambience. The air-conditioning wasn't working, and the windows on an armored truck do not roll down.

Enrique Diaz reflected upon this as he dragged his hairy forearm across his forehead to wipe off the beading sweat. Hell, it wasn't as if he even had enough protection to make the sweat worthwhile. True, the windows were Lexan and molded firmly in place. But the cheap bastards who ran ArmorDade didn't bother to put armor plate in the trucks at all. The oversize vans had merely been decorated with heavy riveting on the outside to look as if the vehicles were bulletproof. A true armored truck cost into six figures. Armor-Dade fielded its vans after putting less than twenty grand into each truck. That was one reason they could afford to undercut the prices of Brink's and the other legitimate armored-car transport services. In the past couple of years, ArmorDade had taken over a heavy chunk of the business in Dade County, Florida.

In the back of the truck, Bobby Washington and Eddie Lemers weren't a bit more thrilled with ArmorDade's management. Sweltering in the heat of the closed box, they felt intimations of mortality as much as they felt the choking, humid warmth.

"They don't give a shit about us," Washington grumbled. He was a heavy man, black, with a gut that spilled over his worn Sam Browne gunbelt. "They gave a damn, they'd give us decent equipment. What do they think we're gonna do with these chicken-shit .38s if we get hit by somethin' like that Shotgun Gang? Ain't even sure the damn bullets'll go off. Can't remember the last time they even give us fresh ammo."

To make the point, he fingered a cartridge from one of the worn leather loops at the front of his belt. The brass casing of the shell showed the moldy green color of corrosion.

His partner, Lemers, ran a gnarled hand through the thinning blond hair of his forehead and flicked his fingers. Perspiration flew. "The .38s ain't their fault," he muttered bitterly. "Blame State of Florida for that one. It's in the statutes, Bobby. Security guards gotta carry .38 Specials. No automatics, no Magnums. Like, they figure we're too stupid to learn to use a real gun."

The black man snorted, looking glumly at the huge circles of dark sweat that were soaking outward from his armpits, stark against the light gray of his uniform shirt. "Even so, they could at least give us some decent ammo, give us some trainin'. Can't remember the last time I even shot this thing."

"You got *that* right," his partner answered. "Friggin' bosses pay off a guy at one of them commercial shootin' ranges, sign us off that we shot our annual qualification the state says we're supposed to have, even though we don't get close enough to the range to smell the gunpowder. Cheaper'n payin' our salary to go out an' shoot, I guess. Don't have to buy no ammo, neither. That's why we still got that old green shit.'' He shook his head. ''Nice to know you work for assholes, don't give a damn if you live or die, huh?''

Washington chuckled mirthlessly. ''Yeah, tell that to Sanderson. Remember when he come in, said, 'Look, we got you these here bulletproof vests, see how we're lookin' out for yer survival out there?' Shee-it. I wouldn't put that raggedy-ass piece a junk on my body, even if the damn Shotgun Gang was shootin' at me already.''

Lemers nodded agreement, glancing at the vests that lay unused in a rear corner of the van. Discolored and tattered, they looked like pieces of old cloth that a ragman would have discarded.

''I found out how the company got them, ya know,'' Lemers said. ''I was down the Top Cop Shop, an' they was talkin' about it. Seems the people that make that bulletproof shit, that Kevlar or whatever it is, done some tests an' found out the vests don't work so hot after like five years. So some department down by the Keys buys all new vests, trades in their old shit for like twenty bucks a vest. Understanding's supposed to be, the old ones get sent back to the factory an' get chopped up for scrap or somethin', 'cause they ain't supposed to get re-sold. Well, in goes Sanderson or some other honcho from ArmorDade, gives the guys at Top Cop Shop some line of bullshit that they're gonna use the old vests for backstops at some new tactical range they're gonna build to train us on, right? Gets 'em for the trade-in value, twenty bucks each, saves Top Cop Shop the freight cost for shippin' 'em back to the factory, right? Then they turn around, give us the junk vests, tell us how grateful we oughta be. God, I hate those stupid bastards.''

Washington's eyes flashed with the same anger. "Shee-it," he grumbled, "Goddamn Shotgun Gang wants every penny we got on board, they can be my guest. I'll even carry the bags to their cars for 'em. Sanderson an' them sure don't pay me enough to die for ArmorDade.''

They heard Diaz's voice through the vent that separated the cab from the money cubicle. "Heads up," he called. "We're passin' the Chart House. Bank's gonna be the next turn, right.''

JOHN BLAISDELL fingered the droopy *bandito* mustache that was glued to his upper lip and smiled into the vanity mirror in the front passenger seat of the Ford sedan. The face that looked back at him was, satisfyingly, totally unlike his own. The combed-forward stretch wig combined with the big mustache and his tanned face to make him look like a thirtyish Hispanic businessman trying to appear young enough to get through a midlife crisis. The mirrored aviator-style sunglasses completed the facial picture.

From the neck down he wore clothing that cried "Attention K mart shoppers!" The jeans were blue, generic, prewashed and new. As new as the running shoes. The dark polyester sport shirt, one size too large, hid the Armo-Tech bulletproof vest he wore underneath. The muted madras sport coat, two sizes two large, hid the sawed-off shotgun in its homemade leather sling under his right arm. Clipped securely inside his jeans in the middle of his back was a loaded .380 automatic pistol.

He glanced at the slim, tense Asian man beside him. With his own narrow mustache and goatee glued on with spirit gum, Chen looked like Fu Manchu with AIDS. A pastel shirt hid a vest identical to Blaisdell's but cut slightly smaller to fit his narrower chest. Chen wore a cream-colored polyester suit, also bought large to cover a stubby shotgun similar to Blaisdell's, and the cuffs of his slacks swelled into a boot cut that was almost a bell bottom, big enough to hide the snubnosed Taurus revolver that was strapped to his left ankle in a holster made of black nylon and Velcro.

The portable cellular phone that rested on the seat between them came to life. Blaisdell picked it up and answered with a curt "Yeah."

"Win, it's Moss," said the voice on the portable phone. "They're comin' up on the Chart House. I can see their silhouettes through the back window. Don't look like they've put nothin' on. We've dropped back about a hundred yards."

"Fine," answered Blaisdell. "It's a go." He pressed the End button, and the phone went dead. He set it back in its cradle. He looked at his driver and saw that Chen's dark eyes were bright with anticipation.

John Blaisdell let his hand drift under the cheap sport coat and touch the heavy hardness of the sawed-off Winchester Model 12 pump shotgun. The guns had supplied him with their code names, and they were almost a mnemonic device to help him keep the names in order. The Winchester made him "Win." Dewey Edmonds in the tailing car—tall, black, armed with a chopped-barrel Mossberg Model 500—was "Moss." Chen carried a trim and similarly cut down Remington LT-20, so his code name was "Rem."

They looked at each other now, and Blaisdell pulled his coat back over his shotgun as he said the words that told his wheelman that the armed robbery was going down.

"Let's do it, Rem!"

JOHN BLAISDELL KNEW the upscale minimall well. He'd spent four days at the Hilton casing it, under the guise of being just another attendee at a motivational seminar. His first thought had been, I say, Muffy, how very chic. It was laid out like a cul-de-sac, slanting slightly uphill. On the right was a newish steel-and-glass office building that housed primarily investment companies. On the left going in was the fancy Hilton hotel and miniature convention center. Next to it was the Merchants' Bank, the rest of the way up the hill were slick boutiques and jewelry stores.

The bank was like the mall itself: out of the way, elegantly understated and richer than hell.

It was 3:25 p.m. Blaisdell had monitored well the comings and goings of the armored trucks. All week the fat-cat conventioneers and their rich-bitch wives had been dropping money at the toney stores in the mall, and all week the stuck-up shopkeepers had been dropping the cash in the night slot at their very own

Merchants'. But it was Friday afternoon now, closing time, and just before three-thirty the ArmorDade truck would glide in to scoop the bags of cash and transport them to the impregnable inner vaults of the downtown headquarters of the Merchants' Bank. His sources had taught Blaisdell that suburban branches were thinly enough constructed to make bank managers worry about enterprising thieves who could burrow inside over the weekend with the acetylene torches that burglars called "burning bars" and be into the vault by early Saturday night.

Chen guided the nondescript vehicle smoothly into the parking lot off Bayshore Drive. The Ford, like the other cars they were using that afternoon, had been stolen from the employee parking lot at the Tasco plant out by Miami International Airport. Blaisdell's prison education had taught him that a car stolen from a workplace parking lot right after lunch wouldn't be discovered until the employees got off work, and the police wouldn't even have a report of it missing until "first shift's" end. Even then, the report would come in during shift change for the cops themselves. No police dispatcher would list it on the "hot sheet" until cops had been to the scene to take a confirming report of the auto theft. By that time, coupled with rush-hour traffic and everything else, the stolen car would have been used for its purpose and already ditched before there was even a chance of a police car spotting it and pulling them over.

Chen glided the Ford up into the cul-de-sac. Looking to his right, where the parking area sloped up, Blaisdell glanced past the finance building and caught a glimpse of the famous Chart House Seafood Restaurant down by the water. In his mind's eye, he could see the overview; he didn't have to glance into the mirror to know that the ArmorDade truck had to be coming in right behind them.

THE PARKING AREA sloped upward in front of the Merchants' Bank inside the minimall. Enrique Diaz pulled in the wrong way, with the left side of the ArmorDade van at the curb, and threw the transmission into Park as he crunched his foot down on the emergency brake. He pulled up on the manual button to unlock the door, then opened it. He was stifling. He had to get a breath of air. It wasn't as if he was getting out of the truck or anything.

Eddie Lemers was the first out of the back of the van. He hitched up his black nylon gunbelt and scanned around, his eyes narrowing in the sun, as Bobby Washington climbed out behind him. "Got ya covered," Eddie said importantly.

Washington just rolled his eyes for an instant. That was his partner. John Wayne, so long as it was his turn to stand outside by the truck while somebody else went in and did the lifting. Washington nodded to the two security guards in their brown uniforms in the doorway. As he walked toward them, he marveled for the hundredth time that they wore no guns. This was supposed to be the crime capital of the Western world, and the bank guards didn't carry guns. Shee-it, he thought.

Then he surrendered himself to the blessed coolness of the air-conditioning as they stepped inside the bank together, and the glass doors closed behind them with a soft and automatic hiss.

THERE WERE TWO BARS inside the Hilton. The lavish one was on the second floor. The one they called a "meeting bar" was off the lobby on the first floor, commanding a view of the wide entry doors and the parking lot outside.

A sad-looking woman sat alone at the bar. The only other customers were two men seated in wrought-iron chairs at a small cocktail table, their backs to the bar so they could face outside. They were each nursing an O'Doul's nonalcoholic beer.

The man on the left, code-named Fox, wore a cowboy hat over a thick head of black hair that was actually a Dynel wig. Even though the hat was woven straw, the combination of the hat, the nonbreathing fake hair under it and his own hair underneath made him sweat. He glanced through narrow-lidded eyes at his partner as the ArmorDade van passed in front of the door.

His partner met his eyes to show that he understood. The partner's name was Juan Diaz, no relation to the driver of the truck, and his code name was Steve. His bulletproof vest didn't show under his loose, dark blue *guayabera* shirt, nor did the Colt .45 automatic beneath its hem, tucked into his waistband on his right side. He glanced reflexively down at the attaché case between his feet that held a sawed-off double-barreled Stevens Model 311 12-gauge shotgun.

Fox knew the drill. They had about two minutes. He shifted, feeling the sweat bead on his skin. He was wearing two-thirds of a cheap three-piece suit. The jacket was folded over his brown leather legal portfolio. The polyester vest of the suit covered the Kevlar and Spectrashield blend bulletproof vest underneath. His necktie was loose at his throat. He and Steve looked like a semisuccessful lawyer and his client discussing their case.

He swigged down the last of his O'Doul's. Fox's real name had been John Swift Deer, but after the final arrest at the Indian reservation in British Columbia, he had changed his name legally to John Swift so as not to shame his family anymore. John Deer would have sounded too much like a tractor.

Steve stood. So did Fox. He draped his suitcoat over his left arm and hooked the Guardian Leather legal portfolio over his right shoulder by its long cordovan strap. In the hidden compartment between its panels was a double-barreled Fox 16-gauge shotgun, sawn off to a little more than a foot in overall length.

Steve reached into the shirt pocket of his *guayabera* and used just the nails of his thumb and forefinger to remove a ten-dollar bill and set it on the table. They'd checked before to make sure there were no prints on the bank note, and a few moments earlier when no one was watching they'd used napkins to wipe their prints off their beer glasses and bottles.

They both withdrew sunglasses from their pockets and put them on as they sauntered leisurely across the lobby and toward the open doors and the bank truck just up the sidewalk outside. The sunglasses would protect their eyes from the glare of the outside sun, as well as disguise their appearance.

THE ONE THING the witnesses would agree on later was that it had happened so fast.

They said the bank door opened, with the two un-armed guys in the brown uniforms pushing the big two-tiered roller table piled on both platforms with money bags, the big black guy in the gray guard uniform with the sweat stains walking ahead of them, his hand on the butt of his gun.

There was no screech of tires like on TV. The blue-gray minivan was just there suddenly, at the back of the ArmorDade truck, almost front bumper to rear bumper.

The driver's window of the minivan was down, and there was a white guy with a salt-and-pepper beard and sunglasses pointing an ugly black sawed-off shotgun with a wooden front grip at the black guard. From out of the right front door jumped a big black guy, also with a beard, pointing a similiar gun at the white truck guard who was standing at the back of the Armor-Dade van. The black robber had a Mossberg shotgun, one witness said later; he hunted ducks with a Mossberg 500 himself, and he recognized it. Of course, he stammered with a weak grin, *his* Mossberg wasn't sawed off and he didn't shoot people with it....

Not all the witnesses saw what was happening at the front of the van. Only the ones inside the bank watching through the windows. They saw the white-suited Oriental-looking man with the Fu Manchu face, his long hair in a pigtail, appear at the left front door of the armored truck just as the blue-gray van pulled up behind, on an angle where the driver couldn't see it. They saw him pull the half-open door all the way open, and he swung something up from under his coat and stuck it upward, into the driver's belly.

There was one more thing the witnesses agreed on, at least the ones who could see what was happening at the back of the van.

Nobody would have gotten hurt if the guard with the thinning blond hair hadn't gone for his gun....

"DON'T MOVE," Dewey Edmonds barked from behind his Mossberg and the cover of the front of the van. His gun was centered on the guard Lemers. He knew his partner, Pete "Savage" Morency had his own pump gun leveled at the other guard.

The guards froze, including the unarmed ones. One glanced furtively over his shoulder as if he thought he could make it back inside the bank. Savage caught the movement and barked, "Don't even fuckin' think about it! Roll that thing to the back of this van! *Now!*"

The two bank guards in the tan shirts obeyed eagerly. Savage stepped back to the rear of the truck, a couple of yards away. From that angle he could see all the guards except the one Rem was holding in the front seat of the ArmorDade van. Moss moved around the front of the caravan, his weapon belly high on the guard Lemers, gesturing him toward the back of the van. He could see the sweat making the guard's ill-fitting shirt cling to his skin. He could tell that the idiot still wasn't wearing a vest.

The trolley with the money bags was at the back of the robbers' van now. "Open it," Savage growled. "Lift the whole fuckin' trolley inside."

The guards tried, but they couldn't get it off the ground. "Can't lift it," one of the bank guards blurted. They were both older men.

Savage knew he didn't have time to fool around. "Then lift up the back end and tilt it in, goddamm it," he commanded.

The two old bank guards did as they were told. The bags on the top part of the trolley poured into the back of the van, but half the ones on the bottom spilled on the ground with a heavy thudding sound. "Oh, Jesus," moaned one of the guards, sure he was going to be shot for the mistake.

Savage and Moss turned instinctively toward the sound. Lemers realized their eyes were off him. He saw his chance.

His hand flashed toward his gun.

The deafening blast of the shotgun came from behind him.

His heart leaping, Lemers spun toward the sound as he tried to jerk the rusty Smith & Wesson .38 from his nylon holster. He saw two men in the doorway of the Hilton. One looked like an Indian with a cowboy hat. He was pointing the edge of a leather case at him.

Then orange flame bloomed from the leather case, and an impact like a sledgehammer caught Lemers in the chest, driving him backward. He could see sky above him. There was another terrible impact, this time in the side of his chest, but he couldn't hear any shots now, only a sound like rushing water. He was aware of his head hitting pavement. Then he was aware of nothing else at all.

Moss had heard the shot and pivoted back toward the guard, saw the man jerk as his chest exploded in red at the sound of the second shotgun blast, saw the guard falling with the gun still in his hand and instinctively fired a shot from his own Mossberg. They were so close that all the buckshot pellets hit Lemers together, making a black hole appear suddenly under his arm as he fell, jerking. Blood rushed out of the hole in the side to join the red mass from the wound on the front of his chest. Lemers's head made a hollow sound as it hit the pavement. The revolver clattered away from his hand. Moss knew the guard was dead.

He reflexively pumped the action of his shotgun and spun toward the other guard, the black guy. He saw the big man's hand going for the holster on his worn leather belt.

Then they were all shooting.

Moss was aware that Savage was firing, and he felt his own sawed-off buck in his hand and saw smoke coming from behind the doorway where the layoff men, Fox and Steve, had to be. Moss didn't know who hit whom. He just saw the big black guy jerk violently and crumple, the half-drawn revolver pivoting out of his holster and falling to the sidewalk with a metal clank. He saw one of the brown-clad bank guards go flying backward, his feet in the air, and land on the tarmac of the parking lot. The other bank guard was running away, straight away from Moss, down the paved incline toward Bayshore Drive below.

Moss raised his weapon, holding it tight to keep the recoil from smashing him in the face, and sighted down the stubby barrel. He pulled the trigger. He saw the man jerk and pitch forward on his face.

Behind him there were gunshots. He turned and saw Chen, on his back on the sidewalk, firing and pumping and firing again into the door of the ArmorDade van.

THE SLIGHT BREEZE had felt good to the guard Diaz as he cooled in the draft of his open door. He saw Washington and the two bank guys coming up to the rear of the ArmorDade van.

Suddenly his door seemed to swing out away from him. He thought the breeze had caught it, and as he reached he saw the face of the little man who looked like a Japanese prison guard in a war movie. He felt a hard thrust in his belly and looked down. The man was holding the muzzle of a stubby shotgun in Diaz's belly with his right hand, holding the door with his left.

"Freeze," the little man grated. "Don't touch your goddamn gun, an' you'll go home alive tonight."

Diaz was no fool. He froze on the command. There was movement and other commands back behind him. *Madre de Dios!* he thought silently. They'll take my job away for this. My door is supposed to be shut and locked when this happens. I'm supposed to put it in gear and floor it when this happens. I'm supposed to save the money when this happens....

Then there was gunfire behind them, unbelievably loud. Diaz winced at the sound and saw the little man turn toward the shots, as well, the shotgun turning with him.

Turning away. Away from Diaz. Here was the driver's chance.

He kicked out with his left leg as hard as he could, catching the gunman in the chest and knocking him back on the pavement. Diaz slammed his door shut and took a second to push down the lock button, secure behind his shield. He was reaching for the transmission lever when there was a banging and clanging sound, the blast of the shot and the clamor of the buckshot tearing through the sheet metal, and burning pain engulfed him.

The terrible blasting sound continued. Something hot and agonizing burrowed under his ribs and lanced through the middle of his chest, taking his breath away. There was an impact down below on his body, but he couldn't feel pain, couldn't feel anything below his chest, and he couldn't breathe.

Another blast. Glass from the side window showered over him. Crystals of broken glass knifed into his eyes. Now he couldn't see, either.

He tried to say, *"No mas, por favor,"* but there was no breath in his lungs to get the words out, and then something hard and round pressed under his ear and the world of Enrique Diaz disappeared into a shocking red explosion.

FOX HAD LET GO of the empty and useless shotgun, and now it hung inside its leather portfolio from the

shoulder strap, bluish tendrils of gunsmoke still wafting from the huge hole both barrels had blasted in the
front of the case. He pulled open a zipper on the outside of the portfolio and clawed out a Colt Trooper
.357 Magnum revolver. He swung its muzzle past the
men on the ground, but there was no movement.

Beside him Steve had his own double-barrel out.
The attaché case that had held it was sprawled open on
the ground, spare 12-gauge shells rolling out of it.

Then Win was there. He had come running down
the sidewalk yelling, "Plan B! Get the rest of it! Plan
B!"

As Blaisdell covered the windows of the bank and
Chen thumbed fresh shells into the belly of his sawed-
off shotgun, the other four set to work. Moss and
Savage let their guns swing back under their coats on
their leather slings as they hand-shoveled the money
bags into the back of the van. Steve held his sawed-off
double-barrel with one hand, its twin muzzles fan-
ning the parking lot against any threat that should
emerge from there, as his left hand scooped the open
attaché case from the sidewalk and tossed it into the
back of the getaway van. He knew there were no fin-
gerprints on the spilled live shells, but there might be
some on the case.

Then it was done. Fox and Steve dived into the back
of the van, pulling the doors shut behind them. Savage leaped behind the wheel, and Moss jumped into
the front seat. He didn't know if there were any live
shells left in his pump gun or not, and he didn't care.
He reached under the front seat for the .30-caliber
Enforcer semiautomatic carbine with its 30-shot ba-

nana clip, and cradled it down below the window as Savage spun the car into a U-turn down toward Bayshore Drive.

Behind them Win and Rem—Blaisdell and Chen—backed up on foot to their white Ford, still running a few yards away. Chen let his shotgun swing back under his cream-colored sport coat as he threw the Ford into gear. John Blaisdell, grinning under his long fake mustache, twisted in his seat so he could fan the muzzle of his sawed-off out the window and make bystanders and witnesses duck out of the way as his wheelman raced the two of them out of there, following the blue-gray minivan.

Inside the bank the clerks had pressed the panic alarm buttons as soon as they'd seen the men pull guns outside. Already sirens were audible in the distance.

It was 3:32 p.m. The robbery and murders had taken just seventy seconds.

IT WAS FIVE MINUTES to four when the intercom buzzed on the desk of City of Miami Chief of Police John Kearn. His manicured, chocolate brown hand pressed the button.

"Yes?"

"Line one, Chief. I think you'd better take it."

"Thanks." Kearn felt a shiver of anticipation. In the four months he'd sat behind this desk, he had learned that Charlene, his superefficient receptionist, only said "I think you'd better take it" when it was something heavy.

He picked up the handset and touched a button and said again, "Yes?"

"Litton, Chief." Kearn recognized the voice of his chief of detectives.

Hiding his impatience, Kearn grunted, "Whaddaya got, Bob?"

"Shotgun Gang again, Chief. Bad one. Merchants' Bank at the mall on Bayshore in Coconut Grove. Hit an ArmorDade truck outside a bank. I'm en route now. Looks like five shot, three dead. None of the wits caught any plates, from what the uniforms on scene tell me now. We put out a BOLO for a white Ford sedan and a blue-over-gray Plymouth or Dodge mini-van. It went down less than half an hour ago."

Kearn closed his eyes for a moment. He'd known it was coming. It was only a matter of when.

"Thanks, Bob," he said. "Keep me posted. Get what you need at the scene, leave your best people on top of it there and get back here to my office as soon as you can. Top level. It's going to be a long night."

After he hung up, he buzzed Charlene. "Have someone notify the deputy chief, the chief of patrol and the commanders of SWAT, training and public affairs. Chief of detectives is already notified. Six p.m., my office. And, Charlene? I'd like it if you could work late, be here with me on this. Also..."

Somehow he couldn't bring himself to say it.

Charlene prompted him. "Also..."

Chief of Police John Kearn took a deep breath and said, "The Stakeout Squad project. I need a copy on

my desk now. I'll need a copy for each of them, on the
conference table, no later than six.''

The phone was silent for a moment before she said
very softly, ''You're going to do it, aren't you?''

''Yes,'' said the chief of police in a voice suddenly
tired and dead, ''I'm going to do it.''

2

Billy Maloney looked at himself in his full-length bedroom mirror. He saw a fifteen-year-old boy who didn't yet have whiskers amid his freckles, a boy who weighed a hundred thirty pounds.

Then he raised the chrome-plated pistol. Everything changed. The figure in the mirror looked down the black hole at the muzzle of the automatic. Now the freckled kid was a man with a gun. A man of power. A man of respect.

A *man.*

"I dunno," said the voice behind him. "This ain't like boostin' cars, Billy. You're talkin' an awful big step here."

Billy turned, his green eyes blazing with anger. "Man, what a pussy you are," he snarled contemptuously. "Your name ain't Pat Michaelson, man, it's *Patti* Michaelson! You're too pussy to live, man! You got no balls at all!"

Patrick Michaelson, fourteen, clenched and unclenched his fists. "Look, man," he hissed, "I got balls big as yours. Bigger, even. I just don't feature bein' in reform school till I'm as old as the hills, okay?"

Billy stuck the pistol into the front of his waistband as a gesture of finality. "Aw, what's the matter, afraid your mommy can't bear to see you gone? Afraid your mommy's gonna run out of welfare and shit when she ain't got you to claim no more? Heck, she's got so many a' you little bastards, she can't keep count who's in the trailer an' who's out. I bet you're *all* a bunch a pussies!"

"Knock if off," Patrick said angrily. "My mom's had a tough time, okay? She works in that motel every day, cleaning up rich bastards' shit, she's got a right to some money from the state. An' it ain't welfare. An' she don't need her oldest kid goin' to damn reform school, awright?"

Billy changed his tone. "Aw, Pat, come on," he wheedled. "That's just the point. You do this with me, you'll have thousands, man! They said on TV last night, they got like a quarter million out a' that bank in Coconut Grove. Now, you figure we get half that, shit, a *tenth* a' that, out a' that little branch bank thing where my aunt works. Shit, man, twenty-five grand even, that's more than your mom *and* my mom make in two years! It's the best thing you can do for your mom!"

Patrick was lost for a moment in reverie. Just last night his mother was crying because their old beater Chevy had bit the big one and she couldn't afford even a secondhand car, because his scumbag father had put them both in bankruptcy right after he ran out on all of them, and how was she going to get to work at the motel? Pat pictured the look on her face when he'd slip the fistful of greenbacks into her hand and say,

"Nothin' to worry about anymore, Mom. I'm takin' care of us now...."

Pat looked at Billy. "Your aunt works at the bank, she's gonna recognize you and rat you out, for Christ's sake."

Billy shook his head violently. "No, no, man, you ain't listenin' to me! My aunt's got PMS like big-time, man. She was on the phone to my mom this mornin' for like half an hour, sayin' how she feels like shit an' can't go to work today. Why do you think I picked today, man?"

Pat played his last ace. "This is Florida, man. You do somethin' like this with a gun, it's three years' minimum mandatory, even if you're a juvenile. Everybody knows that!"

Billy grinned and reached under his mattress. "Yeah," he said, "if you use a real gun. But check this out." Billy withdrew what looked like a huge black pistol.

"Oh, shit, Bill! What is that, a .45 Magnum or something?"

Billy tossed the gun to his friend. Pat caught it, and the surprise was evident on his face. "It's plastic! But, damn, it looks real!"

"You bet it does," Billy crowed triumphantly. "Exact model, U.S. Army Beretta 9 mm. I'll fool a *cop,* man! Nobody's gonna argue with ya if ya stick that in their face, so long as they can't actually touch it, tell it's plastic instead a' metal."

The grin was spreading across Pat's face. "So it's like we got real guns for the stickup," Pat said, "but we get caught, it ain't like goin' to jail for real guns?"

"Hell, no," answered Billy. "See? It's perfect. I'll even let you use the good one. I'll take the little one that looks like a .22 or somethin'. Whaddaya say?"

Pat took a deep breath and nodded, a sly grin showing on his face at last. Billy grabbed him by both his shoulders. "Okay!" he cried. "I knew you wasn't no pussy. Go grab us a couple Cokes out a' the fridge. I gotta go to the john, then I'll be right with ya."

As soon as Pat left the room, Billy closed the door gently behind him and picked up the chrome-plated pistol. He reached under his pillow and withdrew the clip that held six .25-caliber cartridges. He inserted it into the butt of his mother's Raven pistol and pulled the slide back, then let it slam forward as it carried the first live cartridge into the firing chamber.

Billy smiled. It was okay for a kid to use a toy gun in a robbery, but a man would use a real one. Besides, it wasn't as if he was going to get caught or anything....

ORLANDO HERNANDEZ, the mayor of Miami, Florida, didn't like being outnumbered by people who intended to push him to the wall. He liked it less when the people who were doing it were his own appointed department heads. Where, then, did John Kearn get off marching into his conference room in his mayoral suite with his deputy chief, and his chiefs of both detective and patrol divisions, and the academy captain and the SWAT captain and the PR captain?

But he could paste on a smile and wait. Fighting his way up from the barrio to head of the city had been a game of patience. He had learned not to shoot unless the target had revealed itself, and he found that most targets revealed themselves quite well if he just gave them an opportunity. His voice was bland as he asked, "What's on your mind, Chief Kearn?"

The tall black man in the gray worsted suit stood to his full height at his end of the conference table and said, "Mr. Mayor, you and I talked long and hard before I took this job. We both understood up front that Miami had a unique problem with violent crime—some of it real, some of it perceived because of distortions in both the news and the entertainment media. I told you I'd do my damnedest to clean up the real part, and you told me you gave me a free hand to do it.

"We're working on the drug end—our narcs, Metro Dade's narcs and DEA. Hell, we're the biggest DEA substation in the world, as you know, and we're doing pretty well so far.

"You wanted me to work on corruption. I have. In the four months I've been here, you've seen cops fall to indictment because they were dirty, faster than anyone in Miami ever saw it before. No one can say I'm a good ol' boy who whitewashes bad Miami cops.

"You wanted me to work on violent street crime. That hasn't gone so well, Mr. Mayor, and one of the reasons is this damn Shotgun Gang. It looks like they started about a month before I got here, one hit every six weeks or so. It's a real clear M.O., and a real indistinct gang. The descriptions and the bank-camera pictures of the perps are always a little bit different. What's consistent is the shotguns—always the damn shotguns—and the small-unit urban guerrilla-warfare tactics.

"That and the sheer ruthlessness. The hit yesterday in Coconut Grove was the worst yet. They shot five people, all uniformed guards. They killed three of them. They would have killed all five, but the two who worked inside the bank were wearing vests. They had sense enough to play possum and stay down after the shotgun blasts knocked them on their backsides or on their faces. And these five, six, eight perps—whichever witness you want to believe—just stepped over the bodies, threw the money bags into their stolen van and left."

"Wait a minute," the mayor interjected. "Now, I understand from the reporters that there are some things going on that aren't the department's problem. I've heard the truck wasn't armored the way it was supposed to be, and that two of the dead guards and maybe all three would have been alive if the company had given them good bulletproof vests. I don't think that's something the press can blame on the city or the city's police department."

John Kearn held his anger. "I heard the same thing, Mr. Mayor," he said evenly. "I've already got some people in Dade County State Attorney's Office looking into that, with the licensing agency in Tallahassee. Maybe ArmorDade will be put out of business. But it won't bring three dead men back to life. It won't bring back to life the other people the Shotgun Gang has murdered in the last five months. And it won't put the Shotgun Gang and others like them off the streets. That *is* our job, Mr. Mayor."

The police chief took a deep breath before he continued. "Sir, I've made police work my life. You know that. You knew it when you appointed me. I told you two months ago that I was going to look into the concept of a stakeout squad. A couple of days later you called me back and said, no way, your people had looked into it and said it was too much of a liability from the public-image standpoint."

Kearn could barely keep the disgust out of his voice. "After you told me that," he continued, "I was curious as to how the people in my department could have, uh, missed that point. I assigned some of our top people to put their feelers out. I found that three of the major police departments in this country have been using stakeout squads, and that two of them still do.

"It started in Philadelphia, Mr. Mayor. Philly's Stakeout Squad is the most flexible. It handles SWAT team stuff, as well. I inherited an excellent SWAT team when I took over Miami PD, and I'm not going to change a thing with it, except perhaps to graft some of their talent over to the Stakeout Squad. Philly Stakeout has had to kill a share of bad guys, but every single shooting seems to have been proven justifiable.

"The next was New York City. They had a wave of particularly vicious and murderous armed robberies in the late 1960s, the way we're having right now. They took a look at the Stakeout Squad in Philadelphia and made their own. They made up the initial teams from firearms instructors out of the academy.

"NYPD put their stakeouts in place with two-man squads. Each of the two cops had two revolvers

apiece, a bulletproof vest and either a shotgun or a
.30-caliber automatic carbine.

"New York was a lot more rigid in its application
than Philly. They never had the stakeout cops pose as
clerks or patrol outside. They always put them right in
the store they expected to be hit, behind one-way glass,
in ambush positions.

"The squad only lasted four or five years. During
that time they killed thirty or forty armed robbers in
gunfights, wounded more than that and captured a
helluva lot more than that without a shot being fired.
Still, they were disbanded. The department didn't like
the public image of what they were doing.

"LAPD was the third. Los Angeles started their
stakeout team in the seventies. They call it SIS, the
Special Investigations Section. They did it different
from NYPD or Philadelphia. They work in large
teams—six, seven, even ten cops at a time—functioning as rovers in areas where there's reason to believe
there might be a hit about to go down.

"When the robbery takes place, they don't inter-
vene unless lives are threatened. Instead, they follow
the escape car, take it down someplace fairly safe and
make the arrest the way we or any other police department would do a felony car-stop. Obviously they
get a lot more armed resistance. Still, they've been
operating several times longer than NYPD ran *their*
Stakeout Squad, and they've had to kill fewer than
twenty-five perpetrators. They've come under a lot of
fire, but they've weathered the storm."

The mayor raised his hand, palm forward, in a gesture that said *stop*. "Wait a minute," said Mayor

Hernandez. "As you know, my people did check out this Stakeout Squad thing. They told me that the NYPD team was disbanded because of allegations of racist tendencies, and that the LAPD's SIS was under some pretty heavy fire for something similar. Let's address that before we go any further."

"Certainly, Mr. Mayor," the chief said evenly. "Every perpetrator killed by the NYPD Stakeout Squad was black. Every one of those shootings was intensively reviewed by NYPD Internal Affairs and ruled justifiable. Every one of those slain criminals died with a gun in his hand, sometimes a smoking gun. But the local media couldn't get past the fact that a police team that was overwhelmingly white—because the NYPD itself was at that time overwhelmingly white—had shot that many black men. There was a change of commissioners, and an incoming police commissioner disbanded the squad—some said—so he could preserve his own career against any charge of racism.

"SIS? They've killed black, white *and* Hispanic perpetrators. They've been sued again and again, but there's never been a criminal charge against any of the team's officers sustained by a grand jury. One particular lawyer seems to keep chasing ambulances and bringing suits, calling SIS a 'death squad' that 'hunts down and executes' people identified as being violent criminals. But the squad is still in business, and no one can argue that they've saved a lot of lives.

"But hear me out, Mr. Mayor. We're going to do our own thing here. I've sent one representative to LAPD to study SIS operations, one to Philly to get all the intelligence he could from Stakeout there, and one out to debrief some retired New York cops who worked Stakeout for NYPD. We'll take our own approach, using the best of what the others have done and leaving less than the best behind.

"Let's talk about public relations for a minute. That's what did in the NYPD squad and threatened the one in Los Angeles. NYPD Stakeout went down the tubes because it was mostly white guys killing all black guys. For God's sake, Mr. Mayor, I'm your chief of police and I'm a black man. When they attack a police department, they attack its head, the way they went for Chief Gates in L.A. after the Rodney King incident. I am a black police chief, and I am putting black and Hispanic *and* white cops on this Stakeout Squad, and I think I can stand the gaff.

"The other thing is, our primary target right now is the Shotgun Gang. They're not all black or all Hispanic. The witnesses have described a number of different suspects, but the one thing consistent is that every hit has involved all colors of the rainbow on the bad guys' side. The one last night shows black, white, Hispanic, Asian, even a Native American according to some of the descriptions. If and when the confrontations take place, it won't be a massacre of black men or brown men, if that's your concern."

The mayor sighed deeply and rocked back in his swivel chair. "And," he said sarcastically, "I suppose you'll want to equip every member of the team with a machine gun, and an assault rifle and an assault pistol?"

Kearn knew where his boss was coming from. Mayor Hernandez had seized on gun control as an issue in his winning campaign, and had ridden that horse ever since. He was on the board of the National Coalition to Ban Handguns and had appeared in a full-page ad in *Time* and *Newsweek* saying, "When you stamp out the killer guns, you'll stamp out the gun killers. I'm the mayor of Miami, and I know."

Kearn had always found that ironic. He knew that Hernandez had replaced Mayor Estevez, who had not only declined to support gun-control laws but had drawn a gun himself when armed criminals had invaded his home. Put to a vote, Kearn, who always kept a gun at home for his wife and another strapped to his hip, would have gone with Estevez instead of Hernandez. But then, if Hernandez hadn't won the election, Miami wouldn't have needed a new politically appointed police chief.

The chief paused before he answered, "You mean high-capacity plastic assault pistols like the Glock? Mr. Mayor, this city got used to its cops carrying Glocks as standard-issue service weapons in 1985 or so. You mean M-16 assault rifles or MP-5 submachine guns like the SWAT team has had for just about decades?

"You'll be happy to hear, sir, the answer is no to all the above. Every man you see here was part of my study committee. They said that a stakeout squad in Miami didn't need full-automatic weapons that would sweep a wide field with gunfire. That makes sense for a SWAT team kicking down the door of a fortified crack house. It doesn't for a few stakeout cops sitting inside a bank full of innocent citizens.

"They also said that a stakeout team didn't need 18-shot, medium-caliber pistols like our service Glocks. They said that a stakeout cop would be using his pistol half the time or more instead of a rifle or shotgun, because they would often have to pretend to be a bystander to get in close, and that meant a concealed gun. It also meant having to fire down a narrow channel bordered by innocent citizens. They wanted a pistol that shot a lot less than eighteen bullets, so none of the cops would be encouraged to hose the area, but a gun that shot big bullets so they could hit a bad guy once and pull him down without any more shots being fired at all. LAPD SIS seemed to have the handle on this. They recommended .45-caliber semiautomatic pistols, like theirs. My team agreed, and I agree with my team."

The mayor shook his head. "I hate to waste all your planning, Chief," he said, "but I thought I made it clear to you before—we're not going to have a stakeout squad in this city."

The chief grinned and shook his head back. "No, Mr. Mayor, what you told me then was that you didn't want a stakeout squad in your city. I don't blame you. I don't want one, either. Unfortunately I need one. I think this city needs one.

"Mr. Mayor, before you told me you didn't want a stakeout squad, you also told me that you appointed me to be the protector of the innocent in a threatened city, and the protector of blacks in a city where blacks were threatened. You *do* remember that, Mr. Mayor?

It's on video. It was televised citywide the day you swore me in. You also told me for the record that night that you were giving me carte blanche to deal with crime in Miami.

"I'm taking that carte blanche, Mr. Mayor. I'm calling in my white card, as it were. I ordered the selection and training of the Miami Police Stakeout Unit two months ago. They've been ready to go ever since."

The mayor shot to his feet. "Well, then, you can fucking *un*-train them, John! I won't have it! I forbid it!"

Chief of Police John Kearn stood up to face him. "You're too late, Orlando," he said softly.

"Wha— You mean—"

Chief Kearn allowed himself the luxury of a slow grin. "That's right, Mr. Mayor," he purred. "Our first stakeout teams went out on the street this morning."

BILLY AND PAT got off the bus at the Chopin Plaza at Biscayne Bay. They curled up their Windbreakers against the wind coming in off the Atlantic as they crossed the broad streets, heading toward the shopping district.

Pat said, "It doesn't show, does it?" Billy turned and looked at him speculatively. The plastic toy Beretta was completely hidden by the poplin jacket.

"No sweat, man," he said. "Just be cool. Do what I do, an' follow me."

Billy was supremely confident. He knew his mother's little Raven pistol was invisible under his own jacket. Soon he'd have money to buy a 9 mm and a shoulder holster like on TV. His heart was pounding. This was going to be great.

Confidently they walked up the hill toward the shopping center, toward the small branch bank where his aunt worked.

THINGS SEEMED TO BE going as normal at the Bay Branch of the Dade County National Bank. It was Monday, approaching noon. Two of the three teller's booths were closed, though one would have to be opened at noontime when customers started coming in on their lunch hour. For now there was one good-looking black man at the operating window, chatting cheerfully with the customers as he counted out the money for them. He seemed slow, as if he was new at it. In the next two booths were a red-haired woman and a balding, middle-aged man with Slavic features. They appeared to be counting cash and reconciling the money drawers.

To the right as you went in the doors, after facing the teller's booths, were two desks. Behind them sat men in suits, one white, one black. One appeared to be reading reports, while the other was riffling through a stack of papers. Neither seemed preoccupied with what he was doing. Both constantly glanced upward, surveying the patrons of the tiny bank.

Suddenly two compact male figures burst through the door. Each was wearing a poplin Windbreaker, and each had a nylon stocking pulled down over his head and face.

And each had a gun in his hand. The first one in wielded a small silver-colored pistol. The other held what the "bank employees" instantly recognized as a 16-shot Beretta Model 92 9 mm automatic. The one with the chrome gun screamed, "This is a stickup! Don't touch the alarms! Keep you hands up, *up!* Give my man here the money *now!*"

The voice sounded high-pitched. The "bank employees" weren't surprised. Their training had taught them that stress would make men's voices turn high-pitched.

The black man behind the open ticket counter said loud and clear, "Hey, no problem, fellas. Be cool . . . tell me what you want me to do. . . ."

The one with the silver gun threw a maroon gym bag onto the counter in front of the man who spoke, and cried, "Fill it! Everything! Now! None of that red dye or that shit, or I'll blow your face off! Then pass it down!"

The man in the booth seemed to focus intently and obediently on shoving fistfuls of cash into the gym bag.

The robber with the silver pistol seemed to be so excited that he was almost hopping up and down. He looked around jerkily, not seeming to see anything that was going on.

The one with the Beretta lowered the gun muzzle. He looked about aimlessly, as if he wasn't sure what was going on.

Behind the second office desk, the balding man with the Eastern European face knew exactly what was going down. The two armed robbers were obviously spaced out on drugs. They were the most dangerous kind. And now, at this moment, the muzzles of their guns were not pointed at any specific target.

It was the best chance. And he was the man to take it.

The balding guy didn't stand up. Instead, he dropped to both knees, the swivel chair scooting out from behind him, as he drew the SIG-Sauer P-220 pistol from under his pile of paperwork and leveled it at the two gunmen over the top of the desk he was using as cover.

"Police," he yelled. "Don't move! Drop it!"

Startled, the two gunmen turned toward him, the guns in their hands. Still, the balding man did not fire. "Drop 'em," he yelled again.

The first one, the one with the silver pistol, fired. The crack of the pistol shot split the air, and the bullet went five feet over the head of the man behind the desk, embedding itself in the ceiling.

The tiny bank erupted into gunfire.

The bald man fired, and so did the man at the desk next to him, whose hand was magically filled with a stainless-steel Smith & Wesson automatic. So did the "tellers" in each of the two empty booths.

The four shots resounded like one roll of thunder. The gunman with the silver pistol seemed to be thrown backward, his pistol cartwheeling in the air and clattering to the tile of the bank floor. He sprawled onto his back, his arms akimbo. He didn't move.

The other one, with the Beretta, fell straight down. His beige nylon mask was suddenly red with blood. He crumpled onto his back, his knees bent and his ankles crossed, the big black pistol still held loosely in his hand.

He didn't feel the running steps that closed on him or the gun muzzle that pressed against his bloody forehead, or the foot that stepped on his plastic pistol and shattered it with a crunching sound. Patrick Michaelson, age fourteen, had died the moment the hollowpoint .45-caliber bullet had entered his brain.

Six feet away, on the floor, Billy Maloney lay gasping like a fish. He couldn't see, and he couldn't breathe. There was only the awful burning, choking pain in his chest, where it felt as if three separate red-hot rods of steel had been run through. He was aware of someone pulling the mask off his face.

An anguished voice cried, "Oh, shit, it's a *kid!*"

A voice that seemed farther away said urgently, "Stakeout One! Shots fired this location, two suspects down, we need paramedics now!"

Then the sound disappeared into the blackness along with his vision, and Billy Maloney heard nothing else, forever.

3

They sat around the dining room table in John Blaisdell's condo in Coral Gables. Fox and Steve, Moss and Savage, and Rem, and Blaisdell's slender brunette woman, Kimberley. At the head of the table was John Blaisdell, handsome and tan without the wig and the fake mustache, his dark hair moussed back from his forehead in a glossy widow's peak.

He wore Calvin Klein jeans, the SIG P-230 .380 automatic comfortably in the hollow of his spine where the nylon holster held it clipped in place, covered with his salmon-colored Izod polo shirt. He felt as satisfyingly heavy and content as all their bellies felt from the grilled New York steaks they'd eaten, as heavy and content as they felt with the money in their wallets from the Cocoanut Grove heist.

In Blaisdell's hands was the Tuesday edition of the *Miami Crier*. He announced, "You gotta hear this, people. This is their new columnist, Oliver Teasdale, who does the column called 'Miami Justice.' You gotta hear the whole thing."

He began to read aloud:

"Miami Justice
"Death in a Downtown Bank
"by Oliver Teasdale

"Miami is supposed to be the city of violence. Newcomers know it. Visitors know it. Certainly native Miamians know it.

"Sometimes the violence comes from criminals. Sometimes it comes from the cops. Remember Alvarez in the video arcade, and the MacDuffee cops on that dark and lonely road, their big black flashlights rising and descending until Arthur MacDuffee's head was crushed protoplasm, and Officer Lozano panicking with his gun and leaving two black men dead in the streets of Overtown.

"And remember—oh, God, as if a Miamian could forget—remember the riots that followed the MacDuffee incident, and the Alvarez incident and the Lozano incident. The riots that tore our city apart, that marked us to the rest of the world as a city so bestial that the people themselves had to riot against the savage brutality of the police.

"The angry blood of the riots has reached tidal flow, then ebbed, then at last eddied into turbulent subterranean currents that bubbled beneath the surface, waiting to be released by yet the next outburst of police brutality. That outburst has come...but will it overflow the dam?

"Probably not. At least not yet. The only reason is, the latest victims of the Miami Police Wehrmacht happen to be white, and the angry white poor in this city are too subjugated by the police state to throw bottles or light fires to demonstrate their rage.

"But their rage is well earned. Patrick Michaelson was fourteen when he was shot to death yesterday by Miami's finest for the horrendous felony of holding a plastic toy gun in his hand. His friend William Maloney was fifteen. The tiny pistol in his hand was real, but he only fired it over the heads of the cops who startled him, who terrorized him with their show of force of drawn .45s.

"The cops didn't have little Billy's compassion. They didn't fire over *his* head. They fired into his chest, once and again and yet again, with .45-caliber horse pistols, guns so powerful that even the U.S. Army considers them obsolete for modern warfare.

"John Kearn, Miami's new chief of police, says the deadly stakeout squad he had in place in the downtown bank—the squad of people who had to fire bullet after bullet from Dirty Harry guns to shoot the young boys to death—was sent out on its hunter-killer mission in response to the Shotgun Gang.

"Perhaps Chief Kearn would have more credibility with that excuse for the death of innocent youths if he—or his new 'stakeout squad'—or indeed *any* of the thirteen hundred Miami police officers under his command had been at the Merchants' Bank in Coconut Grove last Friday. When half a dozen criminals with deadly assault shotguns murdered three armed guards and shot two more guards and left them for dead.

"With no stakeout squad, and no Miami cops of any kind, and certainly no Chief of Police John Kearn to stop them.

"If we're in trouble, should we call the City of Miami Police? Or should we call the Shotgun Gang for assistance?

"Before you answer that question, consider this: The Shotgun Gang has only shot uniformed guards, uniformed soldiers 'from the other side.'

"Unlike the Miami Police Department under Chief Kearn, the Shotgun Gang has not yet shot and killed any young boys with toy guns."

As he read the last line, John Blaisdell threw his head back and crowed, "Isn't it *great*? Isn't it just *primo*? The *Miami Crier* itself, flat just about comes out and says we're the good guys and the pigs are the bad guys!"

Dewey Edmonds said sheepishly, "Uh, Win, it ain't like the paper itself is endorsing us, you know? This one writer, does his column in the op-ed pages, opinion and editorial, you know? *He* happens to be the only one sayin' it, an' all he's really sayin' is, he be hatin' the cops worse than he be hatin' *us*."

John Blaisdell slammed the newspaper to the floor. "Jesus Christ, Moss," he blurted angrily. "I don't know if you're going to get your head out of your ass or anything, but this is the damn city newspaper, and what is says, *is*. Don't matter if it's a column or front page, so long as it ain't the letters to the editor or something, you know? What's happening here is, this newspaper guy—this guy that's hired by the paper to write for 'em, gets all his shit approved by the editors, you understand?—this guy just came out and said, there's like two teams.

"Team one, that's us. Team two, that's this Kearn character, this no-good nigger police chief, and his chicken-shit cops that can't shoot nobody but young kids!"

He paused. "Hey, Moss, you understand how I meant that, okay? I mean, 'nigger,' it's like a word you use to piss people off if it fits 'em, doesn't mean every black guy's a nigger, doesn't mean *I* have any problem with black guys, understand?"

Dewey "Moss" Edmonds shook his head gravely, knowing that John Blaisdell wouldn't recognize his fake smile even as he looked at it.

"Sure, Win," Edmonds said smoothly through his forced smile. "Sure, boss. I understand. You just pissed at that *po*-lice chief, tried to stake us out to kill us and blew it, is all."

John Blaisdell smiled eagerly. "That's it, Moss! That's it exactly! That son of a bitch has declared war on us. Moss, you been in this city for a while. You know how much the cops mess with black guys. You know I recruited you deliberately, man, give you a chance with this outfit."

Dewey Edmonds nodded with his best "Yassuh, Boss" smile. Sure, he knew that Blaisdell had deliberately brought him into the gang because he was black. He also knew there was at least one other black guy in the gang that he'd never been allowed to meet. He figured that John Blaisdell cared about him being black just about as much as the mayor had hired the new police chief because *he* was black. Either way, it was a white man—and to Dewey, a Cuban guy was as white as a WASP, compared to a black man—who needed a black guy for something. It was obvious why the Hispanic mayor needed a black guy as chief of police in a racially torn city. It hadn't yet become clear to him why John Blaisdell needed a black guy in the Shotgun Gang.

But Dewey would find out. It was only a matter of time.

After one more drink in the nervous silence, John Blaisdell announced, "We all gotta be tired, it's time for bed. Keep the money down and quiet, like I told you. Stay tuned. A few weeks, we'll go out there, make some more headlines."

There was subdued laughter, then they began to leave.

Chen was the last one out the door. He had been telling Blaisdell to be sure to get him another 20-gauge; those damn 12-gauge shotguns were too big and heavy. He probably would have nailed himself into the sidewalk firing one of the big shotguns from his back, upward into the van. He knew he had to lose the sweet LT-20 Remington—it was gone, and he didn't miss it—but he wanted to always still be there, doing his best, doing his best for his boss.

Blaisdell put a hand on Chen's shoulder and smiled a fake smile. "No problem, Rem," he said, then chuckled. "You mind changing your work name to Frank?"

Puzzled, Chen looked at him, and Blaisdell laughed. "Got you covered, bro," he said cheerily.

"You'll see what I mean next time. You're cool. Get out of here, go have some fun, just stay low, you know what I mean?"

Then Chen, the last, was gone. Blaisdell secured the condo door behind him, turning the locks and setting the alarm.

Then Kimberley was behind him, pressing her soft, warm breasts against his back. "Hey, lover, congratulations," she purred. "I love watching a big boss man keep his peasants in line."

Blaisdell couldn't keep the grin off his face. "Yeah, it is like that, ain't it? But, Kim, look . . . I gotta think over some stuff. How about you go get me a Scotch—the single-malt stuff, the private stock, back of the cabinet—and go keep the bed warm, okay? I gotta go out on the balcony, get some fresh air, think for a while."

JOHN BLAISDELL LEANED out over the stony railing of the sixth-floor balcony. He cupped a hand around his Colibri lighter until the tip of his Player's Navy Cut Medium cigarette glowed red. He inhaled the strong smoke deeply, then exhaled it to the balmy Coral Gables wind that took it away.

Life was good.

Blaisdell was thirty-three. He considered himself well along in his second life. His first had ended in prison.

Blaisdell's parents were what had been known as "poor white trash." His dad had been seventeen, his mom two years younger, when they drove north to Baltimore to seek work and wait for him to be born.

He had never known his grandparents in Alabama. If they didn't want to stand by his mom or dad, they sure as hell wouldn't stand by him, and if they wouldn't do him any good, what was the point of knowing them?

Not that he had that much use for his own kin. Blaisdell was an only child. His mother was eighteen-going-on-thirty-five when she got a chance to peel out of Baltimore with a guy she met at the Laundromat where she worked. That left him alone with his father, who was a burned-out cynic after that. Nobody wanted a high school dropout with a redneck Southern accent, and his dad bopped around between odd jobs and petty crime before being arrested for robbery and sentenced to the Maryland State Penitentiary when John Blaisdell was nine years old.

Blaisdell wound up as a CHINS, a Child In Need of Services, and was in his first foster home before he was ten. He lost count of how many foster homes he'd gone through before being sent to the YDC—the Youth Development Center, the reform school—at thirteen. Armed robbery had already become his occupation of choice.

Turned loose at eighteen because the system had no choice but to let him go, Blaisdell hitchhiked west and allowed himself to be dropped off in Indianapolis. He was five-foot nine, a hard hundred seventy pounds, and strong-arm robberies of old people got him by for awhile. He found his way easily enough into the undercurrent of the criminally disenfranchised, and bought a black market .38 in the back room of a sleazy bar in downtown Indianapolis.

The next step was a bank robbery. He was smart enough to do it a considerable distance away from his home turf. He was dumb enough not to plan it all the way through. He was running his stolen car out of Lafayette, Indiana, with the back seat full of money when the state police in their white cars with the blue V stripes blocked his way, all those big blond country cops pointing stainless-steel Magnums and ugly blue-barrel shotguns at him.

No one ever accused John Blaisdell of being stupid. He surrendered, knowing that those Hoosier cops would have killed him for the sheer joy of having a war story if he hadn't raised his hands. They bagged him solid, with his .38 and his money bags, and their Hoosier judge sentenced him to the Pendleton State Reformatory for ten solid years because he didn't have a lawyer worthy of the name.

In prison they showed him the rehabilitation films, the guys on-screen talking earnestly about how glad they were that they'd been arrested, because it had changed their life. Being arrested and sent to the joint, they said, had saved them from a certain plunge to doom and damnation. Now they were fine, upstanding family men with good jobs, they said, and being arrested and sent to prison was the best thing that had ever happened to them.

At first John Blaisdell laughed a hollow and mocking laugh. Later, much later, he realized they had been right.

He was indeed grateful for being sent to prison.

Where else would he have gotten an education like the one he now had?

Prison, he knew now, was the advanced graduate school of crime. Even Pendleton, a relatively low-security reformatory.

It was there he met Luther, a member of the original Shotgun Gang out of Baltimore, where he'd once lived. Luther taught him all about why you used a shotgun in armed robberies.

Nothing scared people like a shotgun, Luther told him sagely. Especially the slide-action kind. You pump that thing, *chunk-chunk,* and everybody's blood ran cold within earshot. You didn't need to be into guns to recognize the noise. Folks heard it often enough on TV when you pumped a shotgun. They knew what it meant. They knew what was coming.

Besides, Luther taught him, a shotgun had many other advantages for crime. A rifle or a pistol or just about any other gun had rifling in the barrel and only shot out one bullet, and if the pigs got that bullet, they had these microscopes that could compare the bullet out of the body to the rifling grooves in the gun they caught you with, and that was that. Prima facie. Guilty as charged, ass in prison, do not pass Go and do not even think about collecting no two hundred dollars.

Not so with a shotgun, though. A shotgun was the most versatile weapon in the world. Most shotgun shells fired shot, not a solid projectile like a bullet. You could have bird shot, hundreds and hundreds of little tiny lead balls. They'd kill somebody in real close, but from any distance they didn't have much power to them. That's why folks used them for shooting birds. Didn't tear up so much meat you couldn't eat the bird afterward.

Buckshot was the way to go, Luther told John. Like ball bearings. Luther told John to cut open a double-aught buckshot shell, like what the cops used to shoot people like Luther and John with. It would have nine lead balls in it, each about a third of an inch in diameter, and going about fourteen hundred feet per second velocity. It was like getting shot nine times with a .38 or .357 all at once Luther explained. People didn't give you a whole lot of shit, no sir, after you nailed them with one blast of double-aught.

And the shot pellets couldn't be identified. Not only were there a whole bunch of them inside the bore of the gun at once when you fired it, Luther explained, but the bore of the shotgun itself, the inside of the barrel, was smooth instead of rifled. That's why the white crackers inside prison—nothing personal, you understand, John—used "smoothbore" when they meant to say "shotgun."

But, Luther warned, there were ways the pigs could trace even shotguns. If you left the fired, empty shells on the ground, you best be getting rid of that shotgun quick, because the brass at the end of the shell would pick up the tool marks from the breechface of the shotgun and the firing pin when the shot went off, and they could match those to your gun, even if there was no bullet to match it with. You either picked up your shucked-out empty shells and got rid of them later or you used a gun like a double-barrel that didn't kick its shells out at all for the cops to find, or you just got rid of the whole damn shotgun after you'd fired it and found another one and started over.

After all, Luther explained, it wasn't that hard. He'd heard on TV there are two hundred million guns in America. You needed another one, it couldn't be too damn hard to find.

Standing on the balcony, John Blaisdell smiled at the memories. His cigarette was down to a stub. He lit a new Player's off the glowing coal of the butt, then flicked the old one away. He saw its pink tip arc and disappear into the wind.

He had learned well from Luther. Over a year ago he and Chen and Dewey had gone into a pawnshop on the Tamiami Trail, drifted in a couple minutes apart as if they weren't together, just before closing time. The cracker behind the counter had been leery about Dewey, didn't trust blacks in his store apparently, and when he wasn't watching Dewey he kept shifting his eyes to Chen.

That's why he hadn't seen Blaisdell's white face at all until it was behind him and Blaisdell was holding a double-edged dagger to his throat. It only took seconds for Chen and Dewey to lock the front door and kill the lights, and help him drag the cracker pawnbroker into the back room.

They relieved him of the cash and jewelry, of course. Luther had taught him to take the records of the gun sales and purchases and pawns with him, too. That way, if they ever found Blaisdell or any of his friends with the stolen guns, no one could ever prove that they'd been taken in that job, because there'd be no list of makes and models and serial numbers of the guns for the cops to work from. Blaisdell had very carefully burned all the record books and receipt books later in the Everglades.

And the guns they'd gotten, oh God, the guns! About twenty magazine-fed shotguns, mostly pumps but a few automatics, and another half-dozen double-barrels. Blaisdell hadn't bothered with the single-barrel shotguns. He didn't see much point in a gun that could only fire once. There were nearly two dozen pistols and revolvers—Blaisdell took them all—and a bunch of rifles. He ignored the .22s. He took the three high-powered bolt-action hunting rifles with telescopic sights, and the two lever-action .30/30s, and the stockless Enforcer that looked like an already sawed-off .30 carbine.

After they'd loaded the stolen Chevy van with everything they'd taken, Blaisdell looked down at the hate-filled face of the white guy who owned the dumpy pawnshop.

"I know your face. I know your nigger friend's face and your gook friend's, face," the man had hissed. "You won't get away with this!"

That expression of angry macho pride had been expensive. Another lesson. Another of his mentors at Pendleton, Bobby Joe, had warned, "Johnny, remember. You'll hear guys say they're gonna get ya, they're gonna kill ya, they're gonna mess you up. Some folks'll tell ya, 'the man says he's gonna do it, don't worry, that means he ain't gonna do it.' Johnny, you hear me now, anybody talks that shit to you, yer listenin' to some asshole who ain't been got *yet,* 'cause every asshole *I* done said it to, I done *did* it to! Man

tells ya he's gonna do somethin' to ya, believe him—
he's gonna! That means you gotta do him first, soon
as you can after he says it.''

Blaisdell heeded that advice, too. When he nodded
his head, Dewey held the cracker down while Chen
sliced his throat out with a big-ass hunting knife he
took out of the cracker's own pawnshop showcase.

Blaisdell had learned those lessons well. He had
learned more. An old man named Pearlie, in for life
as a multiple offender for grand theft auto, had taught
him the subtleties of stealing cars. He'd even taught
him the multiple options for ditching them if you
weren't going to sell them to a chop shop. And if you
had used the car for anything else, you didn't sell it to
a chop shop; those places were constantly being raided
by cops, and the guys who cut up the stolen cars for
parts would give up the guys who brought them their
automotive meat as soon as look at them. If that car
could tie you to a robbery or a murder, whoo-eee, said
Pearlie, talk about penny-wise and pound-foolish.

He learned from most every old head inside the
walls, ''Don't shit where you eat.'' Ever the good student, Blaisdell bought the condo in Coral Gables and
never did one job in the Gables. Coral Gables was a
community separate and apart from Miami, though
on its very edge. It even had its own police department. One thing Blaisdell learned in prison was that all
cops were glory seekers, and if you lived in Town A
and did your jobs in Town B, the cops in Town B
would never touch bases with the ones in Town A unless things got so heavy their careers absolutely de-
pended on it.

But Ian, who used to be a mercenary in Rhodesia and South Africa, taught him the most useful lesson of all. Ian told him of how he'd worked security at the diamond mines in Kimberley, the "badlands" of central South Africa where the stones in the ground were the only thing worth living there for.

Ian told him how the mining bosses had to keep separate the three-man teams that went down into each hole. There would be a Zulu and a Xhosa and a Bantu—were those the exact names? Blaisdell couldn't remember precisely, but it didn't matter—one of each because of the history of tribal wars and tribal loyalty. Two Zulus and a Bantu in the same hole? Before you knew it, said Ian, the two Zulus would band together and screw the Bantu, and next thing you knew, they'd figure they were strong enough to screw the white bosses. That's why they'd had to hire strong-arm mercs like Ian to begin with, he explained.

Blaisdell saw the wisdom in that. Almost everyone he came to know in prison had been ratted out, ratted out when two guys who were alike had gotten together and considered *him* the odd man out. Two black guys screwing the Hispanic guy who put the deal together, or a couple of white cops getting with the white guy they arrested and screwing the white criminal's black connection.

Blaisdell knew instantly that he was going to put together a rainbow coalition as soon as he began assembling his own gang. He smiled at the thought. The stupid columnist in the newspaper had hit on one thing right. And it had kept Blaisdell out of prison so far. Black and white, Asian and Native American, Hispanic, you name it—just don't let two of a kind work the same job together.

John Blaisdell kept this rule inviolable. Of the dozen or so men he had on tap to work with the Shotgun Gang, no two of a kind ever worked together, at least side by side, on the same job. Never more than half the gang did a single hit.

Hell, as far as he knew, he was the only one who knew their real names. He'd taken their names, the code names they called each other not only on the job but even here at dinner, from the shotguns he had issued them. Mossberg became "Moss." Remington, "Rem." Stevens, "Steve." "Fox" and "Savage" took their names directly from their issued, stolen, sawed-off shotguns without bothering with a contraction. So did "Noble" and "Ruger" from the other team.

Chen Ho Lee would get his code name changed. He had to. The yellow spent casings from his Remington 20-gauge had been left all over the scene. His new name would be "Frankie," for the Franchi automatic shotgun that was still in the storage building from the hit on the pawnshop. Chen's little Remington pump gun was already gone, cut up with the acetylene torch and thrown into the bay, along with Dewey's Mossberg and Tony Alonzo's Savage Model 77, which had left their own distinctively marked green Remington 12-gauge shell casings at the Coconut Grove murder scene.

Blaisdell wouldn't even have to change their names. He had another Mossberg in inventory. Hell, he'd stolen four of them at the pawnbroker's. "Savage" would get a better gun than before, a Savage Model

775 automatic shotgun. Its aluminum-alloy frame was even engraved with ducks and pheasants and stuff. It would be a step up.

Blaisdell had carefully picked one of the three Winchesters for himself. He simply liked the code name "Win." Not only did it sound like a champion's name, but it sounded like the kind of nickname you'd have if you could afford to live in Coral Gables without ripping people off.

When he had given one other Winchester, a model 1200 pump gun, to another guy on the second-string team, he had code-named the man "Chester." The guys called him "Chet." That was fine with Blaisdell, so long as there was only one "Win."

His second cigarette was done now, and he flipped it away. His hard-earned education had served him well in the past few days. Pearlie had been right about dropping stolen cars, as right as he'd been about stealing them. They'd only had to go five blocks to find the seedy adult bookstore with the big fence and the sign Park In The Back. They could hear all the sirens converging on the minimall, already swamped now with ambulances and cop cars. But they'd taken their time off-loading the guns and the money bags into the next set of stolen cars, the Chevy Suburban and the big Honda sedan, which had been stolen from the same Tasco parking lot.

Pearlie had been right. The kind of people who went into porno bookstores were the kind of people that "didn't want to call the cops." Anybody who wasn't too busy at the glory holes between the stalls of the peep shows and might have seen them, wasn't up for telling the cops what he was doing there when he saw the guys dumping stuff from one set of cars to the other. According to the papers, they hadn't even found the white Ford or the blue-gray Plymouth Caravan yet. Maybe the porno bookstore owners had driven them into the Miami River themselves to take the heat off *them*. John didn't care anymore.

John Blaisdell took a deep breath. The jasmine was on the wind, Kimberley was waiting nude in his bed, and he had become so strong the Miami police chief himself had singled him out as an enemy and screwed up along the way.

Life was good.

Before he closed the door to the balcony and turned out the lights, Blaisdell decided it would be good to give Kimberley a good slapping around tonight before banging her. That was another thing he'd learned in prison. "The rougher you treat 'em, the harder they cry when you leave."

4

Miami Police Lieutenant Ken Bartlett, tall and slim
and black, stopped at the check-in booth and took a
pair of earmuffs and a set of shatterproof plastic goggles and a key to a locker. He took a few steps, turned
the locker key and threw his peaked blue uniform cap
inside. He fitted the headset and the goggles on, then
looked down sadly at the new pistol on his belt.

Although it looked like the Glock 17 he had been
issued in 1986, it wasn't the same familiar, light-
weight weapon. It looked like his gun with a gland
condition, the same shape and dark gray color, but
distinctly bigger.

This was the Glock 21. Instead of eighteen 9 mm
cartridges, it carried fourteen of .45 caliber. That had
been the chief's edict, the decision of his damn fact-
finding team on the stakeout proposal. Stakeout cops
would be the only ones in the city to carry .45s instead of 9 mm weapons.

And Stakeout, for Bartlett, was inescapable. The
sixteen-year veteran cop knew what was coming. He
had put in for consideration to command a special
unit, and what did he get but the Stakeout Squad. The
instant bastard child of the Miami Police Depart-

ment, which had felt its feet against the fire since its first day on the job, when it had killed two young kids.

Sure, the *Crier* was full of distortions. Bartlett knew that. The reports were as clear as the undeniable videotape that had been recorded on the bank's security cameras when the shooting had gone down. The first robber had turned with what had to be a Beretta. You could hear the cops yelling again and again to drop it. Then the second robber cranked a round from his Raven .25, and there was a one-second volley of gunfire. Four officers fired one round apiece. Three of them shot the kid who'd fired the gun, who died a few seconds later.

The other officer, old Pavlicek, a twenty-year man, fired the one shot that struck the kid with the Beretta in the head, killing him instantly.

Ken Bartlett, newly appointed field commander of the Stakeout Squad, had been the first to respond. Pavlicek was sitting at the desk where he'd been before, pretending to be a bank officer. His head was down on the desk, folded in his arms. His pistol, a SIG .45, was back in the holster in his waistband.

When Bartlett came up to him, Pavlicek sat up, and the lieutenant would never forget the look of unspeakable horror on the older man's face.

"My gun's on my hip," he mumbled to Bartlett. "Take it, Lieutenant. Take it away. He was a kid, Lieutenant. I shot him. I shot him in the face. His gun was a toy. A toy! Take it away, Lieutenant...."

Ken Bartlett gently removed the gun from the older man's holster. He couldn't help noticing that Pavlicek had reflexively decocked the weapon before holstering it. Training would always tell. Bartlett held the gun numbly in his right hand, his left arm around the convulsing shoulders of the sobbing Pavlicek, until other cops did in fact come and take him away, too....

Snap yourself out of it, Bartlett told himself. Too late to feel sorry for yourself now. Damn Oreo police chief figures he's gotta give a body count of bad guys. Needed a black field commander 'cause he knew how this community would handle it when his damn ambush squad started putting notches on their guns. The guy in the paper was right. If those two dead kids had been black, this city'd still be in flames right now. Figured a black commander might put some brakes on his death squad, let him have his cake and eat it, too, let him be good cop and bad cop at the same time.

And I'm stuck with it now.

He took a breath. One of the three teams he commanded was inside the range now, doing firearms training. He had been here before with the other teams; that was where he had qualified with the damn .45 Glock they made him carry, the gun that felt too big for his hand, though he had to admit it shot very well for him. He would choke back his revulsion at his assignment. He would go in there and supervise.

OFFICER BOB CARMODY felt as if he'd died and gone to heaven. The department's training records showed him to be consistently the top pistol shot on the City of Miami Police Department. Marksmanship was a natural talent for the tall, blond police officer. He'd picked it up as a Boy Scout, where his first merit badge had been won in riflery. As he'd grown, working with weights to sculpt the muscular body he had now, weapons other than the Boy Scout .22 rifle proved as natural to him.

He had joined the Miami Police Department at twenty-two, after his graduation from Florida State University at Tallahassee with a bachelor's degree in criminal justice. From the beginning only two cops on the force had ever been able to outshoot him. One was Sergeant Christopher James, the legendary instructor who had convinced the department to dump their old-fashioned .38 six-shooters and adopt the high-tech Glock 9 mm automatic as a standard service weapon. The other was Sergeant Angel Arcaya, who had won national championships shooting the duty Glock against target pistols. Eventually Arcaya had earned his twenty-years' retirement and taken a position as senior firearms instructor at the Federal Law Enforcement Training Center in Brunswick, Georgia.

It was logical to put the top shot on the force into the Firearms Training Unit. Carmody had known his job well. On his first vacation as a Miami cop after filling out his probationary period, he spent his own time and his own money to travel to Orlando with Sergeant James, then head of the Firearms Training Unit, to attend the annual conference of the International Association of Law Enforcement Firearms Instructors—IALEFI. He listened transfixed as James told his peers the subtleties of transitioning a police department more than a thousand strong from the traditional service revolver to a modern semiautomatic service pistol. James introduced him to the other heavy hitters of IALEFI. Bob Carmody had found his milieu.

Less than a year later, Carmody got the midnight call from a friend in the firearms unit: James had been killed in a train wreck on his way to New York to meet his wife and kids, who had been waiting for him there for a holiday that he had had to start late because of work commitments. The news was devastating. It was the first, last and only time Bob Carmody ever called in sick because he was drunk. His grieving binge lasted for two days. James had been thirty-six years old, the father of two young children and the mentor of un-counted young officers like Carmody.

And now Carmody was one of the staff instructors of the firearms unit. The word had come to him qui-etly that the new chief was organizing a new unit that would be somehow interdicting the growing number of armed robberies and robbery-homicides that were plaguing the city. The new unit would have three teams. The chief would very much like it if three fire-arms instructors could be found, one to work with each team in the new elite squad. Of course, this would not be merely a marksmanship coach position; the in-structor would be a member of the team, working with the team in the field, doing what might euphemisti-cally be called "high-risk duty."

Bob Carmody was not yet thirty. He had no wife, no kids. He saw adventure. He volunteered.

And now Bob Carmody stood on the firing range behind his team of Stakeout Squad officers as Ken Bartlett, the unit commander, walked in wearing his crisp blue uniform, set off by the golden circles at the shoulders with the palm trees embroidered on them, the mark of the Miami Police Department.

"Afternoon, Lieutenant," Carmody said, extending his hand. He was surprised at the strength of the lean black man's handshake.

"Afternoon, Carmody," Ken Bartlett answered. "I'm here to see how your team—Sergeant Cohen's team, actually—is shaping up."

"Sergeant Cohen's on the far end, qualifying," Carmody answered. "He put me in charge of the training portion. I assume the designated team firearms instructor is still in charge of that?"

Bartlett smiled wryly. "He is, Carmody. You are. Take me down the line. Show me what your people have got."

THE FIRST COP they came to was Melinda Hoffritz, tan and fit and tawny blond. The weapon in her hand was a Colt Gold Cup .45 target automatic. She stood in the first booth.

Behind her the range master triggered a strobe light. It was her signal to fire. Carmody had never liked the idea of training people to shoot on a whistle or some other audible signal. It was too much like training a dog to attack. In real life people used guns to react to what they saw happening in front of them, not what they heard. Melinda Hoffritz had been told that when the light flashed, it was a gunshot, and it meant that one of the six opponents in front of her, all down behind cover, had opened the gunfight.

When the strobe flashed, the blond woman reacted instantly. Her body snapped forward, her shoulders ahead of her hips and her body weight on her flexed, muscular forward leg. The pistol had come to the center of her body, her arms locked straight out behind it.

She began firing. Fifteen yards away the eight-inch disk on the right jerked and fell as the heavy bullet struck it. Then the next one in, and the next. Six shots, six plates down. Bartlett looked at the brown box that housed the Pro-Timer electronic timing device. Hoffritz had shot down six head-size plates in six seconds from fifteen yards. Bartlett was aware of a metallic clatter. He glanced back to the tawny blonde and saw that she had dumped the nearly empty magazine from her Colt automatic and instantly shoved in a fresh 7-round magazine, bringing her fully loaded weapon back on target.

Carmody said, "Hoffritz is one of the few female officers on the Stakeout Squad. She's—"

Bartlett raised a hand to cut him off in midsentence. "I know about Hoffritz," he said cryptically. "Let's go down the line."

As they walked, Ken Bartlett thought to himself, "Yes, oh yes, I know Melinda Hoffritz. Rolled on a code-three pursuit assisting Metro Dade cops on a chase they brought into the city from the county line. She was the second car to come to a stop behind the armed-robbers' car when they crashed. She stood on her brakes and came to a stop, as the Metro chase car did. The Dade County cop jumped out of his car first, and the shots from the robbers' car blasted him back on his ass. One in the shoulder from a .38, one in the chest from a .357 Magnum—the vest saved his life. Then the bad guys opened up on Melinda's cruiser.

I saw the pictures of her patrol car, Bartlett thought silently. The bullet holes in the windshield, the bullets going on track for her head. But they missed because she had already done what she was trained to do— popped open her driver's door and taken cover behind the door post, and then she fired two shots from her issue Glock. One that struck the guy with the .357 through the right eye. One that struck the one firing the .38 at her between the eyes. Both dead on scene in the front seat of the getaway car, shoulder to shoulder, their heads touching like dead Siamese twins.

As they walked, Bartlett said aloud to Bob Carmody, "I remember Officer Hoffritz very well. I remember why I approved her for the Stakeout Squad."

CARMODY AND BARTLETT came to the fourth booth. Frank Cross stood there, his hands relaxed at his sides, his Smith & Wesson Model 4506 automatic hidden by the shapeless drape of his greenish Banana Republic cotton vest, the kind photographers wore. He faced three silhouette targets.

A light beam from the range control tower flashed on the center target. Cross—tall, broad shouldered, appearing to be strangely uncomfortable with his own size and strength—reacted instantly. His hand flashed, there was a silvery flicker as his S&W came on target, his thumb simultaneously flicking the slide-mounted safety catch into the Fire position. Then twin orange flashes bloomed at the mouth of his gun.

Bartlett and Carmody looked downrange to where the target stood, fifteen feet from Cross's gun. They watched as the tall young officer flicked his thumb, decocking the pistol and returning it to the off-safe and ready to fire position.

Two .45-caliber holes had appeared in the center of the designated target's chest.

"Cross is very good at this," Carmody told his boss. "Good reflexes. I can't ever catch him off guard. He spends a lot of his own time on the firing range. Dedicated. Won the Combat Cross last year, in that shooting where—"

Ken Bartlett cut him off. "I know where he won his damn Combat Cross," the lieutenant snapped abruptly.

I know it well, he thought to himself, and God help me, he's still on my squad. He's six-three, two hundred twenty, and he's still a little weasel as far as I'm concerned. Combat Cross for a gunfight? My ass. He and two other officers on plainclothes assignment are breaking down a door, and the next thing you know both the others are down, one dead and one screwed for life, paralyzed by a bullet in the neck, and all Cross gets is a clean through-and-through wound of the calf muscle? Yet he says he unloaded eighteen rounds from his Glock and never once hit the bad guys? And he still got a Combat Cross medal? Sounded like a coward's bullshit cover-up story to me then, and it still does.

But Bartlett said nothing to Carmody. He himself had been unable to disapprove Frank Cross's application for the Stakeout Squad. He had the distinct impression that Cross had lied about the gunfight in which he'd won his award, but he couldn't prove his suspicion that the Stakeout Squad now had a coward on board, a coward who could only have volunteered for the squad for one reason: to get a chance to make up for his own shameful defeat.

"Let's keep going down the line," Bartlett said gruffly.

OFFICER STANLEY BARANCK was at the next booth down. He was about thirty, solid looking, his closely cropped dark hair setting off his ordinary-looking white face. He was up against half a dozen Action Targets, narrow pedestals hooked up to pneumatic hoses. When the range master touched a certain button, Baranck had one second to react to whichever steel silhouette the air hosed upright, and shoot it back down. He was barely making the second each time, firing two shots whenever a target exposed itself and decocking his SIG-Sauer P-220 at the end of each "double tap."

"Baranck doesn't have lightning reflexes or anything," Carmody told Bartlett, "but it's like he makes up for a slow decision with a fast action. He'll fire right at the end of the time exposure, but he'll never shoot a target he's not supposed to, and he'll always hit the target he *was* supposed to shoot."

Bartlett couldn't help but nod agreement. "I know," he told Carmody softly. "That's why I approved him for the squad. I'd rather have the right decision a second from now than a wrong decision right now."

DAN HARRINGTON was on position seven. He faced a
set of six round plates as Hoffritz had, his Glock 21 at
the low ready position.

Bartlett watched Harrington intently for two reasons. First, he was shooting a polymer-framed .45
automatic identical to Bartlett's, and the lieutenant
couldn't help but wonder how the other man would do
with the gun. The other reason was that his alarm bells
had gone off inside: he didn't trust Dan Harrington
and hadn't for years.

The signal came. Harrington opened fire, left to
right. The first plate fell, and the second. The third
stayed up, and the .45 slug missed the fourth plate
also. There was a distinct pause for an instant, and
then, *blam blam,* plates five and six were down.

There was another brief pause, and then the big,
bald-headed Anglo named Dan Harrington pivoted
back toward the two middle targets that were still up.
Blam-blam-blam blam blam-blam blam blam. The
two targets went down in a spray of .45-caliber gunfire. Both Carmody and Bartlett noticed that the first
few shots had been a panic burst, and then the big man
had steadied down with his gun, one careful shot on
each and back, one on each and back again, but this
time done with the precision of a man who knew he
was being watched.

"Good recovery, Dan," Carmody called to the big
bald man. "A little loss of control there at first, when
you realized you didn't hit what you'd wanted to hit,
but you got back under control and took 'em all
down. Good recovery," he finished, repeating himself.

Bartlett motioned him aside. "I don't *want* good recoveries, Bob," he grated. "I don't want to have to see recoveries. 'Recovery,' like you and I both just saw, means that you that you had to mess up on your first chance. I want a team that doesn't need recoveries at all."

Bob Carmody nodded. "I agree, Lieutenant. At the same time, isn't that what training is all about? Get the bad performances out in practice, get the bad shots out of their system here on the range, so they know what perfect is. Harrington's on his way to that. It's what I like about him. He doesn't screw up and then give up—if he screws up, he gets right back there and fixes it."

"That's what I mean, *Officer* Carmody," the lieutenant answered pointedly. "We're talking about firing guns down very narrow lanes for a shot, lanes that are bordered on each side by the living and breathing bodies of innocent people. Harrington makes a bad shot that hits a bystander, he's gonna get back and fix that somehow by shooting his gun off again? He muffs his one chance to stop the bad guy with the gun from killing the bank teller, and the bad guy shoots that teller in the head. Are you telling me Dan here's going to fire another shot and *then* put down the bad guy, and he's made up for not making his first shot count when he had the chance? Get real, Bob. We're going to be dealing with human lives here.

"And something else—don't worry about Dan, he's got his earmuffs on and can't hear me—you got a man there who's come up to detective rank climbing over the backs of brother cops. Oh, yeah, Carmody, I checked him out before we put him on the squad. He likes to tell you about the four shootings he's been in, but he never shot one bad guy in all but one of them. I know because I went through his record with a fine-tooth comb. Couple of them, he hosed the area with bullets after other cops had been shot—while *he* was safe behind cover—and the two other shootings he didn't fire at all. What happened was, the bad guy had shot a couple cops and then ducked under something solid and said to himself, 'Oh, shit, I just done *what?* I better get myself given up before they send in the SWAT team to come kill my ass.' Dan Harrington always seemed to be the nearest live cop, the nearest up-and-running cop at least, once or twice, for them to surrender themselves to.

"You know how the system worked before they brought in Kearn as chief. Whoever laid hands on the guy was the arresting officer, and the arresting officer got credit for the collar. That's where Dan Harrington got all those arrests, brought him up to detective, carried him so much weight I couldn't turn him down for the Stakeout Squad when he volunteered."

Carmody sighed softly. "Geez, Lieutenant, I didn't know. I mean, I'd heard about him being not quite a hundred percent, but—"

The lieutenant waved his hand, cutting the instructor off yet again. "Look," said Bartlett, "I didn't like it, either. What's done is done. I had slots to fill, mandatory, and I filled them with the best I could get. That doesn't mean I filled them with the best there was, okay?"

Carmody couldn't think of anything to say. And that, Bartlett thought wryly, was just fine; he couldn't think of anything he'd want to hear, either.

"Look," the lieutenant said after a moment, "we got two guys left to watch, right? Tom West and Sergeant Cohen. Let's take a look at them."

TOM WEST WAS SHOOTING Mozambique drills: two shots to the center of the chest, then one in the center of the face in case the opponent had been wearing a vest. The .45-caliber holes had clustered tightly toward the point of aim. His pistol was a Smith & Wesson 4586, similar to the gun Cross used but a little shorter and with no safety catch. Tom West figured that the simpler things were the better. If he had to go for a pistol, he didn't want to have to remember to flip a safety latch. He figured he'd be lucky if there was just time to pull the trigger.

"Improving quickly," Carmody commented. "Record shows he just shot average qualification scores before signing on with the unit. He seems to have really applied himself since he started training with Stakeout."

Bartlett nodded, musing. "Let me talk to him alone for a minute."

The lieutenant walked up to West, who was just pulling an empty magazine from the butt of his smoking pistol. "Hey, Tom."

"Hey, Lieutenant. Haven't seen you since you interviewed me about coming on the squad."

"I know. I haven't had a whole lot of time to get to know you guys. Given any more thought to what we talked about?"

"You mean about the chances of them putting me and the other black guys on point, so when black guys get shot they'll have been shot by black cops? Placate the community, and all that?"

The lieutanant answered, "Did you think I was kidding, Tom? The chief may be new to Miami, but I suspect the first thing he learned was that we have a riot every two or three years, and every single one of those riots has revolved around white cops killing black suspects. A lot of guys we face are going to be black. Not too many of the black officers volunteered for the squad. You're the only one on Team Two. It's important to me to know that you understand what you're getting into."

The black patrolman grinned mirthlessly. "Oh, believe me, I understand, Lieutenant. Why do you think I became a cop anyway? Hell, I grew up in Liberty City. I found out real early that most of the crime in this city is committed by blacks, against blacks. I took this job to help my own kind, yours and mine. If it means blowing away some asshole predator, it doesn't matter to me a whole lot what color he is."

West quickly shoved a magazine into the butt of the gun and thumbed the latch that dropped the slide and chambered a round. He spun and fired three shots. The first two struck the target where a human breastbone would be, and the third hit the center of the head.

BARTLETT WAS BACK with Carmody, and together they approached the compact man with the iron gray crew cut and tired face on the far right of the firing line. "Hey, Sarge, Lieutenant's here," said Carmody.

Mike Cohen shook hands with both of them. "What do you think, Bob? The team look good for the lieutenant?"

"I'll answer that for him, Mike," the black lieutenant answered. "He's doing great. They look like a pistol team out there."

"They *are* a pistol team," said Cohen. "You and I have discussed this, Ken. You got them the training time they needed on dealing with hostage takers, and I appreciate that, but I still think we're going to need a lot more emphasis on controlling these things without bloodshed."

Bartlett nodded. "That's your job as team leader, Mike. Pavlicek almost had it with the kids in the bank. Then the older one lit off a round at him, and it was all she wrote. I'm not sure we can ask for anyone to hold their fire any longer than Team One did in there."

Cohen frowned. "How those guys doing?"

Bartlett answered, "Not great. Pavlicek's off indefinitely. Shrink says killing the kid really did a number on him. The others seem to be getting through it okay. They're back on the street, of course. We wrote it into policy from the beginning that the usual rule—the week of administrative leave to get it together after being involved in a shooting—would have to be waived for Stakeout. We can't take a whole team out of the field after a predictable encounter."

Cohen shook his head. "I don't like it. Every man and woman who volunteered for this went through the toughest battery of psychological tests our people could put together. There was nothing that showed Pavlicek would break after a shooting."

Bartlett put his hand on the sergeant's shoulder. "No," he admitted, "but there was nothing to show that he'd have to shoot a young kid who had a toy gun, either."

5

Bob Carmody locked his apartment door behind him, set down his Waller gun bag and prepared to clean his .45 automatic. He ached for a shower, but he'd do it later. He knew that cleaning a gun would just get him dirty again. Finish the dirty work, *then* shower. Carmody had found that the world of the gun was a pragmatic place, where logic took precedence over gut reflex.

Carmody knew that there were people who used guns as surrogates: surrogate muscles, surrogate penises, surrogate power, surrogate whatever. He took satisfaction in his knowledge that he didn't fit that profile, even though a cop who was into guns seemed always to be suspected by higher command of just such motivations.

In high school he had pictured himself as average. So had his guidance counselors. They had discouraged him from going to college, though he went anyway and passed with grades of C and B. His major was criminal justice, which was what you studied if you wanted to be a cop, and a cop was most certainly what Bob Carmody had wanted to be since his adolescence.

As a little kid he was a Cub Scout. He went smoothly from there into joining the Boy Scouts, and made Eagle Scout at seventeen. Carmody was comfortable being a part of an organization, comfortable and even proud when he wore a uniform, and at peace when he worked within something that had a clearly specified set of goals and parameters.

He thought at first that the military might be the thing for him, the logical extension of uniformed organization and guidelines that had defined so much of his growing-up years. Then a cop from Miami, the city where he'd grown up, came to lecture at a junior high school assembly.

Carmody liked the uniform. Liked the decisive set of values. Liked everything the guy seemed to stand for, as a matter of fact. He pictured himself wearing that navy blue uniform with the golden circular shoulder patches that depicted the palm tree and all that.

In school he realized that he liked sports better than he liked the classroom, and that he especially liked sports he could excel at. He had a swimmer's build, and swimming came naturally to him; he competed for the high school swim team. He never won any significant awards in swim competition, but he enjoyed being a part of a team that did well.

In scouting, he found he enjoyed winning merit badges. His Miami Scout Troop had a session on marksmanship, and his marksmanship merit badge was more than just another medal on the khaki-colored sash he wore proudly at Scout meetings. In marksmanship, he discovered, he not only held up his end of the team but beat almost everyone else.

Carmody liked being first place. He got more serious. The Boy Scouts didn't have a rifle team per se, but their coach knew of a gun club that did. Bob learned that the Pentagon had an office called the DCM, the Director of Civilian Marksmanship, which worked closely with the National Rifle Association. In his high school civics class, the teacher put the NRA in with the Ku Klux Klan as a right-wing organization that endangered the public, but Bob quickly learned to identify with the NRA. They used DCM funds to provide free rifles, free .22 ammo and free coaching for kids who belonged to an NRA junior rifle program.

With his parents' permission, Bob Carmody signed up. He was then a member of a gun club with a facility out on the edge of the Everglades. It was better than the high school swim team, because instead of each member of the winning team getting a trophy— although that still happened on the rifle team—when you went to a rifle match you could also get trophies for high individual shooter.

There were, of course, individual trophies for the single best swimmers at meets. It was just that he had never won one. But in riflery, almost immediately he started to win medals and trophies.

The rifle, Carmody quickly learned, was ninety percent in your head and only ten percent in your body if you wanted to master the thing. It was sort of a Zen game. The secret was, once your body had been taught what it had to do, you had to keep your mind out of it and let your body do what it knew it had to do. Tighten the rifle's sling to your upper left arm…drop into exactly the right sitting position, where the skel-

etal support structure of your lower legs reinforced
that of your arms, with your elbows resting just ahead
of your knees, and the rifle would be dead steady.
Now, all you had to do was take a deep breath, let a
third of it out and hold the front sight on target as you
centered it through the aperture of the peep sight on
the rear end of the rifle. Then your index finger would
gently squee-e-eze the trigger until the shot went off
with total surprise, and fifty feet downrange there
would be a .22-caliber hole dead center in the ten-ring
of the bull's-eye target, a mark that was about the diameter of the eraser on the head of a pencil.

The gun-club people brought different master
shooters in to give lectures and pep talks. One of them
was a cop from the Homestead Police Department, an
Asian guy. Now, many years later, Carmody couldn't
remember the cop's name but he could recall the lecture almost word for word.

"You kids shoot the .22 rifle," the police lecturer
had begun. "I shoot NRA police revolver. In the open
class of the competition, I use tricked-out guns. My
favorite competition revolver is a Smith & Wesson that
has been completely rebuilt by Bob Cogan down in
Clearwater.

"It has the same frame as my .38 service revolver.
It has the same Hogue finger-grooved grips, made out
of a springy rubber substance that absorbs the kick of
the gun when you have to shoot a hundred and fifty
shots in one stage. Other than that, it is nothing like
my issue service revolver.

"The barrel isn't like a regular barrel on a gun.
Here, let me show you. It's like a stovepipe, more than
an inch in diameter. See this sighting rib that's been

installed on top? Part of its job is to give me more weight to hold my gun steady on target. In our competitions you have to shoot at fifty yards, a hundred fifty feet away, and the center X ring on the target is about the size of a human fist seen from the front. Maybe four inches apart from its widest points. About the size of a human heart, as a matter of fact.

"See these little screws on the back sight? They're for adjustment. One click on this sight will move the bullet's point of impact about a quarter of an inch at fifty yards. That, my friends, is some kind of precise.

"You ask yourself, 'Why would a cop have to shoot all that precisely?' That's what they say to us in our regular police training. The average police shoot-out takes place within seven yards and more often than not, within seven *feet*. You'd figure, just shoot from the hip and hit the bad guy somewhere and never worry about your gun sights at all.

"Tell you the truth, that's what they used to teach us in police training. 'Just hit him somewhere, and be grateful that you did.' Only trouble was, that sort of teaching put a lot of cops in their graves before their time.

"Truth of the matter is, the closer you are, the more surgically precise your bullet placement has to be if you are shooting under pressure. Gang, we're talking about putting that bullet someplace where it can instantly shut a guy down so fast and so totally that he can't twitch his index finger and pull the trigger of *his* gun, which might already be aimed at *you*.

"That means that when you're fighting for your life, you need marksmanship a whole lot more than when you're just shooting to win a trophy. You've got to be accurate, but you've also got to be fast.

"I don't know how many of you kids are ever going to become cops. But if even one of you is, you need to know what I'm about to say to you, and all the rest who don't plan on being cops, you all listen, too. The time is going to come when a cop has to shoot somebody in the community where you live, and that community won't understand what happened, and I'd kind of like at least one or two of you guys and gals to know how stuff really works. So when the editorial says that some crazy killer cop shot somebody who didn't need to be shot, you can write a letter to the editor and know what you're talking about when you say, no, as a matter of fact, that cop had to fire his gun when he did or else he would be dead, and maybe a whole lot of the citizens he is paid to protect would have been dead, too.

"Let me put down this target gun. We call it a PPC revolver, in the combat competition shooting world. Watch me take this service revolver out of my holster. You see I handle it real careful. That's because it's a real gun and it's loaded.

"It's a Smith & Wesson Combat Magnum, stainless steel. It's loaded with a 125-grain .357 Magnum hollowpoint bullet that comes out of the gun muzzle traveling about fourteen hundred feet per second. It hits with an impact that has been measured at 583 foot-pounds of energy. That means that the bullet coming out of this gun has enough power to take something that weighs 583 pounds and smash it about one foot back from where it was standing when the shot went off.

"Now, does that mean if you're facing some monster guy who weighs 583 pounds, a hit from this is going to set him back in his tracks about a foot? Naw. That's because the bullet spends most of its energy tearing a hole through whatever flesh it comes into contact with. It's a really narrow, focused kind of energy. It doesn't spread itself out and physically push you back. What it does, it blows up your guts on the inside where it hits, and when you see a man seem to jerk back after getting hit from it, it's probably really just his body's 'alarm reaction' pulling him away from something that caused him pain.

"But, kids," the police instructor concluded, "let me tell you something. Whether the bullet knocks you a few feet backward or not, it's going to mess you up, and there's a damn good chance you're going to die from it. That's why the police department doesn't encourage ordinary people to have loaded guns lying around to shoot people with, and that's the reason why we only want to see people carrying guns who are really trained with them, and know what they do, and know how to hit what they're aiming at. Can you imagine a bullet of this power missing the bad guy you were trying to shoot at, going past him and hitting an innocent bystander?"

There was a long silence after the Homestead cop stopped talking, and in the aftermath of that silence, Bob Carmody was the first kid to raise his hand. The cop smiled and pointed to him, silently commanding him to speak.

"Sir," a fifteen-year-old Bob Carmody said, loud and clear, "do you get paid to shoot for your police department's pistol team? I mean, is that like part of your job?''

The guest cop chuckled and answered, ''It was until lately, son. You see, kids, what it is, it's always good for the organization you work for to be able to show that it's really good at what it does. If you have something where you compete against the other people doing the same job, well, that's something you can use to show that you're good at what you do, right? Assuming, of course, that you *are* good at it.

''Well, how does a police department show the chief, and the mayor, and the city council, and all the voters, that it's pretty darn good at what it does? You can't use the number of crimes committed. If you say there were very few crimes so you must have done a good job of preventing crime, the voters will just say, well, there mustn't have been that much crime in the first place so why should we have to pay to have you cops here?

''By the same token, you'd think that if you prevented a lot of crimes, which is what a cop is supposed to do, the voters and everybody else would say, 'Ya done a good job. Here's a raise. Here's some tax money for some more cops so you can prevent even more crimes next year.' But it doesn't work that way. Instead, folks will say, 'If crime is down that much we don't need as many cops. Let's fire a few of them.'

''Now, let's say that crime goes *up* in the community. Does more crime mean you need more cops? Naw, not at all. People will say, 'If those cops that we've got were doing their job, we wouldn't be having this increase in crime. Therefore, the cops doing the job for us must be lazy, incompetent, bad cops. Why should we pay for lousy cops like that? Let's fire them. The crime situation can't get any worse, right?'

"So you see, son, that's one reason my department has a pistol team. There's no real empirical way for a police department head to show the community how good a job he and his people are doing. Convictions are a function of the court system, not the police department. Arrests are a function of demographics, and even if you make a lot of arrests the public thinks that must mean a lot of crime, and they blame you for all that crime, you see?

"But a pistol team, well, it tests a police-related skill against other departments. If you go to the regional and the national championships like we do, you test those skills against the biggest, best, most prestigious departments in the country. When our team wins a match, it's in the sports pages of the newspaper. When we came in second at the national championships in Iowa last year, we made the front page. Each of those stories was saying to the public, 'You can be proud of your police department. They're the best in the area and one of the best in the country.'

"Something like that creates a bond. When the community feels good about its police department, it's more comfortable talking to its cops. When citizens talk to cops, the cops get more leads and make more arrests and head off more crime. You understand what I'm getting at, son?"

The young Bobby Carmody nodded. He did understand, pretty much, but what he mainly understood was that if he was able to join the right police department, he'd be paid to become one of the best shots in the country and win glory doing what he loved. From that moment he set his sights on being a police firearms instructor and shooting on a big department's pistol team until he became national champion.

The boy joined the Explorer Scouts, in which youngsters became unarmed junior police cadets. After high school he enrolled in the criminal-justice program of the Florida State University in Tallahassee, working his way through on the night shift as an assistant dispatcher, then full dispatcher, at the Leon County Sheriff's Office.

At twenty-one he had his bachelor's degree in criminal justice and more real-world police experience than any candidate his age among the horde of applicants for fifty new jobs with the City of Miami Police Department. By the time both the written and the oral exams were tallied up, Carmody was third highest among the candidates and on his way to the police academy.

The four years of university included more preparation than just the classroom and working the dispatch desk. He volunteered his time to assist at the firing range in Leon County, at first just pasting targets and picking up spent cartridge casings and helping to clean guns at the end of the day.

Soon, however, his enthusiasm for firearms training caught the attention of the designated instructors, and by the end of his first year there he was an unofficial coach. Given a hopelessly bad marksman, some of the instructors would say, "Look, rookie, I want you to go over to Range Two with Bobby here. He'll work on your technique, get you sharp."

Between reading every firearms book and gun magazine he could get his hands on and listening intently during the range training sessions and the pistol team practice drills, Carmody learned the subtleties of stance, balance, grasp, breath control and the myriad other components that made up the art and science of marksmanship. He found that in an afternoon he could take a subqualifying police shooter from under two hundred points on the three-hundred-point qualification course, up past the 225 points that met the minimum score requirement and usually up past a 250 or 260. The designated range masters, who found that patience was the first thing to go in their job, considered Carmody a godsend.

The pistol team accepted him, at first as a mascot. He went along to their matches with them, picking up their brass and helping them tally their scores. Soon, more for their own amusement than anything else, they would lend him their guns and sign him up to shoot. He scraped to pay his own entry fee, but the ammo was the department's, and what the hell, they wouldn't miss another three boxes here or there that could be written off to training.

At his first match, right there in Tallahassee, he won the unclassified category, shooting 1451 points out of 1500 possible with a borrowed heavy-barrel .38 Special. When he was nineteen the team took him along to the nationals, in Jackson, Mississippi, that year, and Carmody placed first in the nation in the police cadet category.

By the time he graduated from FSU Tallahassee, the county sheriff's pistol team was sorry to see him go. He had contributed as many awards to the impressive trophy cabinet in the foyer of the sheriff's headquarters building as any of them.

A couple of the instructors knew Christopher James, the famous head of firearms training at Miami PD. They phoned him to let him know Carmody was on the way, and to advise him to watch out for their promising young student.

James watched out for him, but not exactly the way they'd had in mind. His job was to train cops to survive on the street, not to win pistol matches, and he had no intention of brooking some "watch-me" superstar marksman.

The master instructor was pleased to discover that the blond kid with the fast hands had already absorbed enough from the cops up in Tallahassee to know the difference between survival shooting and target shooting. In the standard range exercises, the kid set records for a recruit class. But in the survival drills, walking and stalking among the bullet-absorbent buildings they called Combat City, he showed that he knew how to take cover, how to spot a threat before he had walked into its cone of fire and how to hold fire when he needed to. Only then did James realize that his friends in Tallahassee were right: this kid had a helluva lot of promise as a police instructor. He instantly absorbed everything James showed him, and the veteran sergeant and instructor knew that the first component of the ability to teach was the ability to learn.

But no recruit begins as an instructor. Like every other cop in his graduating class, Carmody began on the street, working the unpopular midnight shift. James, who was tight with Carmody's shift commanders, kept a remote eye on his progress. He knew there were problems that could show up with a cop at work that wouldn't be evident in the artificial atmosphere of the training range.

Was the cop a coward? Only the brightest shades of yellow showed up in the police training environment. Any cop smart enough not to spill his coffee in his lap knew that the instructors weren't really going to let anything hurt him, only frighten him. But on the street they faced entities that did want to hurt them, to kill them, and a lot of men who were cool as ice against a paper target crumpled like tissue paper when they faced a living, aggressive human who wanted them to die and was firing real bullets at them from close range.

Was the cop a hot dog? In other departments cops who thought Sylvester Stallone was a role model instead of an actor would get the contemptuously spoken nickname of "Rambo." Miami PD didn't use that terminology. Their lead officer-survival instructor was named Bob Rambo, and too many men and women on the department owed their lives to the tactics he'd taught them to use the name as a pejorative.

But that didn't mean the syndrome was ignored. As hard as the police psychologists and the oral board worked to weed them out, there were still people who wanted to join a police department for an opportunity to legally satisfy an inborn streak of not only recklessness, but sadism. It was one of the things field training officers watched for intently when their young charges first came out of the academy and into the street. An unusually intense interest in guns or martial arts was considered an early-warning sign of that attitude, and James knew the field supervisors and FTOs would be watching the kid intently for any such behavior without his asking them to.

Was the cop a showboater? James had known firearms instructors who considered their students nothing more than an audience for their own skills. Their ulterior motive in getting an assignment to the range was to gratify their own hobby and ego, and gain access to more department ammo than they could have blown away otherwise. James doubted that this was the case with Carmody; his sources at Tallahassee had already spoken of the kid's natural talent in sharing knowledge with others, particularly those who needed remedial training, and the sergeant had even seen a little of that during the recruit class. He knew that Carmody had been working during off time with some of the others in his class who couldn't keep up with the firearms program. Bob seemed prouder of getting them up over the hump of the final qualification than the fact that his own score, a new record in the annals of the academy, won him the cherished Smith & Wesson off-duty revolver always awarded to the top marksman in an academy class.

Bob Carmody's first few years disappointed no one, and surprised only himself. Everyone thought that because he was into guns, he would shoot people... and so had he.

Instead, Carmody learned something more important: if you were good enough with a gun, you usually didn't have to pull the trigger.

Toward the end of his second year on patrol, transferred to the active four-to-midnight shift now, Carmody was at the range for bimonthly qualification when one of the instructors told him, "Sergeant James would like to see you in his office before you leave."

When Carmody sat down across the desk from the intense, dark-haired sergeant, he felt more tension than he had any time his gun had been drawn in the street. James was only about thirty-five, but already a legend among police firearms instructors nationwide. It had been he who had managed, against all odds, to replace the obsolete 6-shot .38 service revolver with the 18-shot 9 mm Glock semiautomatic as standard issue, making Miami the first department of that size in the nation to do so.

"I hear you've been doing well on the match circuit. High service revolver at the midwinter nationals over in Tampa, first-place stock gun at the Florida invitational. They give you a decent prize for either of those?"

The Florida Invitational Pistol Tournament was the first big event on the handgun competition pro tour each year, and a good performance there really counted. Carmody blushed modestly. "Just NRA award points for the service revolver thing. FIPT was pretty rich this year, though—I got a combat-customized Colt .45 for high stock gun."

The sergeant nodded. "Nice gun. I always liked the Colt .45."

Carmody blurted, "Too bad we can't carry them."

The sergeant chuckled. "I hear you. Trouble is, we've got to have some uniformity with the equipment. It's hard to train somebody to take a safety off before they shoot if they've been accustomed to a gun without a safety catch like the Glock or the old Smith .38. There's the matter of the recoil, too. You and I know you can handle the kick on a .45, but all those Army stories have cops believing the recoil will tear your arm off. Sometimes the perception is the reality. Say, what gun did you shoot for stock class at FIPT?''

''The issue weapon, sir, the Glock.''

The sergeant beamed. ''Good. A sense of reality at work. When I first saw you in action, I was wondering if you knew the difference between street gun-fighting and pistol-match play. I've pretty much decided that you do.''

''I hope so, Sarge.''

''How would you feel about coming to work out here?''

Carmody had hoped for this moment for years, but never allowed himself to expect it, and now it almost stopped his breath. ''Well...sure! Uh...yeah! You bet! Of course!''

The sergeant asked softly, ''You're what, Bob, twenty-three? You'd be the youngest instructor out here by far. If you were me, what would you worry about in terms of making Bob Carmody an instructor out here?''

It was a question the young officer hadn't ex-pected. He thought a moment, sighed and answered, ''Credibility, I guess. Only twenty-three, two years on, never shot anybody. I can see some of the old harness bulls saying, 'Who's this punk kid to tell me how to do it? I was shooting a gun when he was on mother's milk. He ever blow away some scumbag, like I have?' You know the drill, Sarge.''

James chuckled. ''Yeah, I know the drill, all right. Tell me something, Bob, do *you* think you have to have shot a man to have credibility teaching someone how to shoot to survive?''

Carmody pondered a moment. ''No, not really. I mean, hell, you do a great job, and as far as I know, you never shot anybody.''

The sergeant's smile seemed to fade. ''I know. It's not something I talk about except when I get on the witness stand to speak for a cop. Take that oath, and your life is an open book. If it matters, I did have to shoot a man once.

''I wasn't much older than you, and wasn't on the job much longer, either. He came at me with a knife. I had no other choice at all. I shot him twice. He died.''

He shrugged and continued, ''I've never felt that I needed to begin a lecture talking about it. I'd much rather start a lecture talking about some of the alternatives to pulling the trigger. I've talked with your bosses. They told me about the guy with the shoulder holster. He was yours, bought and paid for if you'd wanted to kill a man. He was going for his gun, and all you had to do was give him another couple inches of rope and he would have hung himself. Instead, you drew proactively, you dominated the situation and you turned what could have been a killing thing into an arrest with no blood spilled.

''They told me about the EDP with the bayonet. I've got a copy of the report, in fact. You used the gun as a deterrent, not a killing machine, and it's always a tricky situation with an emotionally disturbed person. Sure, there are times when you've got no choice but to pull the trigger, but part of our job here is teaching them that there are other options they can use before that last resort.

"You see what I'm saying, Bob? I've never started a lecture talking about the man I had to kill in the line of duty. I can see starting a lecture saying, 'I want you to hear right now from one of our instructors, Bob Carmody, about an incident or two he was involved in where he would have been justified in killing his suspect, but was able to control it instead without a shot fired.' You see what I'm saying?

"What do you think, Bob? Could you be happy working with me as a firearms instructor out here?"

That conversation had taken place years ago. No Miami PD firearms instructor had ever been happier in his job than Bob Carmody. He dedicated himself to the work to the point that he took a sabbatical year away from tournament shooting and devoted the time to attending advanced-marksmanship training schools. He drove up to the Palm Beach County Sheriff's Office when the PBSO training staff sponsored a Smith & Wesson Academy course there, and returned for the special Marine school that PBSO's instructor staff did each year with the Marine Corps.

He drove over to Metro Dade when they hosted a Lethal Force Institute program, and took vacation time to fly cross-country to the American Pistol Institute in Arizona, and the following year, to take the advanced pistolcraft course at the Chapman Academy in Missouri. Because Miami's training program had made them the flagship of Glock sales to American police, the department often hosted Glock training programs, and there Carmody was able to work one-on-one with the elite Glock training staff.

By the time he was twenty-five, Carmody had more advanced training than most police range masters did at the ends of their careers. He was rising fast in the training unit when the shake-up hit.

A Hispanic officer had shot and killed a black man who was trying to run him down. The shooting triggered a major riot. James was pressured by the state attorney's office to testify against the officer they had indicted, saying that he had violated department policy. James refused to damn the cop.

Suddenly he was transferred out of training and into some remote precinct. A new sergeant Carmody had never heard of was brought in to head the unit.

Numbly Carmody stayed at his job. Like the other trainers, he had hopes that James would be vindicated and would be transferred back to where he belonged. That sort of thing had happened with other police supervisors in the past.

And then came the day when he heard the news that Christopher James, his mentor and role model, was dead, killed in an Amtrak train crash. That night he had deliberately taken out two comp days, locked his gun up at home and headed to a bar. It was the worst alcohol binge of his life, and the last. Nothing seemed able to wipe out the loss.

When he came back to the unit, the place seemed somehow empty and haunted by James's ghost. He wondered if he should stay.

Then he heard the rumors about the new anti-armed-robbery unit that was starting up. The Stake-out Squad.

It piqued his interest. Word was that these would be the first cops on Miami PD to be allowed to carry .45

automatics since that kind of gun had been taken away from the SWAT team. Any unit that would have his favorite gun as standard couldn't be all bad. It sounded as if something progressive was going on in the department for a change.

The plan was for each stakeout team to have its own resident firearms instructor. Bob Carmody knew he'd qualify. He would be doing the job he knew and loved best. He would be able to devote himself to training a small, hard cadre to be as skillful with a gun as he was, a much more exciting prospect than working with more than a thousand cops with only enough time and budget to get them to an acceptable skill level.

And, for a selfish moment, he thought about his own career. One of the most famous firearms authorities in the country, Jack Cerio, had been a New York City firearms instructor at the time NYPD's Stakeout Squad had been conceptualized. Cerio had gone on to kill a number of men in that assignment, all in face-to-face gunfights, blasting his way into the all-time gunfighters' hall of fame, if there was such a thing. One expert had called Cerio "the Wyatt Earp of the twentieth century."

Carmody pictured himself doing the same thing, but with a different spin. He found it most satisfying to be able to control a danger scene without pulling the trigger. In this assignment, out in the field with the others, he would have many more opportunities.

He was still the new kid on the firearms-training block. There had still been the question he and James had discussed, usually muttered behind Carmody's back: "Who's that kid to teach us survival shooting? *He* ain't never shot nobody."

Could he do it? He was sure that he could...
reasonably sure, at least. He had been ready to with
the guy with the .357 if the man had made one more
movement with his drawing arm. If the psycho with
the bayonet had fulfilled his promise to lunge, Carmody was sure that he could have blown the man's
hips out before he and his rusty blade reached Carmody or any other cop.

But how could he know for sure until he had been
where James had been that terrible day, in the position where there was nothing left to do but drop the
hammer?

There was only one way to find out.

Carmody volunteered for Stakeout and, as expected, was made a team instructor. He was pleased
with his group's performance.

He pictured them in his mind going up against the
Shotgun Gang. Those people were ruthless and deadly.
They would never surrender like the guy with the .357
or the EDP with the bayonet.

Bob Carmody finished cleaning his Colt .45 automatic. He reassembled it and worked the slide rapidly
back and forth several times, distributing the light
coating of oil he had applied to the frame rails. He
raised the empty gun to eye level, aiming at the bulb
of a lamp across the room. The front sight was steady
in its notch of the rear sight. He applied four pounds
of pressure gently and smoothly, and the hammer fell
on the firing pin with a sharp metallic click. The sight
never wavered off target. If there had been a cartridge
in the pistol, the bulb would have disintegrated with a
dead-center hit.

Carmody wiped the excess oil off the gun with a dry rag. He picked up a magazine of .45 Silvertips and ran it smoothly up the butt of the gun until he felt it snap into place, and then worked the slide one more time. It gave a different sound this time, a much more businesslike sound, as the slide stripped the topmost cartridge off the top of the spring-loaded magazine and fed it into the firing chamber.

He thumbed the catch upward into the Safe position and pressed the button on the left behind the trigger to drop the magazine, now "down one," back out of the gun. He set the magazine on the table, took a fresh one and locked it into place.

The heavy automatic was now fully loaded with its total payload, eight shots. He set it down on the side of the table and leaned back heavily in his chair.

He asked himself the eternal question of all armed men.

Could he really do it?

He had a feeling that he was about to find out.

6

The Tamiami Trail branch of the Citizen's National was the last banking establishment on the road that quickly led from a strip of fast-food joints and car dealerships to the uncharted blankness of the Everglades. Situated in a corner mall with access and egress in three directions, it was as convenient for armed robbers as for bank customers. That was why Bartlett had assigned Team Two to stake it out.

It was the day after Bartlett's surprise visit to the shooting range. The Stakeout Squad was still experimenting with different concepts. The strategy for this job was two team members inside, posing as bank employees, and the rest roving the area a few blocks wide, ready to respond. A module had been added to the bank's alarm system so that a hitting of the panic button would ring, not only at headquarters, but on the monitors in the stakeout team's cars. If possible, the inside team would act as eyes and ears, guiding the responding officers in and keeping them apprised of the situation.

This way, they hoped, they'd reduce the likelihood of a shooting in the bank. They thought a takedown outside in the parking lot—or even following the fugitive vehicle until they could be forced off the road at some safely isolated point—would be most likely to result in capture without bloodshed.

Melinda Hoffritz was riding shotgun with Bob Carmody in the driver's seat in one unmarked Chevy. Stan Baranck and Tom West were in the other, with West at the wheel. In the front of each vehicle was a gun rack installed along the forward edge of the front seat that held two Remington 870 pump shotguns, one pointed either way so each officer could quickly and safely draw his or her own 12-gauge either in the car or while bailing out of it.

All four wore oversize nylon warm-up jackets draped over heavy Hardcorps vests. With overlapping layers of laminated steel over Kevlar, each of these heavy-duty bulletproof vests could stop an armor-piercing rifle bullet. Each also weighed almost twenty pounds, but riding in the car with the air-conditioning turned up made them manageable.

At 2:13 p.m. the alert tone sounded on the alarm monitors. Hoffritz and Carmody, at Southwest Eighth and West Flagler, hit the toggles that made the head-lights flash and triggered the police lights behind the grille of the unmarked unit. They didn't touch the siren since they didn't want to alert the robbers.

Baranck and West were closer, having just circled through a mall parking lot, and turned back onto the Tamiami Trail. As West floored the accelerator, Baranck reached down and unlatched a Remington. "Dammit," he muttered, "we should have just stayed right at the bank."

"If we had, they'd have seen us if they were smart enough to scout, and been scared off, gone to someplace we weren't,'' West said logically. There seemed to be no tension in his voice.

Then they all heard the voice of Harrington over the monitor, in the tone of a man breathlessly trying to control his excitement . . . or his fear.

''Two perps, both five-six, five-seven, look about one-fifty. Gloves and ski masks, short-barrel revolvers, look like .38s. Just headed out the door, making for a cream-colored Chevy Cavalier, double parked outside, looks like the engine's already running. Can't see the plates from here. They're pointed toward the south exit. They're getting in the car now.''

Hoffritz and Carmody were in sight of the bank. ''Ski masks,'' she muttered, chambering a round in her Remington. ''Where the hell do you get ski masks in Florida anyway?'' Bob didn't bother to answer.

The plain Chevy carrying West and Baranck swung into the lot. At that moment they could see the doors closing on the Cavalier. Then there was a *whump*, and the interior of the car filled with a dark reddish haze.

''Die marker blew,'' Baranck snapped into the microphone. ''We're right in behind them. We're going to engage.'' He threw the mike to the car seat and shoved the car door open even as West slammed the vehicle into Park. Baranck felt the ground slap his feet, and now he was looking over his aimed shotgun barrel at the dark figure emerging quickly and awkwardly from the right door of the getaway car. He could see metal flashing in one hand.

West didn't think he had time to go for the shotgun along the front seat. He threw the door open with his left hand as his right drew his S&W .45 automatic from its Bianchi holster. The weight of the bullet-proof vest suddenly felt comforting.

He knew they had them. They were disoriented, blinded by the gas and smoke from the booby-trapped money bag. He heard Baranck yell "Police! Drop your weapons!"

And then, incredibly, it happened.

The figure on his side, still wearing the ski mask, pointed at the sound of his partner's voice and triggered the pistol. West saw the muzzle-flash of the gun, brilliant orange even in the bright afternoon sun, and was aware of how strange it seemed that he hadn't heard the shot.

Then West was firing, the three white dots of his gun sights lined up on the dark nylon of the figure's jacket, thirty feet away. He didn't hear his own shots, either, but the pistol bucked twice in his hand, and when he went to sight for the third shot to the head, he realized the figure was no longer standing.

There was an eerie silence. The person he had shot at lay sprawled on the ground, motionless, the gun on the pavement a few feet away.

"Stan," West yelled. "You okay?"

"Yeah, you?" Baranck's voice sounded distant.

"Yeah. Mine's down."

"Mine, too."

Then the others were there, Carmody and Hoffritz coming in from behind, their shotguns at the ready, and Cross and Harrington emerging from the bank, their .45s in their fists.

"Cover 'em," Harrington barked to Cross, holstering his Glock .45 automatic. Handcuffs appeared from the back of his belt. He rolled the one by the right side of the car into a prone position, brought the hands behind the back and cuffed them. Another pair of cuffs came out of a hip pocket, and he did the same with the other.

Harrington could hear West talking calmly into his microphone. "Two suspects down, repeat, two suspects down. Roll parameds, supervisors, evidence technicians." His voice seemed unnaturally cool.

Hoffritz was the first to say "See if there's anything we can do for them."

Carmody on-safed his shotgun and set it on the trunk of the Cavalier, choking on the pungent red smoke that was only now beginning to dissipate. He gently rolled up the ski mask of the one on the left.

"Oh, shit," he blurted, "it's a woman!"

"Jesus Christ," he heard someone say on the other side of the getaway car, "so's this one!"

7

The bedroom was picture perfect, right out of *Better Homes and Gardens*. Only two things would have jarred a reader seeing the tableau in that magazine.

One was the Glock .45 automatic that lay holstered and fully loaded on the nightstand. The other was the nude brown-skinned man who lay facedown on the bed.

Ken Bartlett had come home exhausted. He had managed to undress, lay his wallet and belt and change and beeper in the bureau drawer, set his holstered pistol on the night table and toss his clothing in the hamper. He had been walking toward the luxurious shower in the bathroom off the master bedroom when the royal blue coverlet beckoned, and he had fallen prone upon it, his muscles more tired than he knew. His arms and legs felt like lead. A tension headache was beginning at the back of his head, and the muscles in his neck and shoulders had knotted fiercely.

First the dead kid in the bank. Now the two women Team Two had blown away. Jesus Christ, who had ever thought that it would have come to this?

Ken Bartlett was an unabashed careerist. When he left high school without enough money for college and without high enough marks for a scholarship—he had been too busy with school activities to work much on his grades—the military looked like the best option. He joined the Air Force at eighteen, since they offered the best college package at the time. Looking down the MOS list, he was struck immediately by the prospect of joining the Air Police. No other job description offered that much power for a young airman at a starting level. To exercise power, he knew, you had to first get power, and power was like money: them that has, gets.

He would never again make the mistake he made in school. In the Air Force he learned to study and absorb. His college credits were all in the area of public administration, not criminal justice; the Air Police program taught law enforcement, and he saw no need for redundancy. He applied the same tenacious study program to his promotional exams, and at the end of his first year had five stripes on his arm.

They wanted him to re-up. He was doubtful. He was already only one stripe away from the highest rank he could get without officer candidate school, and from what he'd seen of the Air Force OCS, it turned its students into followers, not leaders.

Besides, he had second thoughts about having picked the right branch of the service. Serious friends who had joined other armed services seemed to be advancing even faster than him. Bartlett had the impression that a black military man's best chance was in the army, second best, in the Marine Corps. The officer's cadre of the USAF, not unlike the pilots on the flight line, still seemed to him to be disproportionally lily-white.

His girlfriend in Miami had written of how well her brother was doing with the Miami Police Department. It seemed that they and Metro Dade had both accelerated their affirmative-action hiring in the wake of discrimination suits. More to the point, both agencies and especially MPD were aggressively promoting blacks at a faster rate than whites.

Opportunity was knocking.

Bartlett was only a few credit hours away from a bachelor's in public administration. That, plus his Air Police training and rank, would put him on a particularly fast track inside an agency like the Miami PD.

Bartlett had no illusions about his blackness alone carrying him up the career ladder. He knew that reverse discrimination carried a terrible tendency to backlash. He looked at the situation almost mathematically, in simple and logical form.

One, they needed to hire blacks, and he was black.

Two, they needed to promote blacks. He was not only black but promotable.

Three, to prevent charges of reverse discrimination, they would have to promote black men based on strong qualifications. His degree and his Air Police time and training gave him those qualifications.

Four, any black officer they promoted would have to do a damn good job to make them—the promoters—look good, too. Ken Bartlett had learned how to do that. The better he made the bosses look, the more valuable to those bosses he would become, and even as city administrations came and went, Ken Bartlett would be on a fast track upward to power.

Four, three, two, one. They added up to ten, a perfect ten, a perfect job for a hungry young black man on the rise.

Bartlett took his honorable discharge at the end of his four years, pausing only to complete his credit hours and get his degree. Copies of all those papers—he thought of them as entry tickets—accompanied his application to the Miami Police Department.

He breezed through the police academy—studying law enforcement wasn't much different from cramming for USAF promotional exams, and he kept in excellent physical shape in the Air Force by regular PT plus learning to play tennis and golf.

Out on the street with his first FTO, he rediscovered something he had learned in his early days as an air policeman before rising to the rank of noncommissioned supervisor.

Ken Bartlett did not like day-to-day police work.

His own personal hygiene and manner of dress were immaculate. The people you tended to have to deal with on the street were scum. Their bodies stank worse than their filthy clothes, and they reeked of sour alcohol and of the peculiarly fetid sweat that came from ingesting certain kinds of drugs.

To excel in routine patrol, you had to aggressively go after what the commanders called "activity." Chasing taillights struck Bartlett as somewhere between boring and offensive. He knew cops who specialized in catching speeders, and cops who specialized in drunk-driver arrests. They seemed like fighter pilots, looking for another shoot-down of an enemy craft, another decal to put on the side of their sleek fighting vehicle to show they had made ace. They all wanted to be Top Gun.

Bartlett couldn't begin to understand their motivation. Why look for a chance to leave the crisp, air-conditioned coolness of the patrol car and stand in the sweltering Miami sun at roadside, giving a drunk a Rohmberg field sobriety test and trying not to inhale his foul breath, or listening to some asshole with a Fuzzbuster on the dashboard of his Volvo ask you why you were harassing honest citizens instead of chasing criminals.

Of course, there were those policemen who aggressively chased criminals. The less-active officers called them "supercops," who would risk their lives entering the pitch darkness of a hot burglary scene, half hoping that some crackhead with a .22 would open up on them so they could blow him away and earn a Combat Cross to wear proudly on their uniform.

Bartlett had never understood that mentality. Like any other young cop, he'd had to go into danger and hunt armed men. He'd gotten through it, but it had left him terrified and shaking each time. Some people seemed to get off on that sort of thing. Bartlett thought of them as adrenalin junkies, and considered them to be a few cartridges short of a full load.

His first FTO—and to his way of thinking, his best—gave Bartlett advice to live by early on. "Here's the deal, Kenny," the grizzled police instructor said. "You get a call, fight in progress. What you got is two assholes trying to kick each other's balls off, or maybe cut 'em off with a switchblade. Now, there's one kind of cop who'll just put the pedal to the metal, lights and siren, and risk his life and his partner's life and a few dozen motorists' lives trying to be the first one at the scene.

"And for what? So one or both of these two assholes can try to kick or cut *his* balls off. You have to smack one of them down, you got a hundred people at the scene yelling 'police brutality.' And don't think being black is gonna save you from that crap, buddy boy. They'll be harder on you than on me. Least, they ain't gonna call me no 'Uncle Tom' like they're gonna call you."

The FTO took a sip of his Dunkin' Donuts coffee, lowered the cardboard container and kept talking. "So, how do you handle a call like that? Real simple, kid. *You slow down!*

"Take your time. Turn on the lights, maybe, but don't bother with the siren and don't break the speed limit. Good, easy rule to remember—don't go fast enough to spill your coffee.

"Now, about the time you get there, the two assholes will have pretty much played themselves out. You arrest the winner, who is probably too tired and beat up and cut up to give you much noise about it, and you call an ambulance for the loser.

"See, what did you have before, Kenny? A couple guys who were gonna turn all their hostility on you and kick the crap out of you just for being a cop. Maybe at best you get an arrest for assaulting an officer, and you know how *that* goes in a Miami courtroom. It's open season on us. The public defender pleads the asshole down to simple misdemeanor assault, he goes to jail for a few weeks for a reunion with all his scumbag friends at the expense of your tax dollars, and he's out of the Dade County jail before you've even healed from your beating.

"Now, look what you've got when you do it my way, kid. You do a slow response, and by the time you get there, the rest of the cavalry's got there, too. Whatever asshole won is too tired to fight, and whatever asshole lost is gonna be so glad to see you he'd rather kiss you than kill you.

"By now scumbag number one has done a nice dance on top of scumbag number two's head. Maybe he's shivved him in a couple of times. Shit, maybe he's killed the guy. So what have you got now?

"I'll tell you, young Officer Bartlett, and you listen close. Instead of a misdemeanor arrest, you've got a nice felony aggravated-assault arrest. Or maybe an attempted-murder arrest. Sure, then assholes in the state attorney's office are gonna get with them other assholes in the public-defender's office and plead the bastard down to some chicken-shit assault, but you got a quality felony arrest on your activity sheet, *comprendo?*

"And if asshole number one has killed asshole number two, it's even better. You arrest him for manslaughter, or what the hell, arrest him for murder. Looks great on your activity sheet. How can a supervisor give you a quarterly work evaluation anything less than perfect when you been out there pinching murderers, for Christ's sake? Kenny, that's the kind of stuff you get Officer of the Month for, you know?"

The FTO paused to sip more coffee, waiting for questions. None came. Young Officer Kenneth Bartlett stared straight ahead as he drove, but his ears were scooping up every word of the older cop's advice.

At length, the field training officer continued. "Never rat out another cop. You'll be a pariah. Might as well go out to the 'glades and eat your off-duty gun after that.

"Never try to be Johnny Supercop. You want to get promoted? You ever notice that supercops never get promoted? Listen, kid, suppose you were a sergeant. Here's this guy doing as much activity as any three other cops working for you on your squad, making them all look bad by comparison, even though he makes *you* look like a pretty good supervisor. Why the hell should you endorse him for promotion? So he can be one of *you,* and make *you* look bad by comparison? So he can leave your squad, and leave you without all those arrests he's been making, which make you look so good? All them supercops'll tell ya, they don't want to be promoted, they want to stay out on the street doing *real* police work.

"What a crock! They know they been had. They know the boss won't let them get promoted, for the reasons I just told you. And they know they got you, 'cause if you say screw it, then, I'm tired of busting my ass for nothing, when you go back to the same activity level as the other cops, it looks like you been slacking compared to your previous activity. Next thing you know they're sending you to the shrink for counseling, and down-marking you on your qualities because of your deteriorating work product and obviously crappy attitude.

"Take it from me, kid—no supercop ever gets promoted."

For the first time Bartlett spoke. "Okay, then, how *do* you get promoted?"

The FTO grinned. "Real simple, kid. Do something that stands out without making other people look bad. Something different. Come up with some new idea, some new approach, something that makes your boss *and his boss* look good. It gets you attention from the people upstairs who decide the promotions. They see you do all the work and give half the credit to your immediate supervisor, they figure you know how to play the game, so all of a sudden they want to promote you upstairs to do all *their* work for them for half the glory. See what I mean?"

Bartlett seemed puzzled. "Give me an example."

"Sure," the FTO answered. "Look at Captain Sayward. He was just barely on the prospective-sergeant list when he came up with that study report on community-oriented policing. Next thing you know, he's sergeant in charge of the pilot project, then lieutenant in charge of the real project when it takes off, and look at him now. Fat and happy in the catbird seat and waiting for someone to die or retire so he can skip major and move right up to deputy chief."

Bartlett nodded. His plans were set. Now all he needed was a project to call his own.

One day he responded to a call of a lost boy. A filthy little kid with dirt matting his hair, his pants soiled and stinking. The kid was sobbing hysterically and pointing at Bartlett's eight-point uniform cap. One of the gathering crowd of grown-ups said, "Officer, he wants to wear your hat, like police let lost kids do on TV."

Bartlett was stricken at the thought. *His* pristine uniform cap on that filthy head, which was probably infected with cooties? He looked around in desperation and saw a small toy store on the corner. "Sir, ma'am," he said politely, "if you'll stay right here with the little guy, I'll be right back."

The toy-store manager was shocked when the handsome black cop in the crisp uniform strode into his store, pulling a wallet from his hip pocket and gruffly said, "Give me the biggest goddamn teddy bear you got!"

A minute later the child turned instantly from tears to glee as the cop with the forced smile presented him with a teddy bear bigger than he was. The crowd was pleased and touched. As Bartlett vainly pumped the crowd to see if anyone knew where the hell the kid belonged, a Minicam crew from a local TV station happened by.

"Pull over," the anchorwoman in the front seat told the driver. "Kid, crowd, cop, we might have some human-interest stuff here."

Human interest it was, indeed. On the evening news, on late-night news, and even the next morning, Miami citizens got their warm fuzzies from the handsome officer who had bought the poor little lost boy a teddy bear out of his own pocket.

When he came to work, the sergeant congratulated him and handed him a note sent down by the chief that said tersely, "Great job, Bartlett. LC to follow for your file."

An LC, a formal Letter of Commendation, was nothing to sneeze at, and Bartlett instantly sensed that they were onto something. He remembered the advice of that first FTO. "Uh, Sarge, do you have a moment? There's something I'd like to discuss with you."

Within two days Bartlett and his sergeant had talked with the Rotary Club, the Lions and the Kiwanis.

Bartlett insisted on having the sergeant share the glory. All three civic service groups had donated equally to buy a supply of teddy bears for each police car in the city. Every "Officer Bear" would have a miniature MPD uniform, complete with the distinctive yellow shoulder patch with the palm tree.

It was human-interest news. First it hit Miami TV and newspapers, then *USA Today* and CNN. By that stage the then-chief of police was in the limelight. Sometimes the sergeant was in the picture and sometimes he wasn't, but always the photogenic young black officer who looked so spit and polish in the MPD uniform was there, holding an Officer Bear.

The sergeant pulled Bartlett in off the street to make him his unofficial assistant in the office. He coached him for the sergeant's exam.

His next brainstorm was the Sensitivity Awareness Program, or SAP. He was still ostensibly working with the sergeant, no longer through him, but it became apparent to the shift lieutenant and the captain he reported to that it was the sharp young cop, not the drone sergeant who had come up with the SAP program and the catchy phrase that would sell it to the department; SAP—We Shouldn't Have To Be Hit Over The Head With It. It was quite brilliant, because the acronym for the program also spelled the word *sap,* a flat blackjack long since forbidden on Miami PD.

Bartlett had been aware of violent situations triggered when some cop, usually Anglo, got on the wrong side of the cultural values of some ethnic minority they were dealing with. On his off-duty time he went through the clipping files and made up a list of just such episodes.

The Air Force and college had taught Bartlett to cram, and he studied up on his new subject, spending nights at the library.

The sergeant was gone from the picture, but his lieutenant was on one side of him and his captain on the other as he stood before the chief of police's imposing mahogany desk to explain the in-service training that would be the Sensitivity Awareness Program.

"Chief," he began, "Let's look at the brawl where five citizens and two of our officers were hurt last month. It began when an Anglo officer was talking to a Cuban motorist about a traffic ticket. The guy was staring down at the ground, and the cop yelled at him, 'Look at me when I'm talking to you,' and *that's* what kicked everything off.

"Sir, I went through the academy fairly recently, and I cannot blame that officer because I wasn't taught about that phenomenon, either. You see, sir, in many Hispanic cultures the casting of the eyes downward is a deferential sign of respect. What that man was trying to say to our officer in body language was, 'Yes, sir, I understand that I did wrong and I totally accept your authority.' But having only Anglo cultural predispositioning, the Caucasian officer took it to mean that the man was ignoring him, wasn't listening to him, was projecting body language that *he* interpreted to mean, 'I don't have to listen to any of your BS.'

"That kind of misunderstanding happens in many other ways, sir. Many American Indians, Native Americans if you will, are taught that staring a man straight in the eye is a sign of combative challenge. Yet if you are dealing with one of the many Arabic-descended citizens in our community, if you *don't* look him straight in the eye, he has been conditioned to believe that you are being deceitful with him.

"Let's say you're dealing with a family and a little boy comes up to you to say hello. Most of us would reach down and ruffle his hair. To an American of any color, that's a gesture that says, 'Hey, sport, you look like a tough little guy.' The parent takes it as a compliment.

"But suppose it's a child of Thai or Laotian descent and a certain religious background. That seemingly innocent gesture says to them, 'I do not care that the top of the head is the seat of the soul. By ruffling your child's hair, I show that I can steal his soul and destroy it if I want.' Many such parents would consider themselves honor bound to slash the officer's throat in defense of their child's eternal spirit.

"We are as racially and culturally mixed a society as any in this country, Chief. We have to be the leaders in preventing this sort of thing, this sort of terrible misunderstanding, in our community. I understand that you'll be addressing the International Association of Chiefs of Police at their Baltimore meeting next year, sir, and if you don't mind my saying so, I think a far-reaching program like this would be an excellent topic for you."

When the presentation was over and the chief was alone in his office, he barked a memo into his Dictaphone. "Tell the deputy chief I want this Ken Barrett or whatever his name is to have an expedited track. I want him as sergeant as soon as I can, and mark him for lieutenant. I need somebody with his kind of smarts up here, working for me in my office.''

Within a few years Ken Bartlett became the youngest Miami Police Department lieutenant in recent memory. He had been entirely an inside-office man. He had never commanded so much as a midnight-shift squad of field cops. He kept his Glock 19 locked in his desk drawer and carried his badge in a wallet only in case he was stopped for speeding. The uniform was replaced with a wardrobe that would have been suitable for the tropical-menswear edition of *Esquire*.

And then the new chief of police came on board. Ken Bartlett sensed that it was good. John Kearn was *him,* five or ten years older perhaps and certainly with more street experience, but other than that, he was *him.*

Relatively young. Black. Performance oriented, goal oriented, politically inclined obviously, and without question on a fast career track. And he, Bartlett, was already part of the inner-circle staff. Not a captain or a major yet, but that, he knew, was only a matter of time.

The armed robberies had been getting bad. Then this damn Shotgun Gang had gotten the city in an uproar, demanding that the police department hunt the crazed killers down and blow them away.

Kearn assigned Bartlett to do the research. He had him flown to New York City—and around the country to talk with the old vets of the now-disbanded NYPD Stakeout Unit. Then to Philadelphia and Los Angeles.

Bartlett hated the idea. He knew that killing would come out of it, and killing was incorrect; it destroyed careers, especially with a collective media as hostile toward police line-of-duty shootings as that in Miami. But the chief wanted it, and the chief would not look with favor on anyone who shot down his first pet idea, and Bartlett knew he would have to make the best of a bad lot.

He would have to put together the best possible Stakeout proposal he could, bring together the best possible procedures and tactics that had been developed by the three precedent squads in other big cities and make them work in Miami with as little force exerted as possible.

As averse as he was to guns—Bartlett considered firearms the mark of the troglodyte and secretly wished that they could be like British bobbies, patrolling unarmed—he listened carefully to the arsenal recommendations from New York, Philly and L.A. The .45s seemed shocking at first, until the L.A. cops explained that the more-powerful bullets meant fewer shots fired and fewer gunshot wounds inflicted. With the heat they'd been taking lately from the *Miami Crier* about the number of shots fired every time a city cop had to light off his 18-shot Glock, that started to make sense. He was at first horrified by the recommendation of heavy reliance on the shotgun, until the Philly vets told him how many bad guys who might have shot it out against pistol-armed cops had dropped their weapons when faced with the cavernous muzzle of a police shotgun.

And then came the bombshell.

Kearn sat Bartlett down in his office and told him bluntly, "Ken, for some reason we haven't had nearly the response I had expected to the opportunity to volunteer for the Stakeout Unit. I'm particularly disappointed that no one in lieutenant grade seems interested."

He flashed the lieutenant a fatherly smile. "Your record shows you to be on a fast career track, Ken. There's only one thing lacking in your package. No real time commanding cops doing real police work, and no time in a heavy-action, high-crime assignment. I think we can solve all these problems at once."

Bartlett's stomach knotted in dread. He knew what the chief was about to say. His prediction was correct.

"You've worked the Stakeout project from the ground up," Kearn began. "You're the logical man to head it. All right, you happen to be light on field-command experience, but no one else on this department is experienced with Stakeout, either, so that's a wash. I sense that you don't have any John Wayne syndrome in you, and that's good—that's the attitude that I want to pervade the squad. I want them to know their commander will take a very dim view of any recklessness, of any use of force that is not absolutely necessary.

"Ken, it'll be great for your career, and I think you're the best man for the job. What do you say?"

Good God, what *could* he say?

And now that was history. Now Ken Bartlett lay facedown on his bed, too tired to move, the muscles cramping in his neck and shoulders and the headache spreading from the base of his skull forward. Dead kids. Dead women. The Shotgun Gang still out there laughing at them.

And everyone, from the police chief to the press to the cops who had pulled the triggers, looking to him for the answers.

Bartlett heard the bedroom door open. "Eugenia?"

"Yes," came his wife's cool, soft voice. "You okay?"

"I've been better." Bartlett sighed. "Honey, you think I can talk you into a back rub?"

Eugenia Gibson-Bartlett, tall and slim, cool and striking, sat primly on the side of the bed and reached forward. Her long, slender fingers, the color of creamed coffee and surprisingly strong, began to knead his deltoids and lats.

"My God, Ken, you're tight as a drum. I heard about the shooting on the radio coming home."

He just grunted. He could feel the tension breaking up under his wife's unrelenting fingers.

She asked, "What are you going to do about it? Take them off duty and put in counseling like the one that killed the kid?"

"Hell, no," he almost snapped. "Look, they had to do it. I went to the scene. I heard some of the witnesses. Those women were dressed like men and trying to kill them both. Tom and Stan didn't have any choice."

Eugenia was so startled her hands stopped moving for a moment. "Ken, they shot women!"

"They shot people with guns."

"You sound like you're defending them."

"I have to defend them. They're my men."

Eugenia tossed her hands in the air. "They're your subordinates. They made you look bad. They made your unit look bad. You should be disciplining them, not defending them."

She didn't seem to understand, and he was too burned-out to explain.

He and Eugenia Gibson had married when both were nearing thirty. It had been the culmination of a slow and cautious dance. Both were devoted to their careers. Neither cared for children. Both hungered for success, fame and power. They were less lovers than allies.

Eugenia Gibson-Bartlett was attached to the city attorney's office, and on as fast a track as he. As an attorney, part of her job was handling lawsuits against the city based on police actions. She had come to see cops as brutal, low-intelligence racists who, if they beat up or shot a white person at all, seemed to do so by mistake. The thought of even dating a cop would have been abhorrent until she met Ken Bartlett at a city function. Ken was different.

Ken understood. Career was more important than family. Leaders were more important than followers. Money was good, but power was better...and you never let anyone make you look bad.

"For God's sake, Ken, I'm probably going to wind up having to do the out-of-court settlement on these two idiots. Are you going to tell me two big, strong men, two trained cops, couldn't have simply disarmed these two ditzy housewives with guns?"

Bartlett sighed, missing the hands on his back. "It's pretty hard to take guns out of people's hands from a car length or two away, when they're shooting at you."

Her voice became insistent. "You *are* defending them, aren't you? What is this, a male-bonding thing?"

"No," said Bartlett. "It's a cop-bonding thing, maybe."

"Oh, *shit*," she exclaimed, exasperated, bouncing to her feet. "Since when did you become a cop?"

For the first time his voice rose. "Hey," he snapped, beginning to turn over.

"Don't you 'hey' me," she snapped back. "Don't forget it, Kenny, you're no damn cop. You're a police executive. You're a member of the Police Executive Research Forum, right? You're a graduate of the FBI National Academy, right? That's the Harvard MBA of police. They don't send cops to the FBINA, Ken, they send police executives.

"You're on the fastest track at police headquarters! All you need now is to have this dirty little trigger-happy Stakeout Squad drag you down with it. You can't let it happen, Ken! You *can't!*"

Bartlett was up on one elbow now, his voice turning grim. "You're right. I can't. I won't. Those two cops, Baranck and West, are looking to me right now to stand behind them. I'm not going to let them down."

She threw up her hands. "Will you *listen* to me? You have to think of yourself!"

He dropped himself onto his back, resting his head on the silk-covered pillow. "I *am* thinking of myself," he answered quietly. "Will *you* listen to me for a minute?"

Eugenia folded her arms and glared at him, but she was silent, and he spoke again.

"Honey, one thing Kearn made clear to me was that if I want to advance any further in this department, I need some time in grade in actual field command. Doing that with a high-risk unit like Stakeout is as fast-track as you can get.

"Now, you mentioned the national academy a minute ago. One thing the FBI teaches—which is a little bit hypocritical, since they don't do things that way with their own agents most of the time—is that when you're in charge of people, it's a parent-child thing. A parent who abandons his children when they're in need is seen as a bad parent. He won't get any parent-of-the-year award, if you catch my drift.

"Now, I happen to think that these guys today did what they had to do. For that matter, the guy who shot the kid didn't have much choice. I didn't send him away for it, and frankly I don't think I would have. *He* spaced out over it, and he'll go out on a stress pension and get swept right under the rug.

"Now, this damn Shotgun Gang is still out there. They're going to keep hitting until they're interdicted. If we do this right, it's only a matter of time. From what I've seen so far, my people have what it takes to deal with them."

Eugenia muttered gruffly under her breath, "'Your people.' Humph." He ignored her and kept talking.

"The public wants the Shotgun Gang to go down hard. Shit, you read between the lines with that little dweeb, Oliver Teasdale, even *he* admits it's time for them to go down. When it happens, it's going to be redemption day, you understand? Redemption for me, for Kearn, for the whole damn squad and the whole damn concept. We've all got too much invested in it now to turn back, honey.

"I've got to keep the squad loyal to me. That means I have to take care of them. Remember that parent-child thing I told you they pounded on at the national academy? If you don't take care of them, they don't take care of you. They haven't fucked up yet, not really, but they're going to if I'm not there to let them know I'll back them up when they do their job. Or, just as bad, they'll slack off and when they do have the chance to take down the Shotgun Gang, they won't be there. *Then* talk about making me look bad."

His wife shook her head angrily. "Okay, okay, I see what you're saying, Ken. I suppose you *would* look bad if they perceived you as throwing them to the wolves. But understand what it makes *me* look like at the city attorney's office. My husband's leading the goddamn killer elite!"

Bartlett dropped limp on the bed. "I don't know what to tell you, Eugenia. All I know is, we're going to come through it. You'll see."

"I hope so," she said, only partially mollified. She began to undress. "Join me for a shower, Ken?"

He smiled at her as she slipped out of her prim business suit. Damn, but she was a great-looking woman! As the black panties dropped away, his eyes went to the shaved edges of her pubic mound. He wasn't sure why she trimmed it; she almost never wore a swimsuit. Like him, she was more of a tennis person.

He was becoming aroused. It seemed like a good time to change the subject. "You know," he said with a leer, "you ought to think about shaving the rest of it."

"Ick!"

"Hey, why not? If it was good enough for the First Lady, it's good enough for you! You're a Democrat, aren't you?"

"Gross! Who told you the First Lady shaved there?"

"I thought everybody knew it. You know why she did it on Inauguration Day?"

"Why?"

"So she could pull up her dress and say, 'Read my lips. No more Bush.' "

Eugenia burst out laughing and threw her panties at him. He caught them and pretended to munch at the damp black lace.

"You are disgusting," she laughed. "I am married to a disgusting, perverted cop."

"A disgusting, perverted police executive, I thought." He pointed at his tumescent organ. "Hey, I got somebody here who needs you, babe."

She pretended to pout. "Gee, I dunno. If you're about to turn into some Cro-Magnon cop, the next thing, you'll be naming that thing."

He grinned. "Tough to think of a name. If it was white, maybe I could call it Moby."

She shook her head, unable to stop smiling. "Why do guys name their dicks anyway?"

"Common sense," he answered cheerfully. "Hell, if something was going to make ninety percent of your decisions for you, wouldn't you at least want to be on a first-name basis with it?"

She laughed again, shook her head and moved slowly toward him. Straddling her husband, she guided him into her, and they began to rock together gently.

It was long and slow and mutually satisfying. When it was over, she rolled beside him and dropped her head against his shoulder. "Eeew. Ken, you do need a shower."

"This is true," he answered.

"What are you wearing tonight? I was thinking of your brown worsted suit."

He looked at her, puzzled.

"Dinner, dummy," she purred. "Remember, we're going to dinner with the city attorney and his wife."

Bartlett winced. "Oh, hell! I forgot!"

Eugenia's diamond-studded Concord watch was still strapped to her slender wrist. She glanced at it and said, "No big deal. We've got time."

Bartlett groaned, "No, we don't. I've got to be at professional standards tonight."

"What?"

"Aw, honey, the shooting. The headhunters wanted to take Tom and Stan right down, and Cohen told them, 'Get fucked. My guys are gonna have time to come down from this and get their shit together, and get a PBA lawyer there. See you in four hours at the soonest.' That's about an hour from now. Eugenia, I've got to be there."

Furious, she threw herself to her feet. "Yeah, right, you've got to be there! Never mind I'm going to look like a widow to my boss! Never mind I've got to tell him, 'Gee, my husband is busy patting two of his cops on the back for shooting two women today.' He's in there doing male-cop-bonding crap, and swearing over and over again. Ken, you never used to talk like that!''

He dropped back, exhausted, on the bed. ''I thought we'd been over this,'' he said softly.

''Not this, we haven't!''

''Honey...''

''Don't you 'honey' me! If you want to strap on that damn gun you're lying next to and go down to internal affairs and play cop, you be my damn guest! Go ahead! Become a cop, if that's what you want!''

She flounced into the bathroom, slamming the door behind her hard enough to turn his headache up another notch.

He lay there feeling helpless and angry. ''Be a cop,'' she'd said, as if ''cop'' was an epithet.

Maybe he should. Maybe it was time. He was a police executive, a leader of cops, and how could you lead the troops if you weren't a soldier yourself?

He was the leader of the Stakeout Unit, and the overboss of Team Two. A couple of his people were in trouble tonight. They had a right to expect that someone they were loyal to should come to their aid, to stand up for them under the questioning of the internal-affairs cops from the Professional Standards Unit.

He shook his head. Did Eugenia think he could be a police executive without being a policeman? Hell, did *he?*

Maybe he did; at least, for a long time that had been his identity and his career plan. Maybe she was right. Maybe he was changing.

He wasn't a parent because he didn't like kids. Perhaps, he realized, he hadn't been a field commander until the chief forced him into it because he didn't like cops.

If Eugenia got pregnant and they couldn't abort, he thought, he'd just get used to the idea and be the best dad he could be, even if he wasn't cut out for it. That was pretty much what had happened at work. The control mechanism had failed; he had become the adopted father of three teams of cops and their three sergeants, and he had to make the best of it. After all, there was such a thing as responsibility, and you couldn't have power without it.

And he *was* feeling a bonding with the men and women of Stakeout. They had risked their lives. Would Eugenia have felt better attending the funerals of West and Baranck if they hadn't fired when they did?

He forced himself up off the bed. It was time to go to work. Time to get used to being a police commander with responsibilities to his troops.

His eyes fell on the pistol. It might even be time to get used to actually wearing a gun again.

8

Alone at the wheel of his pickup truck, Stan Baranck steered onto the highway entry ramp and toward home. As he drove through the darkness, the words of the interrogator kept coming back to him.

"Now, Officer Baranck, you are certain that you identified yourself before firing?" the investigator had asked.

Baranck replied, with almost exaggerated slowness, "Yes, sir. I did."

"Tell me again what exact words you used."

"I issued the standard challenge we were told to use. I said, 'Police' very loudly in command voice. Then I said 'Drop your weapons' in the same tone of voice."

"Just like that? 'Police, drop your weapons?' Or was there a long interval in there, like, 'Police... drop your weapons.'?"

"No, sir," Baranck answered patiently. "It was the way I told you. 'Police! Drop your weapons!'"

Baranck said it in command voice, and the Professional Standards Unit detective jumped, startled.

The flustered detective took a moment to gather his wits. "Okay," he said, "let's go over again how many shots you fired."

At that point Lieutenant Bartlett stood up, looking crisp and professional as always in his brown worsted suit. "For Christ's sake, knock it off," he snapped. "Look, this man has been through this three damn times. So has his partner. Nothing has changed in either of their stories, and I don't think anything is going to change. They interdicted an armed robbery in progress. They were fired upon and they returned fire. They were totally within policy, and I resent the inquisitional atmosphere that this is taking on!"

The detective began to sputter. "Who the hell are you to talk to me like that?"

The lieutenant leaned over the table, his lips coming back from his teeth in a wolfish grin. "I'm their unit commander. I'm their lieutenant, *Detective,*" he said acidly and pointedly.

The detective caught the drift. A few more perfunctory questions, and it was over.

It had been good to see the lieutenant stand up for him and Tom that way. Some of the guys had privately wondered if the boss wasn't something of a pogue, an office ass-kisser. It sure hadn't looked that way tonight.

Stan Baranck shifted uncomfortably in his seat. He was wearing his Glock again, taken from his locker, the standard-issue 9 mm he had worn on patrol before volunteering for Stakeout. His SIG .45 had been confiscated—no, wait, that wasn't the right word—taken for evidence. Even though it hadn't been fired, the Professional Standards Unit wanted to make sure. They had taken his shotgun, too, and Tom's Smith & Wesson .45 automatic.

It didn't bother him. They had a job to do, too. He'd get the SIG back tomorrow, after the crime-lab guys had fired a few bullets into the water tank for comparison and gone over it for signs of its having been fired today.

He sat back in the seat as the pickup carried him forward into the looming darkness and thanked God that he was still alive. Hail Mary, full of grace, he thought. Pray for us sinners now and at the hour of our death, amen. Without thinking, he brought his right hand off the steering wheel and crossed himself.

Stan Baranck began to feel the full impact of what he had done, and it surprised him that this burden wasn't heavier.

He had killed. He had shot a human being to death. He had killed a woman.

It didn't seem to bother him a lot. He thought he knew why.

As a young recruit in the police academy, he was told flat out that the day might come when he had to kill a suspect in the line of duty.

"They'll refer to you having killed a citizen," the instructor told them, "because your shooting of a suspect will be recorded by society as 'a citizen killed by police.' But, ladies and gentlemen, I tell you now that this is bullshit. A person who attempts to murder a police officer is no 'citizen.' Such a person, if convicted instead of being shot, would go to prison. They would have no taxes to pay, no vote to cast, no vestige at all of the powers and responsibilities of a citizen.

"Why," the instructor continued, "should it be any different when the officer is forced to fire in self-defense and kill a person who was about to kill them?

It is the act and not the court conviction that means a person who tries to murder a police officer is not a citizen. Don't let anyone make you feel guilty for going home to your family when someone tried to put you into the ground for the worms to nibble on.''

Baranck took that advice to heart, as he always did with anything he was taught by a credible authority. As a youngster growing up in Catholic schools, he took the words of the nuns as gospel. It was the same at the police academy, and at MPD in-service training. Those who knew would be assigned to teach you, and unless you were a fool or a maverick you would listen and learn what they had to impart. This was the natural order of things.

And Stanley Baranck believed in nothing more than the natural order of things. Organization, logic and chain of command were the cornerstones of his existence.

He had grown up in a big family in a blue-collar neighborhood, the son of a factory laborer and a waitress. His parents had taught him not to presume, but to reach instead for things that were reasonably within the realm of possibility. No, they said, you certainly won't be a brain surgeon or a rocket scientist— ''Not the way *your* report cards are coming in, boy!''—but there was no reason not to plan for a nice civil-service job. The post office. The fire department. Sanitation. The police department. ''Someplace,'' his father roared at him, ''where you don't have to worry where your next paycheck is coming from. Where they take care of you and your family with a good pension and good medical benefits and sick time and all that! Someplace that isn't going to go bankrupt and fire you from a job you worked at hard all your life, because some rich, fat-cat executive spent too much of the profits on yachts and limousines and the country club!"

Baranck took that as gospel, too.

His whole family was, to a greater or lesser degree, devoutly Catholic. As an altar boy, he took the catechisms seriously. He learned painstakingly to understand the words of the traditional Latin Mass, because his family would no more have taken Mass in English than they would have eaten meat on a Friday, the shocking new rules of the church notwithstanding.

He was never comfortable in school. Things always seemed to go too fast for him. It was maddeningly frustrating, but he was stoic about it. He was big and strong for his age, and the nuns appreciated the chores he would do when the other kids were at recess.

Sister Mary Catherine told him one day, "Aw, Stanley, don't feel that bad about your report card. There are times in life when a strong back and a good heart mean a lot more than math or spelling or history!" He almost cried as he basked in the glow of her tribute.

The day came—he was twelve years old, the second-biggest kid in the fifth grade, because he'd had to endure the shame of being kept back a year behind the others when he was nine—when he had to fight *the* biggest kid in the Catholic elementary school, a sixth-grader nearly the size of a grown man.

Tim O'Hara was a bully of particular cruelty. Baranck didn't know the word *sadist* then, but later, when he did, Tim's face immediately floated up from his memory.

Tim O'Hara would extort money from the little kids. There were rumors that he had made some of the little boys go into the boys' room with him and do dirty things, unspeakable things. Baranck stayed away from him as much as possible.

But the day had come when he couldn't stay away. Stan Baranck's little sister Ann was playing with a couple of friends when Tim sauntered up to them. He whispered something into the ear of one of Ann's friends. The little girl turned a bright red, an expression of shock on her face, and she tried to slap Tim O'Hara.

O'Hara caught her arm easily in one big hand, laughed boisterously and punched her in the face as hard as he could.

The little girl fell onto her back, semiconscious, her hands coming up instinctively toward the blood that poured from her broken nose.

Stan Baranck was already running forward when his sister Ann jumped between the bully and the fallen girl. Ann was only ten, but her voice was as loud as a grown-up's when she cried, "You stay away from her! You stay away, you dirty thing!"

Tim O'Hara threw back his head and laughed out loud. Then he snarled a string of invective and vile suggestions. He started to reach for Stan's little sister. "Get your head over here. I don't want her gettin' blood all over me now anyway!"

A moment before, Stan Baranck hadn't known what he was going to do. But now, hearing the words spoken to his sister, he did know. With a greater certainty of purpose than he had ever felt before, he knew exactly what he was going to do.

He charged into the bigger boy like a steamroller, his shoulder catching O'Hara in the armpit, bowling him over. The big kid landed on his side, a shocked expression on his face. Somehow Stan Baranck managed to stay on his feet.

"You take that back," he cried. "You can't talk to her that way."

The look of suprrise turned into an evil leer as the big kid lurched to his feet. "Oh, man," he snarled. "You stupid Bohunk! You stay-back retard! I'm gonna kick the shit out of you! I'm gonna kick your balls in, and then I'm gonna make your precious little sister do what I want!"

Even as the big boy swung, Stan Baranck experienced something terrifying. It was as if there was a great pressure inside his head, and a red haze seemed to appear before his eyes.

He caught the powerful punch full on the cheek. He felt a terrible impact but no pain. Everything was clear in front of him, except everything was red.

And he waded into Tim O'Hara.

He could feel the other boy's punches. Impact, but no pain. Yet he felt the shock waves go up his own strong young arms as he punched back, driving his fists into the other boy with every ounce of his strength.

Tim O'Hara staggered back, still flailing, but the look of confidence gone from his face. Baranck followed him, his fists hammering like pile drivers. The impacts felt good, satisfying.

The bigger kid's belly seemed to soften the more he hit it. O'Hara was making "oof" sounds with each of Baranck's punches. He was starting to double over.

Stan Baranck brought his punches higher, going into the ribs. He dug his right heel into the ground as he brought his right fist up into the boy's side in an uppercut, and something crunched under his knuckles. He knew it wasn't his own fist. The bully let out a strangled cry.

He was dimly aware that the other kids were crowding around, cheering him on: "Hit him, Stan!" "Kill him, Stan!" "Don't stop, Stanley, ya got him now!"

He kept punching. The big boy was bent over almost in half, and at last his head was in range of Stan Baranck's fists.

He swung vengefully, swung with every bit of hate he had ever directed inward toward himself for being stupid. With every bit of hate he had ever felt from his father's self-loathing. With every bit of hatred the church had taught him to righteously feel against the forces of darkness.

The impacts were harder, bone on bone. He saw blood erupt from Tim O'Hara's nostrils, saw it pour from his mouth, saw a part of a tooth fly from between the bully's raw, split lips.

And still the red haze was there, and the madness that fueled his arms. He kept punching.

He saw the penguin suits, the black-and-white habits of the nuns. He knew they were watching and he knew they would punish him, perhaps expel him from school. But he didn't care. The red mist seemed to pull him inward after the retreating Tim O'Hara, who stumbled now and fell on his back.

Baranck followed him down. He was on top of the big kid now, his knees pinning O'Hara's heavy arms to the ground. Stan's fists had a mind of their own. He pummeled the boy again.

The shock waves up his arms were harder now with each punch. O'Hara's head was on the ground, and he couldn't roll with the punches. Baranck felt something else break beneath the force of his blows. He saw Tim O'Hara's eyes roll up into their sockets until only the white part showed.

And then, at last, strong hands were dragging him up and back, away from the tormentor. His arms seemed clasped by iron hands, and now they felt suddenly and terribly tired. He kicked out at the boy's unprotected crotch—the filthy things you said to my sister!—but he was being pulled back and away, and the tip of his shoe missed its target harmlessly.

The nuns were dragging him toward the building, backward. He could see another nun pushing the kids away from the bloody and unconscious form of Tim O'Hara. Some of the little girls were hysterical, and Ann was screaming, "You killed him! Stan, you killed him!"

And Stanley Baranck, gasping for breath, screamed back, "I don't care! I hope he's dead! God damn him! God damn him!"

That was when he had fainted.

Even now, as if it were yesterday, he remembered waking up in the dispensary of the Catholic elementary school with Sister Ellen leaning over him, daubing at the cuts on his face with a cotton puff soaked with pungent witch hazel. His jaw ached from the punches he had absorbed when O'Hara hit him, and so did his abdomen. He hadn't felt the brutal blows then, but the red haze was gone now. He realized there had been something awful in the red mist, something that turned him into something different, something that didn't feel pain, something that could destroy and kill.

"Hush," Sister Ellen said soothingly. "It's all right, Stanley. Your parents are here. They're in Mother Superior's office. They and Mother Superior are waiting for you."

He felt overwhelming dread. His parents *and* Mother Superior, waiting for him! Surely this would be the punishment of the damned! He would be expelled! Maybe even excommunicated!

Numbly he let Sister Ellen lead him into Mother Superior's office like the guards leading a condemned man to the execution chamber.

His mother and father were sitting together in front of Mother Superior's big desk. Mother Superior was saying in her stern voice, "Expulsion is the only answer. I am sorry that it has come to this, but he's simply a little animal, a godless little animal! Whether the public-school system has a cage suitable for him, or whether it will have to be the reform school, I don't know. But I do know there is no place for such a wicked little beast here!"

Stanley Baranck felt his heart almost stop and his jaw fall to his chest. "Mother Superior," he squeaked, "No! No! Don't expel me! I—"

Something seemed to choke off his throat, and he couldn't speak anymore. Everyone had turned to stare at him.

And suddenly Mother Superior laughed!

She rose from the desk, sweeping toward him, an intimidating mass of black and white. He knew she was going to strike him, and he closed his eyes and tensed himself for a blow that never came.

Instead, he felt her strong arms gather him toward her in a big hug. "Heavens," she chortled. "*Heavens!* Stanley thinks I was talking about *him!*"

She put her palms on his shoulders and held him at arm's length. "Look me in the eye, Stanley," she said.

He did.

He saw not anger, but a benevolent smile.

"Stanley," she began, "I was talking about Tim, not you. Before you came in, I was telling your parents about some of the things we suspected that wicked little bully of doing. We couldn't prove it—the children he did it to were too afraid to tell—but after they saw you beat him up, they weren't afraid to tell anymore.

"Tim O'Hara will never be seen in this school again. He will be a matter for the police."

She looked at him sadly and shook her head. "I'm sorry. You thought I was going to punish you, not him. Why?"

"Because...because we're not supposed to fight, Mother Superior," Stanley Baranck blurted.

The nun clucked her tongue. "I suppose we don't make that clear enough, do we, Stanley? No, you shouldn't fight for the sake of fighting. But when you face injustice, when you face evil, you should fight. You must fight!

"What you did today, young man, was right. It was just. You fought against evil, and because I think you believed you would lose, I know it took all the more courage for you to do it. I can see the wounds on your face. I know it must have hurt. But you fought as you had to fight, and you prevailed.''

She paused. "Punish *you?*" She hugged him again. "Not hardly, my brave young man, not hardly."

She took a step back and looked at both his parents pointedly before she stared back at him. "Stanley, do *you* feel that you did anything wrong?"

"Well," muttered the boy sheepishly, "I said I wished he was dead. And, God forgive me, Mother Superior, I meant it! That's a sin, isn't it?"

She nodded sagely. "I know, Stanley. And you don't want him to die now, do you? Of course not. You seem to have far more compassion than most grown-ups. Timothy's own father is quite ready to murder him right now, even as we speak. But you forgive. You are a wise young man."

He looked down at the floor and shook his head. "No, Mother Superior, I'm not smart at all. I'm stupid. Even Tim said so."

Mother Superior laughed out loud. "That's not what I said, my boy! I said you were wise! Smart people are a dime a dozen. Timothy was smart, in his way—he was certainly able to get away with his evil long enough, thanks to his cunning.

"No, Stanley, don't worry about being smart. You are *wise*. You know what is important and you do what you must do. That is more important."

Stanley Baranck looked up at her. "Sister Mary Catherine said I have a strong back and a good heart," he said hopefully.

Mother Superior laughed. "Well, Stanley, I don't know about the strong back, but the wisdom of the good heart should be more than enough to get you through this world of ours. You know what? I think one day you might make an excellent policeman.

"No, don't look at me with such surprise. Many, many policemen in this city were in this school once. You don't need a lot of book learning to be a good policeman. You need the strength and the courage to protect others, and the sense of justice to know when you must use force and when you mustn't.

"It's time for you to go home with your parents now, Stanley, for you've had a very difficult day. But some time a long time from now, you remember that I stood here today and told you that you would make an excellent policeman."

It had been years and years since Stan had thought of that day, but the memory came to him now unbidden, and it was welcome. Welcome and timely, as he reviewed his past.

After graduating high school, Stan Baranck tried college, but that wasn't for him. He got a job in the factory where his dad worked, but he couldn't see the same grind that had reduced his father to weekly binge drinking just to get away from the daily slavery. He was considering the military when the girl he loved, Sharon, became pregnant.

Abortion, of course, was out of the question. They were married. He was twenty by then, and he remembered Mother Superior saying that he'd be a good policeman.

He passed the MPD exam by the skin of his teeth and managed to get through the academy. He wasn't first in his class or even in the middle.

On the street, however, the FTO's gave him top grades. "Probationary Officer Baranck has excellent street judgment," said one.

"Probationary Officer Baranck seems to have an intuitive sense of what it is that we do, and a natural ability to defuse potentially violent encounters by talking calmly and slowly," said another.

"Probationary Officer Baranck seems slow at first," wrote a third, "but after a day or two with him you realize that he is not slow, but deliberate and methodical. It is this FTO's experience that the deliberate and methodical officer is the officer least likely to make mistakes. Therefore, this writer wholeheartedly endorses Officer Baranck's early removal from probationary status to full-police-officer status."

Their comments defined the man. Slow at first in the eyes of those who didn't know him, he was methodical and deliberate to those who had worked with him on the street. No cop who worked with Baranck even as a raw rookie could remember him making a serious mistake or a hasty judgment.

But Baranck always feared the day he would.

He never even thought of taking the sergeant's test. He knew he was not cut out to be a supervisor. Telling others what to do was something he wasn't comfortable with. Advice he would give. Orders were something else.

He worked his station competently, never missing a day except when Sharon was giving birth again and when Sharon's father died and he had to go to the funeral. He never seemed to catch anything infectious. If he had, he would have taken his sick time for fear of infecting brother and sister officers. If it was just an injury and he could still work, he would come in. He saw no point in suffering at home when he could be suffering no more doing his job and pulling his weight and fulfilling his responsibilities. It took a year for the union steward to convince him that he should take his accumulated sick leave and compensatory time and be with his family like any other sane cop.

The only extraordinary leave time he took was when he got the fractured skull.

He still remembered that night, most of it anyway. He was a fourth-year patrolman, responding to a bar fight in Liberty City. The initial cops on the scene called for backup, but it wasn't an urgent signal zero—officer under deadly attack—so he hadn't been too worried. Still, as his partner drove he reached into his attaché case and pulled out the steel insert for his Second Chance bulletproof vest.

Sharon had made him swear that he would always wear his vest to work, and he would never have violated such an oath. The bullet-resistant Kevlar seemed enough; the steel "trauma plate" was heavy and awkward, so he had reached the personal compromise that he would keep it in the attaché case every MPD cop used for his paperwork, and open his shirt and tuck it into his vest any time he was going in on something unusually dangerous. This seemed to fit the criterion.

There were already two other MPD cars and a green Metro Dade county unit on the scene when they pulled up in front of Fat's Bar and Grille. Making sure his gun was securely snapped into his holster, Stan grabbed the PR-24 baton and tucked it under his arm. He followed his partner inside, after the cops who were already there.

The place was in an uproar, as wild as a kaleidoscope and as loud as the Tower of Babel.

He'd seen bar fights at Fat's before, but nothing like this. The place was up for grabs like a John Wayne movie. Everyone was yelling, and the din was unintelligible. The mirror behind the bar had been blown out, and only shards remained of what had been row on row of liquor bottles on the many wooden shelves behind the counter area.

The floor was slick with beer and blood. He could smell both.

Of the people he could see, at least half a dozen were down, sprawled under the tables. Some of them were bloody and silent. Some were bloody and moaning.

There were only eight cops there to deal with what looked like fifty brawlers. Stan saw that one green-uniformed Metro cop and one blue-clad MPD officer were dragging one huge man with a shaved head back out the door. Another green and blue pair was struggling to pull a big, bearded black dude off some downed victim he couldn't see. His own partner was behind him. That left two city cops unaccounted for.

He peered through the smoky craziness. There, toward the back! Two guys in blue, one with his hat knocked off, overwhelmed by what looked like a tide of angry black men. One of the cops was black, one white.

He yelled to his partner, "Come on!" Then he waded in.

Someone grabbed his left arm. He swung the baton with an upward chop, catching someone's wrist with a painful crack. The man cried out and fell away from him. Baranck pressed forward.

A fist came at him from nowhere. Instinctively he brought his right arm up, the baton already reinforcing the arm. A fist hit the unyielding polycarbonate surface of the baton, and there was a crunching sound as the knuckle broke.

Baranck pressed forward.

He saw a muscular, dark bare forearm holding a long-necked beer bottle. Baranck spun the baton forward, the handle turning in his palm as the long end snaked out viciously from under his elbow in an arc that intercepted the threat. The bottle disintegrated into a shower of broken glass and beer and blood, and the lacerated hand that had been holding it seemed to disappear into the darkness.

Still, Stan Baranck drove forward. He kept the baton slashing in front of him, like a machete cutting a path, with forward and reverse spins. People scrambled out of the way. Every now and then there was the blunt smack, usually followed by a cry of pain, but a path seemed to clear miraculously in front of Stan Baranck as he doggedly plodded toward the two embattled brother cops.

He was only a few feet away now. The white cop emerged from the crowd, his face covered with blood. A brutal blow from something hard and sharp had ripped open his forehead, dropping a crimson flap of scalp down over his eyes. He was shaking his head like a blind man, both hands clutching his service weapon into his holster to make sure no one took it away from him.

Baranck's partner moved in from his left. "I got him, Stan," he yelled. "I'm gettin' him out of here! Follow us back!"

"I can't," Baranck screamed. "They got the other cop!"

Someone yelled, "Come back, Stan! You can't save him!"

And he yelled back, "The hell I can't!"

The L-shaped black side-handle baton that someone had taken from the white cop loomed up and over the crowd, slashing down like a tomahawk. Baranck couldn't see who was wielding it, but he heard a thud and a cry and saw the black cops's face seem to disappear under a sea of surging bodies. He heard someone scream, "Kill that Uncle Tom pig!"

For the second time in his life, the red haze descended before the eyes of Stanley Baranck.

It was like the time in the school yard. An unnatural power seemed to surge within him, churning his arms forward. With his left hand he punched someone in the face and saw the guy stumble back. With his right hand he slashed the baton sideways, forward and back, feeling the old, familiar impact shock traveling up his arm.

People lurched, grunted, fell away from in front of him. He was now only a few feet away from where the gang of scumbags was piling on the cop. He saw fists rise and fall, and then he saw that damn baton arc upward again and slash back down toward the officer.

The red haze grew more intense.

Baranck slogged forward. Something tugged at his holster, and he chopped viciously downward with the baton. He was rewarded by a shriek of pain and a sudden release of pressure as something went crunch at the moment the baton struck home.

He was almost there. He saw the baton rise above the crowd again. He swung his own PR-24 again as hard as he could, and he met the intersecting sweep of the stolen baton with a crack as loud as a pistol shot. The vibrations quivered up his arm from the impact, but he saw the offending baton arc lazily away into the darkness behind everyone, torn from the hand of the offender.

He heard someone scream "Get his gun! Blow them pigs' brains out, man!"

He didn't know if they were talking about him or the black cop.

He didn't care.

The rage drew him forward, the baton still slashing unabated. Two more men felt its sting and staggered back, clutching their traumatized arms.

Someone jumped in front of him and grabbed the extended end of his baton with both hands, trying to wrench it out of his hands. It was a black man, big, his eyes bloodshot. Or was that just the red haze?

There was no time to think about it. Baranck brought his left hand down on the man's two fists, which were holding the end of his baton. That created a leverage point. Then, with every ounce of his weight, Stan Baranck crush-gripped the handle that stuck out from the side of his baton and swung it up and over, bringing the short end of the L-shaped stick into the man's face.

He saw rather than felt the short end of the PR-24 peel the man's nose halfway off and break away the two buck teeth that protruded from his mouth. The movement continued, and he felt the end of the PR-24 rake down the man's sternum. There was a ripping sound as cartilage gave way.

With a choking scream, the man fell back and down, clutching at his chest, unmindful of his ruined face. Baranck charged forward like a tank, realizing that his feet were stomping into the man's already broken rib cage as he went over him.

He didn't care.

Now he could see the black MPD officer. The man was down, almost out, his face a bloody mask. He had curled himself into a fetal position, lying on his right side to put his body weight onto the gun he was trying to keep in the holster with both hands. At least four different arms were clawing at the gun, and someone screamed again, "Get his gun! Blow his fuckin' brains out!"

The red haze grew darker. The rage inside him grew darker, too.

He remembered thinking, You can't do that to my brother!

Only later, when it was long over, would he read the statements of the witnesses and realize he had said it out loud.

There were four of them, crouching over the downed officer like wolves. They looked up to see the maddened, bloodied cop who was bearing down on them.

But it was too late.

Forward spin! The PR-24 caught the first one on the ear, cracking the skull and breaking the jaw at the mandibular notch. The man toppled back, unconscious.

Reverse spin! The backward swing caught the second would-be cop-killer square in the forehead, creating a hairline skull fracture and a massive concussion. His eyes rolled up into their sockets as he fell backward, senseless.

Forward spin! The third suspect was rising to meet this new cop threat when the baton smashed into the side of his neck with enough force to dislodge the sixth cervical vertebra and traumatize the spinal cord. The man fell, temporarily paralyzed, his arms going up into the same Thorburn's reflex as President Kennedy's had when the first bullet struck him. The hands fluttered at his throat even after he passsed out.

Reverse spin! There was another batlike crack as the heavy polycarbonate baton shattered the fourth man's lower jaw and blasted his false teeth in a ten-foot arc of bloody porcelain powder. The agony was unbearable, and he fell on his face clawing at his ruined mouth.

There was no one over the semiconscious cop anymore, and Stan Baranck stood over him, straddling him defiantly, waiting for the next one to attack him.

He didn't have to wait long. One man lunged with an expert uppercut to the solar plexus. Baranck's arms had grown tired from the exertion, and he couldn't swing the baton fast enough to intercept.

Instead, the man's knuckles smashed full power into Baranck's steel trauma plate. The man screamed as the proximal joints of his fingers turned into shards and dust against laminar steel that was rated to stop .30-caliber M-1 bullets.

Baranck threw a short jab with the end of his PR-24 into the man's belly. The attacker's stomach closed in on itself so violently that his projectile vomit seemed to throw him back like a jet engine. Baranck was oblivious to the vomitus that sprayed over him. He had been puked on by drunks in bar fights before.

It seemed to be over. Baranck was facing the door of Fat's Bar now, and that door burst inward with what seemed like more blue uniforms than the Seventh Cavalry.

Stan Baranck took a breath. The red haze was beginning to thin to pink. He looked down at his feet. The bloodied black cop he was straddling was out cold, but at least he was breathing.

He heard someone yell "Look out!"

He snapped his head up just in time to see the blunt end of a pool cue coming in toward his skull. It seemed like slow motion. He tried to raise his PR-24 to block it, but his arms were too tired.

He saw stars like an explosion when it smashed into his head. He heard a crunching sound and he knew instantly that his skull was fractured and he was going to die.

The PR-24 was gone from his hands, and he couldn't remember dropping it. But the face of the black man in front of him was twisted in rage, and he saw the man cock the cue again. He knew that the other cops couldn't reach them in time to stop it, and that this time the blow would spray the brain matter right out of his head.

Suddenly both of Stan Baranck's hands were around the man's throat, and he was crushing full force, and the red haze was back, a darker crimson than ever and growing darker still.

Then they were both on the floor, even though Baranck couldn't remember them falling, and the man's eyes were bulging in horror. He didn't have the pool cue anymore and he was clutching impotently at Baranck's hands. But Stan didn't care; he just crushed and crushed and crushed with his hands until the red haze grew so dark that it became black and almost everlasting.

Stan Baranck woke up the next day in Jackson Memorial Hospital. The doctors told him he had sustained a fractured skull but he was going to be okay.

The cops, who were sitting patiently waiting for him to regain consciousness, told him the rest. How he had saved the black cop's life. How even after he was out cold it took what seemed like the whole rest of the precinct to pry his hands from the unconscious guy's throat. Baranck had crushed the guy's larynx, and the paramedics had had to do a tracheotomy to save the dude's life, which seemed like a waste of good paramedic training in their collective opinion.

He had also set what every cop present believed was the record for the number of bar fighters ever laid out flat by a single cop in the city of Miami.

His sergeant told him, "They're kind of still counting, Stan. Put it this way—when the chief paramedic got there, he said 'Holy shit, we ain't got enough ambulances for all these assholes! We gotta set up a M.A.S.H unit here at Fat's!'"

It was funny...afterward.

Baranck was given plenty of time off to get better. The recovery was uneventful. He didn't even have headaches anymore.

He never felt badly about the men he had hurt. They were all trying to hurt him worse. And they were going to murder his brother officer if he didn't stop them.

Mother Superior would have approved, he knew.

Eventually he went back to work and rebuilt his exemplary record of almost no sick time. He enjoyed his job. What he enjoyed most was going home at night to Sharon and the kids. Taking the kids to church. He never wore his off-duty gun into church, because it struck him that it would be vaguely sacrilegious. Church was to watch his children learn about peace and fairness and the natural order of things. Not about guns and hitting and killing...

Killing. He had killed someone tonight. He had killed a *woman.*

He shook his head, as if to clear the memory. But he could still see the flash in front of the muzzle of his Remington shotgun, could still see her falling back, the way the man he'd hit had fallen back from his baton that night at Fat's Bar and Grille.

But this was different. Those men had gotten back up, at least eventually. This one wasn't getting up again. *She* was dead.

Stan Baranck scowled. It wasn't his fault she was a woman. He had thought he was shooting a man. Would it have been different if he had known his target was female?

He didn't know.

He didn't care.

All he knew was that he had done right; he had been a good cop, and he was going home to his family to be a good husband and a good father. A *live* husband and a *live* father.

He was coming up to his exit. He flicked on the turn signal and glided onto the exit ramp. He was less than a mile from home now.

It occurred to him that he could get back on the highway, go up two more exits and be at the church. It was late, but the priest would always answer if he rang the bell at the rectory.

He dismissed the thought. There was no need to bother Father Dunn.

It wasn't as if he had committed any sin that needed to be confessed.

Baranck steered toward home. He suddenly felt very tired.

He wondered how he would tell Sharon about having shot a person to death. A woman. He wondered how he'd tell the kids.

He shuddered. It seemed as if Sharon was right and he was wrong. They had spent a lot of time talking about it, alone, after the kids were in bed, before he decided to volunteer for Stakeout.

"Stan, I'm afraid," Sharon said earnestly. "It's bad enough you could come up against armed robbers any shift when you're on patrol. With this, you'll be *hunting* for armed robbers. Men with guns, ready to kill! You might be dealing with them every day!"

Clasping her hands gently, he replied, "Darling, I've thought about that. You know what the difference is? If I have to deal with an armed robber tomorrow, I won't be expecting it. We don't even have shotguns in the cars, and a lot of us are working just one to a car now. If something happens to you alone, when you're not expecting it, you're not prepared to deal with it.

"Now, with this Stakeout Squad they're talking about, it would be teamwork. A whole bunch of cops, all expecting the worst, all equipped with heavy weapons and heavy armor and all of that. All the turf scoped out and everything. Probably knowing what was going to happen beforehand, 'cause they would have gotten a tip or they wouldn't be there in the first place, right?

"Honey, you know how important it is for me to come home to you and the kids every night. You don't think I'd risk that, do you? We'll have more control, not less."

There was a long silence.

"Tell me the truth, darling," Sharon said. "Is there some special reason you want to take this assignment?"

He took a deep breath and answered, "Yes. Yes, there is.

"Sharon, I've never been a fast decision maker, you know? Regular police work on the street, well, it's unpredictable. You never know what's going to happen, when, how quick. I always worry that sometime, something's going to happen so fast I won't have time to think it out, you know? That I won't have time to figure out the right thing, the just thing.

"You know what I like about Stakeout? The way they're talking, everything is going to be all planned out ahead. All set up for dealing with the worst-case scene that could ever happen, you know? All the decisions made beforehand.''

He took another breath. ''It's so much better that way, you know, Sharon? You know?''

She lowered her head and after a moment said, ''Yes, darling. I love you. And I know. And if it's what you want, it's all right.''

Replaying that conversation in his head, Baranck pulled the pickup into the driveway of their suburban home. All the lights were out except the porch light, Sharon's signal to him that this portal was lit for him, only for *him*.

It made him feel warm.

He thought back to the shooting. To the orange ball of fire that came from one of the guns they were facing. Then he was looking down his own gun barrel and through his own sheet of orange flame, and the person with the gun was falling away. He pumped the action and swung toward the other one but he...she...*it* was already down.

Not until later, after they talked about it at the station, did they realize that Baranck hadn't heard West's gunfire, and West hadn't heard his partner's shot.

Baranck was satisfied. He had made the right decision. They had had a plan, and they did what they were trained to do, and they had followed the proper order of things.

He and West had done the right thing.

He wondered what would have happened if something like that had come upon him on patrol. Could he have reacted as quickly as he had with the Stakeout training? Probably not.

Could he have fired one perfect shot in that one unforgiving moment with the department-issue Glock pistol, and stop the threat as decisively as he had with the one easily placed blast from his Stakeout shotgun? Probaby not.

Stan Baranck stood in the cool night air, looking at his house, his family's house. He remembered that orange flash from the woman's gun. He wondered what it would feel like to have a bullet burn through you after you looked at one of those. To have the red haze turn black and never turn light again. To go into death forever.

He believed in an afterlife. But he believed in life, too. He wasn't ready to leave Sharon and the kids. He didn't think they were ready to have him leave, either.

People had told him that after you shot somebody, you were going to have nightmares and sleepless nights and all kinds of other problems. He figured he'd take it as it came. He should have had the same things with all the other people he'd had to mess up, according to those same experts, but he hadn't. He had always gotten a pretty good night's sleep once all the adrenalin from the fight got out of his system.

He didn't see any reason that tonight should be any different.

He would go to church on Sunday. He would say a Hail Mary for the woman he had shot. It was the least he could do.

But he felt no burden. He had done his duty. It was the natural order of things. He had followed the rules. There was nothing to feel bad about.

He looked up at the night sky. He still wasn't sure what he was going to say to Sharon. What he was going to say to the kids. How he would explain shooting some woman to death in the line of his duty.

He wondered, for the first time, if *she* had had any kids.

He dismissed the thought. There was nothing he could do about it now.

Should he go to church tomorrow? Take confession?

Baranck couldn't see a reason why. You only took confession for a sin. He couldn't see anything he had done wrong.

It was over.

Stan Baranck squared his shoulders and began to walk toward the front door of his and his family's home.

Slowly. Carefully. Deliberately. Methodically.

At least there was one good thing about this time.

This time there had not been any of that terrible red haze. . . .

9

John Blaisdell could not contain his elation. He read the *Miami Crier* column for what must have been the tenth time in an hour.

Miami Justice
Police Death Squad Strikes Again
by Oliver Teasdale

Shots rang out in the parking lot, and two women lay dead. Police say they are victims of the crack cocaine habit that drove them to bank robbery.

Others say different. Others say they were the victims of the police themselves.

Miami Police Department's Stakeout Squad has struck again. Announced by Chief John Kearn as a crime-fighting measure, the squad is comprised of some twenty officers forming three teams.

All, say police, are volunteers.

You have to wonder what makes a police officer volunteer to ambush and shoot to death the citizens they are sworn to protect. That happens in South America. It happens in the Philippines.

Now it is happening here, in Miami.

Sure, cops have to shoot back sometime. That's why they carry guns. But they are supposed to shoot only when there is no other resort.

The die marker with tear gas in it had already gone off. The witnesses describe the cloud of red smoke that enveloped them moments before the police opened fire with sawed-off shotguns and large-caliber assault pistols. The two women had to be blind and helpless at the moment of their slaying.

Chief Kearn admits that NYPD abandoned their stakeout squad more than twenty years ago amid allegations of racism and excessive force. All of their victims were black.

LAPD still uses a stakeout squad. But one courageous attorney, Chip Haldahl, is trying to sue it out of existence with lawsuits on behalf of the people it has killed. He has not yet succeeded in that, but he has succeeded in identifying what a police stakeout unit really is.

Haldahl calls them death squads.

So far, twenty men and women with enough assault weapons to take over Third World countries have stopped a grand total of two bank robberies, committed by amateurs. Robberies that almost certainly would have been solved anyway.

And at what price? Two young boys are dead. One was armed with nothing more than a toy pistol. Two young women, slaves of a drug habit this city's police could not or did not protect them from, are dead, too. Police say they shot first, though they might have fired to frighten away the people they couldn't see in the swirling red smoke. The people who were firing high-powered bullets into their bodies.

It *is* certain that temporarily blind people cannot pose a credible threat of marksmanship to police officers behind the cover of their cars and wearing their bulletproof vests.

Perhaps our Stakeout Squad just can't resist an easy target, the way some "sportsmen" can't resist a sitting duck.

At least they haven't shot any innocent bystanders yet. But perhaps that's just a matter of time. So far, the only thing you can credit the Stakeout Squad with is marksmanship. They have fired seven shots in action, and inflicted seven fatal wounds, killing four victims. If that doesn't add up, it's because some were shot more than once.

Roseanne Palisi was shot twice. Little Billy Maloney was shot three times. That figures out to about seventy-five percent overkill.

But what do you expect from a death squad?

John Blaisdell threw his head back on the plush sofa and cried aloud, "I *love* it!"

Curled up next to him on the sofa, nuzzling his shoulder, Kimberley gave him an eager-to-please smile. It hurt only a little. The bruises on her face were starting to go down.

"Hey, John," she said, trying to be part of his cheerful mood, "you think I ought to do like those two broads? Do a little bank robbery? How do you think I'd do?"

Blaisdell sneered at her. She cringed. That usually meant he was going to hit her again. "Hey," she squeaked anxiously, "I didn't mean nothin'!"

And then his grin was back. He ran his fingers idly through her hair. "Tell you what, Kim," he said softly. "I've got an idea. I think you absolutely *can* make a contribution to our little team, a bigger contribution than you've been making."

She smiled nervously, hopefully. "Sure, John! Whaddaya want me to do?"

He grinned ruthlessly. "I'll tell you in a minute. First I need you to make your primary contribution to the well-being of our organization."

She looked puzzled. "I don't think I understand."

Suddenly the smile was gone from his face. He grabbed her by the hair and jerked her head back until she cried out.

"I mean give me some head, you stupid bitch," he growled, and forced her head brutally down into his lap.

ALONE WITH THE CHIEF in his office, Ken Bartlett handed him the *Miami Crier* section with Teasdale's column in it back to Kearn and shook his head. "Where does he get that garbage?"

Kearn chuckled without humor. "The stuff on the other stakeout squads? I doubt the little weasel had the journalistic initiative to do the research himself. The mayor or one of his punk lackeys fed it to him. Orlando hasn't been too happy with me since I pulled this on him."

"It took balls to do that," the lieutenant said. "He could have fired you. He still might."

"This is true," said Kearn. "And it would bother me if I cared. You see, what I believe His Honor the mayor has realized is that this city is fed up with violent crime. I didn't see the Stakeout Squad as any kind of gesture. I saw it as a final answer to some of the particularly vicious maggots that are preying on the people of this community. Maggots like the Shotgun Gang. I absolutely believe that the rank and file of the people are behind us on this, just as they're in favor of mandatory sentencing, and the death penalty for certain crimes. If Orlando fires me, so be it. I've built up enough cumulative retirement in my career to sustain me. I can always get one of those fat director-of-security jobs with a Fortune 500 corporation. I'll survive, and so will my family.

"I would also, once fired, be free to run for mayor myself when Orlando comes up for reelection. Every violent crime between my firing and election day would be another campaign issue for me. It didn't take me four months here to figure out that the two primary voting blocs in this city are first the Hispanics, and second the blacks. The Hispanics who voted in the mayor hold one issue higher than any other—law and order. I could take his constituency right away from him, and I think he knows that. Combined with me being a truly credible black candidate who would have been fired for using strong measures to protect the overwhelmingly black victim population from violent crime, I would have the second major bloc. The polls show that violent crime is also the overwhelming fear of the white voters. It would be a landslide.

"So I don't think Orlando will be stupid enough to fire me just yet. Unless, of course, the whole community turns against me, and against us. Unless, of course, the Stakeout Squad kills a few more kids and a few more ladies.''

Kearn stopped talking and stared pointedly at Bartlett.

''That's not fair, Chief,'' the lieutenant said. ''Did you say 'ladies'? The two that went down outside the bank were scum. Their records showed everything from assault-and-battery to child abuse and child neglect to welfare fraud. They were a couple of vicious bitches who thought *Thelma and Louise* was a training film. The kids? The Michaelson boy had a clean record. It's obvious the Maloney kid put him up to it. *That* one had a rap sheet that would have taken two file drawers to hold when he turned eighteen and they closed his juvenile record. If he'd ever made eighteen, the way he was going.

''Both those cases, my guys were looking down gun barrels and being fired on. Look, I command the damn Stakeout Squad, and I've got mixed feelings about the whole idea, but these were clean shoots. It rubs me raw to see this garbage like Teasdale's column.''

Kearn smiled gently. ''I agree. And I don't think anyone can say that I haven't stood by your people on these two. What I am saying is this—a couple more dead kids, even one incident that just *looks* like a bad shoot, and the Stakeout Squad is dead and so am I.''

''And so is everyone connected with it, is that what you're saying?''

''Let me put it this way,'' the chief replied. ''I saw an interesting corollary when I studied up on this and compared the stakeout unit in New York City with the one in Los Angeles. In New York the team members were patrolmen who were promised promotion to detective if all went well. All *didn't* go well. Press like these Teasdale columns killed the squad. The commissioner who had approved Stakeout was out on his ass, and the very first act of his replacement was to eradicate the squad. Not one of those members became detectives. Not one of them ever saw a promotion to the end of their careers.

"In L.A. it worked. Not until around 1990 did they start getting crap from the media. The department stood by them, and every damn one became detectives, and their commanders were on excellent career tracks. You hear what I'm saying, Ken?"

"Sure," the lieutenant answered cynically, "but don't worry, sir, I won't take it as a threat."

"I think," the chief said evenly, "it would be better if you did."

TO REACH THE GHETTO of Liberty City, John Blaisdell and Chen Ho Lee drove north out of downtown Miami as if heading for the Hialeah Racetrack, and then cut northwest. "We're looking for the check-cashing joint at Northwest Twenty-Second Avenue and Ninety-first Street," he told Chen. "Moss says Thursday's the time to hit it. All the welfare checks come in in the morning, and there's a big supply of cash there by ten a.m."

"I don't like it, Win," Chen muttered. "We're talkin' about ghetto blacks that run a tough business. They gotta be armed to the teeth in there. We'd be askin' for a firefight."

"That can be arranged," Win answered tersely, "but don't worry about it. I got an idea from that Teasdale guy. Wait till you see it. By the time they've figured out what's goin' on, we'll be long gone."

SERGEANT MIKE COHEN and Lieutenant Ken Bartlett locked the unmarked Chevy behind them as they got out onto the steamy sidewalks of Liberty City. They were wearing plainclothes and had left their jackets in the car. They wore their .45s openly on their hips, next to the gold Miami Police shields clipped to their belts.

The ambulances were already gone. The crowd still pressed against the yellow strips of plastic marked Police Scene—Do Not Cross. They were at the corner of Ninety-first Street and Northwest Twenty-second Avenue.

Sergeant Dan Boyle, Miami Police Homicide, met them in the doorway of the check-cashing office. "Mike, Ken," he greeted them. "Too bad some of your Stakeout people weren't in here this morning."

"I wish," Bartlett grunted. "What've we got?"

"Two dead, two wounded. Shotguns. Got away with close to a hundred grand that we know of. Word is, the place is a bookie joint, too. The check-cashing business gives them a cover to be running money through here. The hundred grand is pretty much official, according to the books. It's the day to cash the welfare checks, and around here that sounds like the right volume."

Cohen asked, "Perps?"

"You'll love it," Boyle answered. "Females. Mostly tall. Two black, one white, one Asian on the inside. Nobody got a really good look at the two in the getaway car. Apparently three of them waited in line at the counter, and the fourth, the Asian, kind of stood back. She was the layoff person.

"The first three put a shotgun round into the ceiling, yelled that they knew the clerks had guns, anybody went for one they'd blow their heads off. Scooped the cash into the same big cloth shopping bags they'd apparently had the sawed-offs hidden in when they entered.

"It went smooth at first, from what we gather. They took the money and ran. They were getting out the door when two of the clerks vaulted over the counter with pistols to chase them. That's when the Asian broad opened up. Twenty-gauge. Come on over here."

Stepping into the foyer of the check-cashing office, they could see the two men on the floor. Both young, both black, both dead. They lay in what seemed to be a lake of gelid, congealing blood.

One was facedown, head toward the door. There were tiny holes clustered in the back of his neck. The head itself was exploded. Bits of bloody gray brain matter and glistening skull fragments were sprayed around the corpse in a five-foot radius. There was the chalk outline of a pistol on the floor, marked by the evidence technicians before they'd picked up the gun the man had dropped.

A step and a half behind him lay the second body, sprawled faceup. There were bloody holes across the shoulders and neck. The upper part of the head seemed intact, but the face had been blasted apart, split down the middle as if by a cleaver but with the flesh spread as if the blow had somehow come from inside the head. The eye sockets were empty pools of blood.

The homicide sergeant continued, "The Asian apparently figured these guys would be wearing vests. All the shots were high—shoulders, neck, heads. The witnesses say she fired faster than hell. Five shots. They both went right down.

"Then one of the white ones, outside by the car, turned around and ran back. Shoved the muzzle of a pump gun against the first one's head and just exploded the skull. Pumped once, stepped over the body, stuck the muzzle in the mouth of this second guy that was lying on his back and pulled the trigger again."

The detective gestured to his right. There were two spent shotgun shells, green plastic with gleaming brass bottoms, lying near the wall of the foyer where they'd been ejected from the weapon that had issued the coups de grace. None of the cops needed an evidence technician to recognize them. They were Remington buckshot rounds, the same as the department issued them for their own shotguns.

Cohen shook his head. "And these were *women?*"

"Looked that way at first, Mike," the homicide sergeant answered. "But the more you get into it with the witnesses, they talk about the real harsh voice the leader used to tell them they knew they had guns and they'd better not touch them. Remember, it was mostly women in here cashing checks when it went down. Couple of them said the killers didn't walk like women, didn't move like women."

Bartlett said, "It's the Shotgun Gang."

Cohen cocked an eyebrow. "The Shotgun Gang in drag? That's bizarre, Ken."

"Bizarre, hell. Asian woman with a 20-gauge. One of the killers in the Grove robbery, the ArmorDade thing, was an Asian man with a 20-gauge." He gestured inside. In the middle of the office floor, chalk circled by the technicians, were five slim yellow shell casings. Yellow was the ammunition industry's color code for 20-gauge shells.

"It gets weirder," the sergeant said. "They left a note for you guys. Evidence people have it in the back, not that they'll get any useful prints off it. Come on. Step over the blood puddle and I'll show you."

As they walked, Bartlett said, "You told us two dead, two wounded. How bad?"

"Not too bad, thank God," the detective answered. "One woman had a helluva bloody contusion on her face, looks like she was hit by the wadding from one of the 20-gauge rounds. Guy behind the counter took a couple of stray pellets in the shoulder, probably from when the Asian hosed the two armed clerks with the 20-gauge."

In the back room jumpsuited evidence technicians were going over the letter that had been left. They held it by the edges with tweezers. The letters had been painstakingly picked out with a penknife from a newspaper, pieced together and glued to a sheet of paper.

The note read:

Dear police death squad
Sorry we missed you Here's some women you won't kill today Sorry we didn't have any kids for you to kill either

                        Killer shotgun bitches from hell

CHIEF KEARN looked across his desk at his Stakeout Squad commander. "What do you make of it, Ken?"

"Shotgun Gang, no question in my mind," Bartlett answered. "You know where it said 'police death squad' on the note? The words were cut out of the headline for Teasdale's column in the *Crier* the other day. These bastards are local, right under our noses, and they are some kind of arrogant. Looks like they've taken the Stakeout Squad personal."

"That's fair," the chief answered sarcastically. "I take *those* bastards personal! What do you think about the angle, hitting the check-cashing office?"

"Good point," answered Bartlett. "It's almost a pattern of guys trying not to have a pattern. Couple banks. Couple armored trucks. Now the check-cashing service. Maybe they just now figured out how damn much money they got in those places certain days. Be a good bet for some stakeouts."

"I agree," said the chief. "Go for it."

"Well, now, sir," said Bartlett, unable to keep the sarcasm out of his voice. "Let's not forget the Shotgun Gang hits have been coming faster than usual, but before, their M.O. was one robbery about every six weeks. Now, in the next six weeks, I'm not too sure how many white guys are going to be dumb enough to knock over armed stores in the heart of the ghetto. Most anybody we interdict is likely to be totally unrelated to the Shotgun Gang. And they're most likely to be black. You *sure* that you're ready for the squad to start smoking African-American folks? You sure it'll be politically correct?"

The chief's hand slapped down hard on the desk. "Goddammit, Ken! You're as black as I am! You about to tell me we shouldn't put stakeouts in to protect African-Americans? Every one of the people shot in the check-cashing hit was black. One of the guards they murdered in the Grove was black. They don't get protection?''

The lieutenant met his angry gaze. ''Is this where you give me the lecture about how seventy percent of the crime in this city is black on black, and we're going to protect the people from whatever color scumbag comes after them? Tom West gives me the same stuff. But weren't we in here a few days ago, talking politics and survival? Talking about how the Stakeout Squad in New York got flushed down the toilet, and the careers of every man on it, because everyone they had to shoot was black? You told me the other day, you had enough pension built up from your police jobs before you came here that you could afford to get fired. Well, I *can't,* Chief, and neither can any of the three sergeants and the eighteen cops and detectives I got working with me on this!''

Kearn shook his head. ''I was hoping the man I picked to command a unit as sensitive as this one would have a little more enthusiasm for it.''

''Yeah,'' spit back the angry lieutenant, ''because you got four months with the Miami Police Department. Well, I got more than that! They ever actually fill you in on how police shootings go on this job?

''Every riot in this city, like we discussed the other day, came out of a white cop shooting a black suspect. Every one of those, except maybe when Mac-Duffee got beat to death, was a justifiable shooting. And every one of those cops went to trial for manslaughter. Damn near all were acquitted. And not a one ever got back on the job, not on this department and not on any other. This department throws you to the wolves if you're in a shooting that gets bad press.

"I've got eighteen line cops out there who know their job is going to make them get into shootings. Every shooting so far has been controversial. All four went down with guns in their hands—hell, even the plastic one looked real as hell till the shooting was over—so there probably won't be any indictments or offers of proof coming out of the state attorney's office over them. But they know what's in the wind. You want them to be enthusiastic?

"See, you got a catch-22 here, Chief. We had to take people into this unit that I didn't want. On Team Two alone, Harrington strikes me as a snake, and I've got real strong suspicions that Cross has a yellow streak. And I've got precisely one black guy on Team Two, Tom West.

"You know why it's like that? Because out of thirteen hundred to pick through, we didn't have enough volunteers to make up the kind of team I wanted. You know why we don't have too many black cops on Stakeout? Because there's one fundamental difference between black cops and white ones, and you see it from the first day of the academy.

"Your white rookie joined the force for excitement, adventure. TV showed him life was going to be fights and shoot-outs and car chases and all the female flesh he could handle. They're in it for the adventure, the young ones anyway.

"But you talk to one of the few black kids you can recruit for this job out of Overtown or Liberty City, and you know what they'll tell you? They've seen the streets the white kids haven't seen yet—the vicious punks that sold their souls for crack and would kill you as soon as look at you. The kids who have to steal to eat. They join the job to help, because the job gives them a power to help that they wouldn't get any other way. And you expect them to volunteer for an assignment that will have them killing their own people? To blow some seventeen-year-old kid's face off because he couldn't get a job, and the welfare check got stolen, and his momma asked him to get some food, feed his little brothers and sisters?

"Come *on*, Chief. I see the reason for Stakeout. I'm managing it the best I can. I'm just not sure how much enthusiasm you're expecting, and if I don't have enough, I guess you can just fire my black ass."

The chief looked at him evenly. "If I was going to fire your black ass, I would have done it about five minutes ago," he said softly. "As of now, I got a feeling that if any black asses get fired around here, it's going to be yours and mine at about the same time. That, goddammit, is why we have to do this together!"

10

There were few banks in the ghettos of Miami. Fear of robbery in high-crime areas was only one reason. The clearest answer, some finance experts would tell you, was simply that when you built a bank, you built it where the money was. Florida First Bank had opened a branch on Northwest Third Avenue in Overtown shortly after the government funding had come in for the huge Southeast Overtown & Park West Redevelopment Project. The branch was located within sight of the Miami Arena, the home of the Miami Heat, the hugely successful NBA expansion team that brought tourist and upscale local money into the area in a way that only Overtown and Park West jazz clubs had done before.

There were half a dozen teller's booths as you walked in, and on the left, an array of desks for loan officers. At one of those desks sat Bob Carmody, looking slightly uncomfortable in the tropic-weight sport coat that hid the Colt .45 automatic in the Bruce Nelson custom holster snapped inside his waistband.

Tom West and Stan Baranck were in teller booths two and four, along with the regular cashiers. They appeared to be teller trainees. Each wore a light cardigan sweater to hide his .45. Mike Cohen stood perhaps thirty feet away from the teller area, watching the scene through the glass of the door that led to the vault area. Outside, cruising in an unmarked Chevy and in both radio and monitor contact, were Harrington and Cross. In their car were Remington Model 870 12-gauge shotguns with short barrels and rifle sights. The men in the outside rover car wore heavy Hardcorps bulletproof vests under their oversize nylon jackets, which were lettered Police in Day-Glo orange on the back. The letters were invisible to anyone until they got out of the car.

All the Stakeout men inside wore Second Chance Deep Cover vests, made of soft and thin Kevlar aramid fiber held tight against their bodies under their dress shirts by a special spandex carrier that looked like a glossy sleeveless T-shirt. Melinda Hoffritz also wore a vest. Her Colt automatic was holster clipped inside her jeans at the appendix position and was concealed by the same oversize, off-white men's T-shirt with a Florida State University logo that hid her vest.

Most men looked bulkier when they wore a vest, as if they had been working out. Hoffritz looked slimmer. The tight-fitted vest had a flattening effect on her substantial bust.

She was an inside rover, and appeared to be a customer. She would slowly fill out a deposit slip at the customer-service desk, then stand patiently in line with the real customers. Alone among them, she stood sideways instead of facing forward, which allowed her to inconspicuously scan the lobby. No one but the cops noticed her except to flirt. When she finished her deposit, she walked to the service desk as if to study the deposit slip and repeat the process. She had lost count of how many cycles she'd been through. It was almost noon.

Hoffritz took her deposit slip, and the bankbook she'd been issued this morning, and slipped them into a hip pocket to keep her hands free. As she joined the two people who were in line at the first booth, she turned sideways with a casual cocking of the hip.

She saw the robber come in then.

He was young, black, clean shaven. She made him for sixteen, seventeen. Plese God, she thought, not another kid. Don't make us have to shoot another kid.

A blue Miami Hurricanes baseball cap was pulled down over his eyes in an unusual way. His eyes glanced rapidly in all directions.

If someone had asked her at that moment how she knew this man was a bank robber, Melinda Hoffritz probably couldn't have answered except to guess that it was intuition. But a police psychologist would have had the answer. He would have explained in one word: precognition.

Cops learn early the arts of violence and the techniques of those with things to hide. They subconsciously file away the indicators and the body-language cues. When they see something that reminds them of criminal behavior, their survival instinct goes to an instant alert status, sending a warning racing through every computerlike circuit of the brain until it finds the right file. It happens subconsciously, so fast that the only conscious awareness is the final printout: "Man with gun! Danger!"

Melinda Hoffritz had seen the nervous, almost desperately furtive eye movements. She had seen that the shoulders were forward of the hips, almost hunching, and that the knees were flexed, and that the man was almost up on the balls of his feet. Those, her subconscious knew, were things the body did when it knew it was about to enter a potentially dangerous conflict. The doctors called it by names like "body alarm reaction" and "fight-or-flight reflex."

It was too hot a day for the long, dark jacket. Only three types of people wore such garments in weather like this in Miami. Cops, and robbers, and CWIPs. A CWIP is a private citizen licensed to carry a concealed, loaded handgun in public, who is by definition law-abiding. The coats were worn for the same reason. To hide a gun. In addition, this man was holding his coat shut with his left hand as if to hide something. Police officers, and citizens with gun-carry permits, never did that. They carried daily and had long since become confident that their guns would not flash in public and frighten people. Most criminals carried guns only when they intended to use them, and were acutely aware of their presence and of the mandatory year in jail Florida law stipulated for the offense. Thus, mannerisms that indicated carrying a gun one was nervous about indicated an armed felon to a seasoned police officer like Hoffritz.

She could not have articulated any of this until later. All she knew now was, "Man with a gun."

She glanced toward the other officers. Without anything so obvious as a nod, they allowed her to read their eyes: Yes, we've seen it, too. We're right here to back you up.

The shortest line was in front of booth number two, with only one person in front of the counter. The suspect walked nervously up behind that person, an elderly black lady. He shifted his weight uneasily. Hoffritz was now behind him to his left, little more than a step away.

Her left hand toyed with the hem of her frayed T-shirt. That was the hand that would rip the shirt up to clear a pathway for her right hand to draw her .45, but she made no overt move yet. Forcing herself to be calm, she slowly and casually surveyed the area to see if the suspect had a layoff man, an accomplice who pretended to be another customer and lie in the weeds, prepared to use gunfire to rescue the primary robber if he got caught. It was a common armed-robbery tactic, one the Shotgun Gang was raising to a high art lately.

She saw no other suspects.

Behind the second teller's cage, the one the suspect was in line for, stood Tom West and a smiling, efficient-looking young black woman. Hoffritz could see that the cashier had not picked up on the suspect . . . and that Tom West had. He had very casually set down the paperwork he'd been holding and moved as far as he could from the woman to his right, Hoffritz's left. Now his hands were free, ready to flash his gun at the first signal.

The cashier handed a thin envelope of cash and a slip to the old lady with a sweet "Have a wonderful day, Mrs. Baker!"

The woman smiled gently back and said, "You, too, dear." She tucked the envelope in her purse and walked slowly away. Now the suspect was at the head of the line.

The cashier hadn't lost her smile. She was starting to say "good morning" when she saw something in the man's face, something terrible, that made her freeze in midword.

And then the world seemed to go into slow motion.

A long, black gun barrel snaked out from under the coat. It was attached to a revolver with a white handle. It pointed straight at Tom West's face, as if the robber instinctively knew that the man, not the woman, was the one he had to watch.

Melinda Hoffritz's hand had already closed over the walnut stock of her Colt automatic, familiar and warm from the heat of her body.

And suddenly, as suddenly and mysteriously as she had instantly recognized the robber, she knew what she had to do. It came in a blur of thought that had no time for words, only images.

She let go of her still-holstered gun.

And lunged for the robber's.

As THE MAN APPROACHED behind the old woman, Tom West mentally kicked himself for not having drawn his pistol earlier and laying it under the counter. That way he could reach it instantly without a telltale movement of the gun arm. After all, the cashiers knew that these were plainclothes cops in the booths with them. But the bank management had been adamant: they didn't want any guns lying around. They had insisted that if deadly weapons had to be on their bank premises, they would absolutely, nonnegotiably, be on the persons and under the complete control of the officers who had carried them in.

The man's eyes were on him. West tried not to meet

the stare. He'd been taught that a predator would take that as a challenge, and perhaps open fire in panic. He also knew that he didn't dare go for his pistol under the suspect's watchful eye, or the same thing would happen.

The cashier—her name was Estelle—handed an envelope of money and a slip to the old lady and said some pleasantry to her that didn't register in West's mind. He saw the woman smile back, place the money in her purse and turn to go.

Then the man was there at the window, and Estelle said something like "good—" that choked off abruptly.

The man's eyes were wide, white showing all the way around the pupils. His lips were drawn back from the teeth. And the gun was up, pointing at West, its muzzle looking as huge as a Pilgrim's blunderbuss.

The man cried, "This is a stickup, mother—"

He never finished the word.

Suddenly two slender white hands flashed onto the gun, driving it away from West and down, and he saw Hoffritz's face, red and tight and angry. There was a surge of movement, a blurring of colored clothing and flying blond hair, and the two of them went to the floor, disappearing from view on the other side of the teller's cage.

West didn't consciously reach for his gun. Suddenly it was just there in his hand, and he was leaping upward, trying to get straight up and over the cage to help Melinda Hoffritz.

And then from below him came the blast of the robber's revolver firing.

THERE WERE TWO MELINDAS when it happened.
There was a passive part of her that watched through
the windows of her eyes as her hands flashed forward
to the weapon.

And there was the active part, the creature of the
countless hours of training in the police gym, the part
whose hands unerringly found their target.

Her left hand closed over the cylinder of the gun to
keep it from rotating and firing, and the thumb of the
same hand locked behind the hammer to keep it from
rising and falling. Her right hand locked solidly on his
wrist.

She weighed about a hundred and twenty pounds.
He weighed at least forty more. But the fury of her
movement had caught him unprepared.

She jerked the gun muzzle down, toward the floor,
down and away from Tom West and the cashier. The
robber struggled. Her legs tangled with his, and they
went down together.

He punched her in the back. She felt a breathtaking impact, but no pain. He thrust his hand forward,
then jerked it back. She could hear the sound of her
skin ripping as the sharp, serrated hammer tore past
her thumb, coming free. The cylinder slipped from her
grasp now, and all she had was the narrow metal tube
of the gun barrel. She forced the muzzle to the floor.

A searing heat flashed through her hand and burned
her wrist. The gunshot, so loud to West, sounded distant to her, like a pop.

The man was somehow on top of her now, making
guttural sounds she couldn't understand. He tugged at
her left hand, which was locked around his right wrist.
He tried to bring the gun muzzle toward her head.

Her left hand was still secure on the gun barrel, but she could feel the muzzle coming toward her. Gritting her teeth, she pulled his wrist in toward her chest and, with every ounce of strength she could muster, drove her entire weight forward against the warm barrel of the revolver.

It went back like a lever, the sharp spur of the hammer gouging through the skin, the muscles, the tendons at the back of his hand. Blood splattered.

But the gun was free.

Hoffritz pulled it back toward herself, preparing to roll over on it where he couldn't get at it again, when she felt more than heard a heavy thudding impact, and suddenly the man's weight was gone from her.

She shook her head and looked over. The robber lay facedown, Tom West standing on his right hand and holding his gleaming Smith & Wesson at his ear, and Stan Baranck kneeling with both knees on the center of the man's back, the muzzle of his black automatic touching the base of the suspect's skull. They were yelling, "Don't move!"

And now Harrington and Cross were barging through the door, shotguns held ready, yelling, "Police!"

Someone was helping her to her feet. It was Mike Cohen. "It's okay," he was saying. "It's over. Give me the gun, Melinda.... It's over."

She looked down numbly. Cohen's words were almost drowned out by the ringing in her ears from the close-range gunshot that had seemed so soft at first.

The revolver was in her hand. It was covered with blood. Some of it came from the laceration on her thumb, but most, she knew, must belong to the gunman. In that slow-motion instant, she had felt the hammer of the gun plow its deep furrow through his fist as she'd levered it loose.

She tried to give the gun to Mike Cohen. She couldn't. Her fingers were cramped on in a death lock. She had to reach down with her right hand to peel her fingers away from the gunmetal. When the gun came away, she saw her palm was bloody, too, torn open and burned black by the blast of the exploding gunpowder that had escaped from between the barrel and the cylinder.

She turned her head. Carmody was standing with his back to the prisoner, and Baranck was holding Harrington's shotgun while Harrington cuffed him. Carmody's gun was up. She realized that he was guarding their backs against any layoff men.

But she knew intuitively that there weren't any.

Through the ringing in her ears, she caught snatches of excited talking.

"Where'd the bullet go?"

"Into the floor at the base of the teller's booth. No harm done."

"Where's the gun?"

"Mike's got it. Looks like a .22 Harrington-Richardson, I think."

"Melinda, I've told them to roll an ambulance. You okay? *Melinda!*"

She shook her head violently to snap herself out of it. "I'm—I'm fine, Mike. Really. I'm okay."

She felt dizzy and breathless. But she would be damned if she would let herself faint in front of these men.

IT WAS AFTER FIVE by the time the last report was written. Sergeant Cohen came into the squadroom, beaming. "Lieutenant Bartlett and the chief are delighted," he said. "The chief's first thought was a TV news conference. Then, of course, the lieutenant reminded him that if you guys' faces get on TV, you're burnt for future stakeouts. So I'll be going down to his office with him and the lieutenant to work on the press releases."

He fished out his wallet and peeled off a fifty-dollar bill. "Listen, I owe you all drinks. I wish I could take you myself, but you know how it is. Anyway, drinks are on me. Gang, congratulations! Quit early, get a good night's sleep and be here at seven in the morning. Looks like we'll be covering one of the check-cashing operations." There was a spring in his step as he turned and walked out the door.

Carmody reached down and picked up the fifty. "I give this little guy an hour," he pronounced.

IT WAS 8:30 p.m. Everyone was too "up" to eat. All of them were there except for Dan Harrington, who'd said curtly, "I don't drink." The bar table was ringed by their Buds and Miller Lites.

They felt safe. They were in the 10-7, the favorite downtown cop bar, run by a retired Metro Dade sergeant who named the bar using police radio terminology for "out of service." Even so, each of them was carrying an off-duty gun.

"I can't believe it was only a .22," Tom West said. "That muzzle looked so big, I didn't know if it was gonna shoot me or eat me!"

"I didn't notice how big it was," said Melinda Hoffritz pertly, "but it sure was hot and sharp." Her left hand was bandaged from the cut and the flash burn.

"When it went off, it sounded like a goddamn .357 Magnum," West insisted.

"Sounded like a popgun to me," said Hoffritz, "but it sure *felt* like a .357 Magnum when it went off. The ripping sound was louder."

Frank Cross looked perplexed. "What ripping sound?"

"When the hammer tore through his hand. When it went through my thumb, too," she answered softly.

No one spoke for a moment.

"Tom," she said, "thanks for getting him off me."

West's eyes widened in surprise. "You *kiddin'*? Wish I did! Pay you back for savin' my brains from gettin' blown out. Naw, that was Carmody, here. When I came over the teller's cage, I was just ready to shoot him when he rolled on top of you, and I didn't dare risk the bullet goin' through and hittin' you. I was fixin' to jump on his back, and then up comes this big ol' quarterback here, looked like he was airborne, give that boy a punt to the chest like an NFL kicker."

Everyone turned to look at Bob Carmody, who glanced down into his beer, embarrassed.

"Shoulda' kicked him in the goddamn face," said Frank Cross vehemently.

Carmody looked up sheepishly. "I tried," he said. "What the hell do you think I was aiming for?"

They all burst out laughing.

"Just as well," said Baranck after a moment. "Little bastard turned out to be, what, seventeen? All screwed up on crack? Wouldn't the *Crier* have just loved to have put him on the front page with his face all split open? Teasdale would be writing something like, 'Death Squad Stomps Disarmed Teen.' Bob, Melinda, you done *great!* Even Teasdale can't twist this one bad on us.''

"True story," West said in agreement. "Man, I saw the blood *splash* when you dug that thing out of his hand! That gray-haired guy from Kansas City, who came in to teach us the disarming and stuff, he woulda loved to have seen you this afternoon.''

"I wish he *could* have seen it," Hoffritz said earnestly. "Jon Letterman. I remember when they had him in here working with us when we were still a pilot project, telling me how a woman didn't have a man's upper-arm strength so she had to go to where he was strong, bring it up from her hips, put her whole body against his hand that was holding the gun. It was weird. It was almost like I flashed back to that day in class, heard him saying it, when I did the move and got the gun away from him.''

Frank Cross raised his glass. "To Jon Letterman," he said.

"Amen! Yeah! Right on," the others chorused, clicking their beer glasses together.

Carmody said, "After today I will never again doubt the natural superiority of females.''

"I dunno," said Hoffritz. "You guys have one advantage. You've got bigger bladders. I'm heading to the ladies' room.''

None of the men spoke as she walked away, but each had his private thoughts.

"She saved my life today," said Tom West to himself.

Stan Baranck's mind flashed back to the moment when he had vaulted the teller's counter, hoping that he'd be able to shoot past his sister officer without hitting her, then jumping on the suspect after Carmody kicked him loose from Melinda Hoffritz. The mental image was crowded out by another: the figure in the swirling red smoke that jerked backward in a slow-motion fall, seen through the gunsights of a Remington 870. She kept me from having to kill that kid today, he thought gratefully.

She's beautiful, thought Carmody. She's strong. She even says 'ladies' room' instead of 'little girls' room.' No bullshit to her at all. He remembered the rage he'd felt toward the guy on top of her as he'd rushed up. He *had* tried to kick him in the face instead of the chest. He had wanted to kill him, kill him for hurting Melinda Hoffritz.

Frank Cross stared down into the dying traces of foam that swirled across the top of his beer glass. It resembled the foam in the water of the Miami River when you looked down at it at night from the bridge. A familiar sight.

I could have disarmed him, he thought. If only I'd been there. I could have taken him. I could have been the hero! Damn. Damn! *Damn!*

11

Melinda Hoffritz leaned her damp blond head back against the recliner chair, fingering a glass of Blue Nun. The after-work shower had made her more wide awake, not sleepy.

She asked herself how the hell she'd gotten into this business....

She and her sister, who was a couple of years older, had grown up in Jacksonville. Melinda was always the tomboy of the family, even though people told her she was the prettiest. She would go fishing and golfing and playing tennis with her active dad, while her sister spent more time with Mom at the hairdresser's and shopping.

In high school, instead of following her sister onto the cheerleading squad, Melinda went out for judo, one of only two girls on the team. She enjoyed the hard, aggressive contact. She discovered that boys were easier to throw to the mat than girls, because they had a higher center of gravity.

By the time she graduated high school, she didn't have a handle on what she wanted to do. All she knew was that her appearance wouldn't have anything to do with it, it would be challenging and it would be some kind of "man's work."

She enrolled in the liberal-arts program at the University of Florida in Gainesville. Learning that the university had one of the finest law schools in the southeast, she audited a couple of law classes. She was nineteen the year she decided to take her two-year associate's degree in liberal arts and switch her major to the pre-law program.

At twenty she was driving downtown one night to do some shopping when her eye was caught by the blue-and-red flashing lights atop a white police car up ahead. Hoffritz assessed the scene. An Alachua County deputy sheriff had pulled over a battered old station wagon. The lone deputy stepped out of the vehicle, her forest green trousers and white uniform shirt looking crisp and sharp. The female deputy was hatless, about Hoffritz's height and a little heavier, her glossy black hair done up in a buisnesslike bun on the back of her head.

As Hoffritz watched, her little VW gliding her closer to the scene, three bulky black men jumped out of the car, advancing on the woman officer. Hoffritz saw the cop's white-shirted arm come up in a stop gesture that the men ignored. They were almost upon her as the woman stepped wide, like a martial artist going into a cat stance. She grabbed the projecting side handle of the long black baton and spun it out of the ring.

Instinctively Hoffritz's foot went to the brake. She didn't know why. All she knew was that she was pulling her Volkswagen to the roadside behind the police cruiser, drawn to the action like a moth to a flame.

The deputy swung the baton like a scythe. It caught the first man on the side of the knee and buckled his leg. He staggered half a step and collapsed to the street, rolling, clutching at his knee.

The second one took a wild punch at the woman, and the black baton arced again. Hoffritz heard the whooshing sound as it cut the air and then the crack as it impacted his arm. It was the sound a baseball made when you connected with the bat. She heard the man cry out in surprise and pain.

The third one jumped the deputy from behind, hooking his arm brutally under her chin and jerking her rearward, at the same time driving his knee into her back. He was bending the female officer backward like a longbow, trying to break her spine. The one she had just hit, his arm hanging limp at his side, hooked a punch into the deputy's breast with his good arm. He swung again and punched her full force in the other breast.

By then Melinda Hoffritz had closed the distance.

She hit the man who was holding the officer, from the side, in a shoulder block, the way her father had taught her when they'd played touch football. The impact knocked the big man off-balance. He let go of the deputy, stumbled, caught himself and turned to face Hoffritz.

She saw him drop his shoulder and cock his hip, telegraphing the punch, and by the time he launched his powerful, looping right cross, she was already ducking beneath it, moving in.

She grabbed the arm with both hands and pivoted, her shoulder slamming into his armpit as her hip caught him at the waist. She spun in the direction the momentum of his more than two hundred pounds was already carrying him.

He sailed effortlessly over his shoulder. He didn't know how to fall. He landed flat on his back in the street with a heavy thud.

The man seemed to be motionless, dazed. Hoffritz turned to help the woman deputy. She looked just in time to see the woman drive the long end of her baton into the second man's abdomen, folding him in half like a jackknife.

But the first one had crawled behind her on his hands and knees, and Hoffritz saw him reaching for the black rubber handle of the silver-colored revolver in the deputy's holster.

Hoffritz shouted, "Look out! Behind you! Your gun!"

The woman deputy caught the warning just in time. Even as the suspect's hands closed on the revolver butt, the woman spun the baton to reinforcing position. Now the short handle was tight in her fist, the length of the baton along the length of her arm and underneath. In effect, it turned her arm into a metal bar, and now she swung that arm down.

It struck the attacker on the forearms with a meaty smack. Hoffritz heard him cry, "Unngh!" One hand fell away, but the other clutched tenaciously at the black gun handle. The woman chopped her baton-reinforced forearm down again. This time Hoffritz could hear the distinct sound of bone breaking. The man fell away, rolling on the ground, pulling his injured arms in toward his belly in a sort of fetal position.

Suddenly she was grabbed from behind, lifted off the ground. Two big arms had wrapped around her middle. The force was crushing. She couldn't breathe, and it felt as if her ribs might break at any moment.

Melinda Hoffritz looked toward the deputy and realized instantly that she'd be no help. The second suspect had gotten back up off his knees and punched her full in the face with his good hand, knocking her against the side of the police car. Then Hoffritz lost sight of her as the man who had lifted her off her feet began to swing her around.

There was no fear, only reaction. She looked down and in the dimness, with the eerie glow of the red-and-blue police lights changing the color of everything crazily, she could see that the man had wrapped his right hand around his left forearm to get more leverage to crush the breath out of her.

Deliberately she reached down and grabbed his middle finger in her whole fist. Using her other hand for extra power, she bent his finger back as hard as she could.

It broke with a crunching snap. Suddenly his middle finger was pointed back up his right arm.

And just as suddenly he let go. She heard him cry "Bitch!"

She jumped forward and away, then pivoted back to face him. His nostrils were flared, his eyes narrowed. Were those eyes red, like something out of a vampire movie? Maybe it was the lights from the police car.

He lowered his head and charged like a bull.

Her years in the judo dojo had not been spent for nothing. She stood in place until the last instant, then wheeled gracefully aside. His clumsy momentum carried him past her, and as it did, she jumped on his back, her slender left arm snaking under his chin and around his throat until the crook of her elbow was just under his chin and her left hand was up near his right ear.

She brought her own right hand up, cupping the heel of her left, and then she used the force of both arms to pull in tight. Her slim but firm left bicep was now biting into the left side of his neck, while the hard upper edge of her forearm scissored into the right side. Together they compressed his carotid arteries and occluded them almost completely.

Judo players called it *shime-waza*. Wrestlers called it the sleeper hold. Cops, she would learn later, called it the lateral vascular restraint in training, and the choke-out on the street.

The suspect jerked violently, his and Hoffritz's combined weight driving him down to the pavement on his knees and elbows. He bucked like a wild horse, trying to throw her off. She held tight, pushing her cheek into the back of his head to stabilize him.

He threw himself into a roll, trying to peel her off. She felt the asphalt roughly raking skin off her bare forearms, but didn't feel any pain. She hung on even tighter, wrapping her long legs around his waist, hooking her feet instep to instep.

She hung on grimly, forcing herself to breathe, squeezing the forearm to bicep as tight as she could with her neck in between. She was on her back now, his massive weight on top of her, and it was all she could do to suck in a lungful of air.

He tried viciously to elbow her in the ribs, but she was in too close. His elbow skidded harmlessly off her side and smashed painfully into the asphalt. She kept applying the pressure.

He was weakening. She wasn't.

He clawed at her hands and arms. She felt his fingernails rake her forearms. Again that surprising sensation of feeling her skin rip without feeling pain.

Suddenly the clawing stopped. His arms fell away, thudding heavily to the tarmac. His weight went dead on top of her. She heard him make a gurgling sound.

But she didn't let go. The first time she'd thought he was out of the fight, she had turned her back and he had jumped her, could have broken her ribs. She wasn't going to make the same mistake a second time.

How long had she been applying the sleeper hold? She had lost track of time. It seemed like forever. *Sensei* had warned her that almost anyone would lose consciousness from the *shime-waza* in no more than fifteen seconds, and that if it was applied for a minute more, brain damage or even death was almost certain.

She realized that she didn't care. She felt no personal anger, only a sense of total determination that this man would not get up again to hurt women this night.

She made the conscious decision to maintain the pressure.

Melinda Hoffritz was more worried about the embattled female officer. She twisted her head and glanced toward the cruiser.

The first suspect, the man who had been hit in the leg and then had tried to grab the cop's gun, was still rolling around in a fetal position, nursing his broken arms.

The other one, his injured arm still hanging at his side, was a few feet away from the woman officer, bobbing and weaving, his good arm tentatively trying to dart in to rip the baton away from her.

The officer herself was balanced in a semicrouch, moving confidently on the balls of her feet. Her hair had been torn loose from the bun and fell in a black cascade over her shoulder to her elbow. Olive-colored skin showed through. Hoffritz couldn't see any blood. She couldn't see the baton, either.

Then suddenly she did see it.

The female deputy's right arm seemed to flick upward in an effortless gesture, and again Hoffritz heard the whistling sound of the baton cutting the air. She could barely see it as it spun, vertically this time instead of horizontally.

The long end of the black metal baton blurred upward between the suspect's legs before he could react to stop it. It hit him flush in the genitals, so hard that his feet seemed to lift off the ground.

Hoffritz saw him double over forward. Both his hands, even the one that had hung useless before, clutched at his crotch. She heard him make a gagging sound, and then he was puking, the projectile vomit spraying around his head like a halo as he rolled on the ground clawing at his ruined privates.

It was over.

Hoffritz realized she was still crushing the neck of the man with the dead weight on top of her.

She planted the sole of her right foot on the asphalt and pushed mightily with her whole body, rolling toward her left. The man sprawled off her, facedown, motionless. She scrambled to her feet.

She could hear sirens. The female officer was talking rapidly into her portable radio—it was the first chance she'd had to use it—but Hoffritz realized that someone in one of the many suburban homes on both sides of the street had called the police anyway.

Sucking in air, she glanced around. People had come from nowhere, lining the sidewalks, and many more stood in the protected safety of their doorways or windows, watching.

At least one of them had called the cops. That was something. But none of them had come forward to help, and for the first time time she felt anger. Half of the onlookers were able-bodied men. Why had none of them stepped forward to assist?

She heard the screeching of tires. Looking around, she saw two white county sheriff cars and a blue Gainesville patrol unit. Cops were bailing out, batons in hand.

The cavalry had arrived. Better late than never, she supposed.

She heard the female deputy cry "Leave her alone! She backed me up!" A cop who had been moving toward her aggressively stopped, looked back and forth, then thrust his baton into the ring on the left side of his belt.

A man with sergeant's stripes on his white-shirted arm said, "Holy shit. Nice going, Brenda. Mike, roll a meat wagon, make that two. These assholes are messed up big time. Get some cuffs on 'em and search 'em."

Now the female deputy had materialized at Hoffritz's side, putting a hand on her shoulder. "Thanks, hon," the woman said, her breath ragged. "You saved my ass out there."

Melinda Hoffritz couldn't think of anything to say. The sergeant was standing by her other shoulder now. The lady cop said to him, "I had one down, then one was holding me from behind and the other was hitting me. She knocked him off me and choked him out. One of them would've got my gun if she hadn't warned me in time."

The sergeant, a white male about forty, looked at her gruffly and said, "Good job, kid. Who you with?"

Catching her breath, Hoffritz said, "University of Florida."

The sergeant answered, "Yeah? Hiring their campus cops a little young these days, ain't they?"

She realized he thought she was a police officer.

"No," she said, shaking her head. "I'm not with the campus police. I'm a pre-law student."

The cops looked at each other. "You ain't a cop?" The sergeant was incredulous. "You risked your ass for Brenda, and you ain't even a *cop?*"

Hoffritz couldn't understand the question. "Look, it was three against one, and they were all bigger than her. It wasn't fair. Anybody would have done it."

A sardonic smile appeared on the sergeant's face. "Yeah, right, kid," he said, glancing pointedly around at all the men on the sidewalks and on the porches who had watched and done nothing. "Sure. Anybody would have." He glanced down at her arms. "You're bleeding. Brenda, so are you. I want you both to get looked at, down to the hospital. C'mon. We'll go in my car. Ben, take Brenda's patrol vehicle back to the station."

They spent almost two hours at the hospital. The lady cop's face was puffing up badly from the punch, but the E.R. people couldn't do much for her but ice packs. Hoffritz's chest X rays showed no broken ribs, but her midriff was badly bruised. Her arms were oozing blood from abrasions, but there were no lacerations that needed stitches. Just to be safe, they gave her a tetanus shot and slathered her forearms with antibiotic salve.

The emergency room was full of cops. They were all asking questions of the emergency-room doctors, and it didn't take long for Hoffritz to hear enough of the conversations to piece things together. The three black men had gotten the worst of the deal by far.

She heard a tall, slim black man who had a single gold bar on the collar of each lapel of his white sheriff's uniform shirt give instructions to his men regarding the various bookings, ranging from attempted murder to aggravated assault.

Then the man paused before going on. "And Thompson, I want a complete report from the blonde. I want her to be a complainant, not just a witness. The son of a gun attacked her when she was the only person on the scene with the guts to help a cop in trouble. I also want her taken home and treated like royalty, understood? Sulieman, I want every witness debriefed before midnight, and I want a stack of their signed statements on my desk when I get in tomorrow afternoon...."

It was after eleven before Hoffritz got back to the dorm. There was a message waiting for her. It said, "Deputy Brenda Aguilar wants to meet you for lunch tomorrow at Harry's Steak House."

She slept poorly that night, suffering what she would later learn was known to cops as "adrenalin hangover."

She sailed through her morning classes, not comprehending the course work, constantly flashing back to the events of the night before. She left "Principles of the Legal Canon of Ethics" early to make it to the steak house.

Brenda Aguilar was already there at their table for two. They shook hands warmly.

"I wanted to thank you," the cop said. "I've been a deputy for three years. I've been in fights before. I thought I was dead meat this time. You were the first person who ever came out of a crowd to help me. I just wanted you to know how much that means."

Hoffritz smiled, a little embarrassed. The side of Aguilar's tan-looking face was swollen and discolored from the powerful punch she had taken.

"I don't know what to say," Hoffritz replied. "It just didn't seem fair."

They exchanged small talk. Hoffritz learned that the female cop was twenty-eight, a single mother of Portuguese-American descent, who had joined the Alachua County Sheriff's office at twenty-five because it was the best salary and the best civil-service benefits package she could find.

Hoffritz asked, "Was it something you always wanted to do? I mean, did you grow up wanting to be a cop?"

"No," Aguilar laughed. "If you'd asked me when I was twenty-four if I was gonna be a cop, I would've said, 'Yeah, right, like I'm gonna be a brain surgeon or an astronaut.' But I was in a nowhere job . . . they had the ad in the paper...and I figured, what the heck. I've got a little boy to bring up. I don't have a man to earn a salary. That means *I've* got to earn a man-size salary. This was the best shot I had at doing it. I took the shot and I hit the target. What can I say? It works for me.''

Hoffritz asked, ''Isn't there a kind of sexist thing? I mean, being a cop is pretty macho. I'm not that old, but I can remember where there weren't any women cops, except for matrons and crosswalk guards.''

The deputy replied, ''Yeah, it's sexist. A big majority of the other cops are still male, you know, and there's a lot of the male-ego thing going on there. It's tougher for a woman at first. They want you to prove yourself. So what's new? Show me where a woman is doing what used to be a man's job, and the men *don't* make you prove yourself. Shit, the men have to prove themselves, too. No big deal.''

Hoffritz was awed. ''You were great with that baton with the handle. What is that thing, anyway?''

''It's called a PR-24.'' Aguilar smiled, taking a sip of her coffee. ''I love the thing. Last night wasn't the first time I've used it. My instructor at the academy told me it would be my best friend out on the street, and he wasn't kidding. A regular baton, a straight stick, the stronger you are the harder it hits. For people our size, the PR-24 is where it's at. You hold that handle and spin it, and it creates its own momentum. You and I are more flexible than most guys, and we can really whip that thing and get some spin behind it. Same as a gun. You don't have to be strong to use it— you have to be dexterous to use it, and gals are more dexterous than guys. I fugure my PR-24 and my .38 are my equalizers, you know?''

"Wow," was all Hoffritz could say.

"So, honey, tell me about you. That was a helluva choke-out you put on that big bastard last night. Where did a nineteen-year-old pre-law student learn that?"

"Oh, it was just a *shime-waza.*"

"She-may-*who*-zit?"

"Shime-waza," she repeated. "You cut off the blood to the brain. It's a judo thing. I took judo in high school."

"She-may-waza, huh? At the academy we called it LVNR, lateral vascular neck restraint. Cops have a way of putting big words on everything they do. I didn't know it came from judo. You a black belt or something?"

"No," Hoffritz said shyly. "I only got to first *kyu,* brown belt."

"Cue? What's cue? You play pool in judo or what?"

Hoffritz laughed. The *kyus* are the levels in the different belt ranks until you get to black belt. In black belt the different ranks are called *dans.*"

"Well, whatever it is, I'm glad you knew it. If that bastard had got my gun, we both would've been dead. If you hadn't got that guy off my back, I would have been dead before that. Did I say thanks yet?"

Hoffritz shook her head. "You don't have to. I just did what I thought anybody would have done. I couldn't believe all those big, strong guys, just standing around on the sidewalks and in their doorways, watching and not doing anything to help."

The deputy took another sip of coffee. "Welcome to the world, kid. It's called 'don't get involved' syndrome. Hell, Sergeant Sulieman thought *you* were a cop. He's been doing it a lot longer than I have, and until last night he'd never seen a citizen do anything but gawk when a cop was in trouble. He was still talking about you when I went home. Feel free to drive as fast as you want, Melinda, so long as it's on his shift. You can do no wrong as far as my sergeant is concerned."

Hoffritz just blushed.

"So," the female officer continued, "tell me—have you ever thought of becoming a cop?"

Hoffritz was taken totally aback. "Me? A cop?"

"Oh, come on," said Aguilar. "You got into the shit, didn't you? Tell me the truth. You crave a little action. You're tough. What're you gonna do instead, be a lawyer and spend your life filing chicken-shit briefs and motions and all that?"

Hoffritz couldn't think of an answer.

The deputy continued, "Look, we've got a ride-along program. Our community-services unit is in charge of it. I can get you in, if you like. See what the job is about. It isn't usually like last night. It's fun, really. And it's satisfying. It's about helping people in trouble. It isn't just a job, once you get into it. It's like a calling, you know?"

Hoffritz took a deep breath. "Wow. I don't know. Is the county sheriff's a good place to be a cop? I mean, if you had to do it over again, is one police department the same as another?"

Brenda Aguilar chuckled. "Not really. I'm on the job here, I like it here in Gainesville, my family's here . . . you know the drill. If I wasn't stuck here, would I go someplace else? Sure."

"Like what? Highway patrol?"

The cop snorted. "Gimme a break. The state troopers I know are good, really good, but they don't get paid worth shit. Cops I talk to who've done policing in other parts of the country, they all say state police have the most prestige and all that, but in Florida it's like the FHP said, 'Hey, if we've got the most prestige, that means troopers that work for us don't need salary or benefits or anything.' Christ, they don't make any money at all. They've got a helluva turnover rate.

"No, if you seriously wanted to get into being a cop in Florida—hell, if I was going to start over again—I'd go to Miami. It's a coin toss between Metro Dade and Miami PD. They both have really good salary-and-benefit packages. And if you want to talk about really being a cop, well, a big city is where it's at. You'll get more action in a year in Miami than you'll get in ten years on a small town or rural police or sheriff's department.

"Which one, Metro or city? That's another coin toss. If you were a man, I'd say, go with Metro. It used to be a regular sheriff's department like here in Alachua County, but years ago they made it a civil-service thing and took the politics out of it. Metro Dade County has a county police department with a chief of police who is appointed, instead of an elected sheriff. Metro tends to stand behind the guys when they get in trouble for doing something that isn't politically correct. Like a white cop hurting a black guy, for instance. All three of those guys who came down on you and I last night just happened to be black. If you and I had been Metro Dade cops and kicked the stuffing out of three white guys like we did last night, it wouldn't have been a problem. If they were black guys, there would have been trouble. But if we were white male cops, the Metro Dade PD would have stood behind us like they would for any cops, any color, any sex.

"But then, you take Miami Police Department. They're very politically correct. Same incident as last night with us, but white male cops? The cops would have been thrown to the wolves in a heartbeat. Taken off duty, fired, even criminally prosecuted. The whole bit.

"Black male cops do the same thing on Miami PD? No problem. Miami doesn't see 'police brutality.' They see 'white-on-black brutality.' But you and I don't have testicles, right, Melinda? I think we both got balls, but we don't have testicles. Two poor little women kick the crap out of three big, bad men, it doesn't matter that the men are black, it matters that they're men. You and I would walk away clean.

"Miami versus Metro? One big thing. Miami Police Department is getting a whole lot of heat for not hiring enough minorities, and they consider women a minority. Same with Metro Dade, for that matter, but for some reason, it doesn't seem to be as bad.

"So, as a white female, where would I go? Miami PD, in a heartbeat. They need women integrated in, not only at starting patrolman level, but as supervisors. That means a woman officer on Miami is going to have a real fast career track, and she's not going to have to worry about the shit a white male cop would have to."

Hoffritz nodded. "So, if I was going to say screw being a lawyer, I wanna be a cop, Miami PD would be where I should go?"

Aguilar nodded in the affirmative. "If I was you, kid, I'd sign up for Miami PD in a New York minute. And you'll have something none of the other applicants will, no matter what color they are or what's between their legs. The sergeant and the lieutenant told me last night they're going to try to get you a hero's medal for helping a cop who was in trouble."

After their conversation, Hoffritz had taken Aguilar up on her offer to get into the ride-along program. It wasn't long before Hoffritz realized that she was spending her days in class looking forward to her ride-alongs at night.

Melinda Hoffritz received her bachelor's degree from the University of Florida, Gainesville, the June she turned twenty-one. Her parents expected her to stay there and enter the law school.

Instead, she had to tell them that she had taken and passed all the exams to join the City of Miami Police Department, and had been accepted and would enter the police academy the following August.

The family reaction was starkly mixed. Her mother almost fainted. Her father beamed his supporting approval. Her sister rolled her eyes and looked as if she was going to vomit.

The entry class was almost one-fourth female to start. By the time the police academy had reached its fifth week, only nine women were left.

Each day the physical training involved heavy running. The women got shin splints and even marching fractures in their lower legs and feet. The men didn't.

There were the unarmed-combat and defense-tactics and arrest-techniques classes. These were little more than semicontrolled fights. The men who didn't like women doing the job they had invested their ego in were particularly vicious when it came their turn to be the bad guys getting "arrested" in training by female officers.

Hoffritz would never forget the hulking redheaded guy in her class who would tell anyone who'd listen that women weren't up to the job and didn't belong doing men's work. She watched helplessly one day as he played the role of a suspect, and when another female student, a petite Hispanic, moved in to handcuff him, he pivoted and smashed her in the face with his elbow hard enough to knock her unconscious and break her nose. He walked away laughing. A day later the Cuban woman became one of the female students who dropped out of the program.

Hoffritz bided her time. She knew eventually that she'd be paired with the big redhead. One day she was.

The role play forced her to put him against the wall in a search position. When he spun to do to her what he had done to the tiny Hispanic woman, Melinda Hoffritz was ready.

She dropped her hips, coiling her power even as she ducked under his savagely swinging arm and grabbed it by the wrist. Then she executed the technique her judo *sensei* had taught her as *osoto gari,* the greater outer reap. As she pivoted at the hips, she kicked his legs out from under him. He didn't know how to fall, and they were role-playing in the parking lot, not on soft mats.

In the dojo she would have let go as soon as his body went airborne. That was the code of Bushido, the "martial spirit" in which you didn't hurt your training partners. But Melinda Hoffritz remembered the sickening sound of the little Cuban girl's face collapsing under the redhead's elbow smash, and at that moment she "forgot" to let go.

Just before his head hit the asphalt, she both heard and felt the cartilage in his shoulder tearing itself apart. It sounded like canvas ripping. Then his head hit the sidewalk with his whole body weight behind it, knocking him unconscious. He never knew that Melinda Hoffritz had ripped his arm out of its socket until he woke up in the ambulance. By then it was too late. He never returned to the police academy, and Hoffritz never saw him again.

She graduated fifth in her class in overall standing. She began her career as a patrol officer working downtown. Not long after her first night on solo patrol, she was involved in the shooting in which she ended two men's lives.

The aftermath of that incident subtly changed things for Hoffritz at work. There had always been men hitting on her. She was beautiful and she couldn't change that. But she had also decided early on that she would never use her looks or her body for any sort of advancement within the police department. She turned down all advances, even the ones she wanted to accept.

Before the shoot-out, men had wanted to bed the beautiful policewoman just because she was a beautiful policewoman. She had seen that coming and she could cope.

Before the shooting, there had been men she met in worlds that didn't involve law enforcement, men she was attracted to, who suddenly turned frosty when they found out she was a cop, a person of power, someone who could do a man's job without compromising her femininity.

But after the shooting, it was different, all different, in a bad kind of way that went completely across the board. Now, all of a sudden there were men who wanted the ego trip of sleeping with the killer bitch.

Now the handful of men who could take a woman strong enough to do a man's job, couldn't seem to relate to a woman strong enough to kill a man like them. Boyfriends stopped calling. Men stopped flirting, at least the ones who knew her and weren't into the "dominate the killer bitch" syndrome.

The worst problem was her shift sergeant. She'd seen him staring at her from the beginning. When he made gentle advances, she had fended them off gently. When he made hard advances, she fended them off firmly.

After the shooting, when she just wanted to be left alone or maybe contacted by a few brother officers who would have said "Hey, that could have been us where you were, and we still care about you," the damn sergeant had kept intruding. Telling her that she couldn't lose her identity as a beautiful woman by getting into identifying herself as a woman who had killed men.

She needed to get back in touch with her womanhood, he would tell her when he cornered her alone in the squad room, his hand reaching first to her shoulder in a person-to-person gesture of humanity, and then dropping down toward her breast where she slapped his hand away. "C'mon, Melinda," he beseeched her. "Don't be overcompensating in a man's world. *Be* a woman. Let me show you how to be a woman."

She resisted the urge to draw her weapon and shoot him down like the others.

She considered going through the union and filing a sexual-harassment suit. She resisted the temptation. She knew she'd be labeled a politically correct liberal bitch by the other cops on the shift, at least some of them.

Hoffritz had been wondering what to do about it when she saw the circular that was going around the department, cautiously explaining the Stakeout Squad and inviting interested officers to apply to join the unit.

She had pondered it. The first thing that struck her was that there would be a higher than average chance of a stakeout cop having to kill somebody. She didn't want to go through that again.

At the same time, she realized, the stakeout cops would already be in location when they faced armed perpetrators. They would control the vertical, they would control the horizontal, they would control everything. They wouldn't be in the position she was when she had been forced to kill those two men, under fire and without any choice except to shoot back. Hell, they'd be less likely to have to shoot people to death!

And it would be a graceful way out of her problem with the duty sergeant. No lawsuit. No recriminations. Just, "Officer Hoffritz is being transferred to another unit."

The following day she called headquarters and wrote up her application for Stakeout.

And now, leaning back in her recliner, the last sip of wine gone from her glass, Melinda Hoffritz was remembering from whence she had come.

Dammit, Brenda, she thought to herself, I know it isn't your fault. I know you never had to shoot anybody as a deputy sheriff for Alachua County.

But you never told me just how tough it could be. You never told me I'd have to retreat behind cover with a shotgun and a .45, ready to kill bad guys on sight, just to get away from assholes who couldn't cope with somebody who had female anatomy inside their police uniform.

12

Eddie "Noble" Stiller got off the MetroRail at the Miami Arena stop and walked the rest of the way to the check-cashing joint. The breeze felt cool on his face and head, both clean shaven down to the skin. Gargoyles sunglasses shielded his eyes. He wore new white running shoes, khaki sport slacks and a salmon-colored Izod polo shirt left untucked to cover the Colt Cobra two-inch-barrel revolver that was snug inside his waistband. Two rubber bands wrapped around the handle of the gun kept it from slipping down inside his pants. He'd figured out that trick from the first detective who arrested him, watching how he carried his gun during the interrogation in the police squad room.

His chocolate brown skin fitted Stiller well to his environment. There wasn't a white face in sight. Overtown was black man's turf.

Eddie Stiller had no mixed feelings about ripping off other African-Americans. He'd been born in Miami's other ghetto to the north, Liberty City. He'd learned early on that there were predators and prey, and being a predator was no less difficult than being prey and a helluva lot more rewarding. Whenever he saw a Bill Cosby or a black athlete on TV saying a black man didn't have to be kept down, that he could pick his own destiny, Stiller would cry, "Right on, brother." Of course, he knew, Cosby and the rest weren't quite clear on the concept, as the white yuppies would say.

You were predator or prey, he knew. That simple. God gave you the power to be all you could be. Strong or weak. If you chose to be weak, then you chose to be victimized. Steal from a white man, you gave him some justice for what his people had done to yours. Steal from a black sucker, you wised him up, gave him some reason to be strong. Either way, they didn't have no comeback on you. What you took was your right to take, because you were strong, and if they were too stupid to learn the lesson and get strong, then whatever color they were, to hell with them.

He enjoyed his life. What he had real mixed feelings about was working with Win. Eddie Stiller instinctively distrusted white men. He'd work with one when he knew it was in the white guy's best interest to take care of him, Eddie. That seemed to be the case so far, and he liked the sense of importance he got from Win telling him that he was the one chosen to do the inside case on the check joint. That little chore was worth an extra ten percent of the profit from the ripoff. One thing about Win, he always paid on time, full up, right there. That much about the man, he liked.

But there were little things. The gun they gave him, for instance. Hell, they were supposed to be the Shotgun Gang. The guns were their identity. That's where they took their very names, man! "Win" for Winchester, and all of that. One guy had a Browning. Browning was to guns what Mercedes was to cars, you didn't have to be no gun nut to know that. So what the hell was the gun Win gave him? A goddamn Noble.

It sounded cool at first. "Noble" sounded like you a prince or something, man. But then you talking with the brothers, you talk about Glocks and Colts and Smiths and Brownings and you say "Noble," and folks say "Noble? What the fuck be a 'Noble'? I ain't never heard of no 'Noble.' "

Then you get curious, you go into a pawnshop, ask about buying a Noble shotgun, and they look it up in they books and say, "Noble, yeah, that be some piece of shit from some junk gun company, went outa business like twenny years ago, man."

Nice guy, Win. Let's you know what he thinks of you. Gives you a junky Noble. Tells you, "Take the MetroRail, don't take your own car or nothin', case you get caught, ain't worth stealin' no car just for a case job. You gotta get outa there quick, they's all kinds of gypsy cabs you can grab. Don't need no vest. Don't need no shotgun. Shit, you just goin' down, case the joint, is all."

Well, screw Win. He wasn't nearly as smart as he thought he was. Make all this big deal about gang members never getting together on their own time, but then you find out he bring the crew that done the Coconut Grove job to his own condo, man. Must be three, four guys know his real name. You gonna find out, too, just a matter of time. Gotta wear you disguises, stick on fake beard with spirit gum, smell like a pine tree. You shave your head, you gotta wear this Afro wig with elastic in it, feel like some French fag wearing a hairy beret or something.

But what the hell. The money good. The money *great*. Don't matter Win say, you can't have no woman be real close to you, because she gonna rat you out and rat everybody else in the gang out with you. Hypocritical prick, some of the guys say he got his own bitch right there in his condo when he bring his *favorite* guys to visit, like the rest of us a fuckin' second-string team, farm team or somethin'.

Least he be right about one thing, Noble thought. Can't trust no bitch. Gotta do like me. You need some, you get some, pay her cash, be rid of her when you done. Don't come back to haunt your ass. Never try to change you, never try to rat you out.

The check-cashing joint he was supposed to case was around the corner. Almost there. But on his right was a bar, and as he looked in through the smoky gloom, he could see a fine-looking fox tending bar. Hey, he wasn't no Stepin Fetchit for Win. He could take his time. All of a sudden he felt like a cool one.

MAXIMILIAN ROGERS looked up from his King Cobra malt liquor and said, "What you starin' at, bitch?" Then he slapped his woman Taneeka across the face as hard as he could, which sent her reeling back through the filthy kitchen of their steamy Overtown apartment.

She was knocked against the wall, her hip banging painfully against the edge of the stove. She caught her balance before she fell. She ignored the stinging pain in her face. She'd gotten used to it by now.

Maximilian was standing up now. His two friends, that fat pig Lamar Johnson and the skinny J. D. Lang, who looked as if somebody had stretched brown leather over a skull and tried to make a face out of it, just sat there staring with grins on their faces. They were enjoying this.

"Don't do it, Max," she blurted. "You all been here drinkin' since last night. You all pie-eyed! Jesus, they got guns in them check-cash places, they ready to shoot you ass, you go in an' mess with 'em!"

Rogers was weaving on his feet. He steadied himself, then staggered toward Taneeka. "Big shit! They fool with us, pull they guns on us, we do 'em like the Shotgun Gang done that other check-cash rip-off joint a few days ago."

Taneeka Roberts shook her head in angry frustration. "You think you the Shotgun Gang? You think the Shotgun Gang gets rollin' drunk, gets to talkin' 'bout somethin' some other gang done, then just goes and does it? Max, please, listen! Them guys *plan*! I seen you an' these two here, you just start talkin' the last hour, all of a sudden you the Bad Ass Gang, you gonna do like that Shotgun Gang they talkin' 'bout on TV! Max, please, I love you Max, I don't wanna see—"

He was on her then, and he cut her off with a savage backhand slap to the face. She spun into the wall, her knees starting to buckle.

"Max, don't—"

Her words ended in a strangled cry as he clumsily kicked her in the kidneys. Now she was down on her knees. She saw blood on the wall her face was pressed against, and realized it was hers.

"No, Max," she cried. "I don't want you to get ki—" He cut off the words with a brutal kick to her lower back that made her gag with the impact.

"Talk in front of my main fuckin' men," he growled. "You need a lesson, bitch!" Behind him Maximilian Rogers could hear his friends hooting encouragement.

"Max, no..." The sound was a wheezing gurgle.

He kicked her hard in the side. He felt something give way. He didn't care. He kicked her again.

"Whoo-eee," crowed the fat one, Lamar. "Show the bitch who in charge, Max!"

"Do it, Max," J.D. joined in, grinning hideously. "Jes' get her done quick. Official ain't open no twenty-four hours, you know!"

She couldn't talk anymore. Rogers kicked her six more times. Now she made no sound at all.

He staggered back, breathing heavily. "Gonna get my .32," he muttered. "Then we the fuck outa here. See if this bitch be little more grateful fo' a good man, once we get back, all that money."

WHAT THE HELL, how do you know that fine-looking bar lady is the bar owner's private stock till you check it out? Eddie Stiller sized up the bar owner one more time. He was standing at the end of the counter, wiping glasses, giving Stiller the bad eye. He was more than six and a half feet tall and weighed three hunderd pounds if he weighed an ounce, very little of it fat.

Stiller shrugged and finished off his draft Carling. A piece wasn't worth fighting for. Every second person you met had some to give, after all.

He got up, left his change on the counter and walked out into the bright sunlight. The postal money order Win had gotten for him—drawn on a false name, payable to the false name on the fake ID card in his pocket—was about to get cashed. He'd take his time, get the lay of the place, do a proper case job.

He put his Gargoyles sunglasses back on. That was one thing you had to say about Win. Noble shotgun or not, he gave them these sunglasses that Win had sworn to them were bulletproof. You couldn't say he didn't take care of his people, at least sometimes.

The warm sun and the cool breeze both felt good outside. And Official Check Cashing was just around the corner.

IT TOOK A LONG TIME for Taneeka Roberts to crawl to the table where the telephone was, and longer to pull herself up to where she could reach it. She dialed 911. What happened then was preserved for the records at Miami Dispatch Center.

"Emergency dispatch," the operator began.

"Oh, Jesus…you gotta help me…you gotta stop him…."

"I can't understand you, ma'am. Where are you?"

"…'partment twelve," Taneeka managed to say, but the rest of the address was unintelligible.

"Ma'am, you sound as if you've been hurt,"

"Oh, God…I'm bleedin'…I think I peed myself…don't matter. You gotta stop Max. Max gon' get hisself killed…."

"Ma'am, please. I can't hear you. Who's going to get killed? Tell me again where you are," the operator instructed.

"Don' matter where I am. Max. Gotta stop 'im.

Gonna get killed. Gonna rob— Oh, Jesus, it hurts...."

"Ma'am, please—"

"Lemme talk. Lemme talk. Gon' pass out again... Oh Jesus... Stop him. Asshole friends...J.D., Lamar, pig Lamar...gonna try... Shotgun Gang...they got guns...the Official, Official Check Cashin'...ain't Max fault, he drunk, they got him drunk...."

"Ma'am, did you say the Shotgun Gang? Did you say they're going to rob Fish Check Cashing? I can't understand—"

"'Ficial, O-fish-ee-al Check Cashin', yeah, don't hurt him, he drunk, he don't mean it, he don' know what he doin', he— Aaah! Oh, Jesus—"

"Do you have that address, ma'am?" the operator asked. "What Official Check Cashing is Max going to rob?"

"Girl, you stupid? How many Official Check Cashin' places they be? Twenny-first, I think— Aaah! Jesus!... He don' mean be this way. The liquor... Oh, God, I peed myself...can't help it. Aw, no... *no* ... I'm peein' *blood*...."

Taneeka Roberts began sobbing uncontrollably, then abruptly hung up.

EDDIE STILLER had scanned it all by the time he got up to the counter to cash his money order. He'd "made" the one-way-glass window on the right that covered the area. The door to the surveillance room was marked Supervisor. No Admittance. Hey, that was cool. Use Win's bitch to charm her way in there with some guy, then take over from inside. Had to be guns on the other side of that one-way glass.

For sure, it'd be Win's bitch that charmed them in. No more of that transvestite junk like the last check-cash hit. They had gone along with Win that one time because it seemed important to him, shoving it up the Stakeout Squad's ass and all that. Not again, though. This place had security cameras. That bullshit makeup or not, you could identify a man's face through what those security cameras would get. Not like when you had a beard spirit gummed to your cheeks and chin, changing the whole shape of your face.

They gave him his money in a nice little envelope. Stiller nodded his thanks. His work was done.

Behind him he heard the unmistakable, bone-chilling sound of a shotgun being racked, and a slurred voice that yelled, "Freeze! We the Shotgun Gang!"

THERE WERE THREE FORMS of communication inside a Stakeout Squad Chevy. The regular police radio hidden inside the glove box, the cellular phone and the Motorola hand-held radios that included the crystal for the special Stakeout Squad radio band. It was the latter that squawked, "Team Two Rover."

It was Carmody and Hoffritz's turn in the outside rover car. Carmody was driving because Hoffritz's hand was still sore. She could have finessed a week of paid leave due to injury, but had chosen to come back to work with the bandages on. That meant she was in the "recorder" position, and it was her job to pick up the portable, key the mike and say, "Team Two Rover, go ahead."

"Team Two Rover, we have a priority-one message from dispatch 911, indicating that the Shotgun Gang is going to hit the Official Check Cashing office on Twenty-first in Overtown. Sounds immediate. No certain time of hit."

Hoffritz keyed the transmitting lever. "What's our status for backup? I make our ETA at ninety seconds, two minutes tops."

"Acknowledged, Team Two Rover. Invisible deployment indicated at this time, per command. Marked units are moving toward interdiction positions. Unmarked units in the area are moving in silently to deploy."

"What about Stakeout?" Hoffritz asked, exasperation evident in her voice.

"Nearest Stakeout units are your team. Unknown at this time if they are moving out of assigned location. Rover Two is definitely assigned to respond to Official Check Cashing, invisible outside deployment indicated."

Hell, thought Melinda Hoffritz as she said, "Acknowledged, will advise when we are in deployment position."

Her mind and Carmody's were racing.

"Invisible deployment" meant that the cops would move in to where perpetrators inside the location of the robbery couldn't see them. Invisible deployment, it was understood, would also be a silent putting in place of patrol cars. No one turned on his or her siren. Robbers caught inside when the sirens were heard had a nasty tendency to take people hostage.

Hoffritz asked Carmody, "Think they'll roll our team out of the other joint they're in?"

"Damned if I know," Carmody answered. "For now, safest thing is to assume we're on our own."

They were coming up to the corner of Twenty-first Street. On the other side on their right, they knew, an armed robbery might already be going down.

The two of them were just sliding out of the car when they heard the gunfire.

THE CAUTION HE'D LEARNED on the streets made Eddie Stiller put his hands up slowly at the commands of the robbers. But inside he was seething. His mind screamed savagely, What you mean, you the Shotgun Gang?

He glanced around cautiously. He identified three black men with guns. A hugely fat man with what looked like a 12-gauge pump gun—it sure wasn't a Noble, and it had a real long barrel, not sawed-off like the real Shotgun Gang's—and a skinny one with a long, slim rifle, and a medium-size one waving a small nickel-plated revolver.

The first thing he realized was that they were just standing around aimlessly, yelling for money. No tactical deployment, the way Win had taught him and the rest. No layoff men, obviously—everybody in the check-cashing office was cringing away from them in apparent terror.

They were being ripped off by amateurs—amateurs who were calling themselves the Shotgun Gang.

A sense of rage grew inside Eddie Stiller. He knew that the check-cashing joints were the latest rage for the Shotgun Gang. He knew how much money the other team, the first team, had gotten out of the previous one, and now these assholes were going to spoil the next hit that he was going to share in!

His eyes narrowed behind the Gargoyles. He assessed the situation in front of him. The fat boy with the shotgun was the most dangerous one. Then the scrawny one with the rifle or whatever it was. Then the swaying one, the one obviously drunk out of his mind, who was holding the silvery little revolver.

Everyone in there was black. That was a shame. Stiller would rather have taken cover behind a white person. But you dealt the hand you were played.

The nearest people to him were a big black woman who had two little kids hugging her close. It was the closest thing he had to cover. *If they weren't smart enough to be predators...*

In one smooth, fluid motion, Eddie Stiller drew his snub-nosed .38, took a sliding step that put the fat woman and the kids almost exactly between him and the big guy with the shotgun and shot the big man three times in the chest.

THE THREE FAST GUNSHOTS echoed through the air just as Hoffritz was getting out the passenger side of the unmarked Chevy. She was about to reach down for the Remington when the concussive sound of the three gunshots split the air. She looked for an instant to Carmody, who was also reaching for a shotgun. They came to the same decision at the same instant. *No time.*

Each slammed shut a car door, pausing only long enough to lock it so no one on the street could get inside at the loaded shotguns. They each drew a Colt .45 automatic, holding it with the thumb on the safety catch and the finger outside the trigger. They sprinted toward the corner, behind which the shoot-out had already started.

LAMAR JOHNSON was on top of the world, the robbery going down in an alcoholic haze, his big J. C. Higgins pump shotgun feeling as light as a toy in his hands.

Then the three fast cracks came from his left, and he felt pain burning deep into him. He was starting to turn toward the threat when the third slug went through the center of his body, and he didn't feel himself anymore as he started to fall. He tried to catch himself, but his arms wouldn't work. He hit face-down.

There was no pain. Just horror. He willed his arms and legs to get himself back upright. But they wouldn't respond to his commands anymore.

Around him he heard gunfire like distant thunder. He tried to scream, "Max! J.D.! Help me!"

But his lungs wouldn't work, either, and he only heard a mewling sound like a kitten, a sound he realized to his terror was coming out of his own body.

Lamar Johnson tasted the metallic salt flavor of blood in his mouth. A lot of it. It was pouring up through his gullet.

Max, he tried to shout. J.D.!

But there was no sound. He was alone.

Dying alone.

EDDIE STILLER KNEW three shots were gone, and he knew the fat guy was spinning and falling. He swung his gun left to engage the other two impostors.

There was gunfire from the other side. A rapid sound, like a terribly loud popcorn popper.

The woman he had ducked behind for cover screamed and jerked. So did the kids who were clinging to her skirts.

Blood sprayed in Stiller's face. The big woman buckled to her knees. One of the kids fell away from her, screaming and doubled over; the little girl was clutching her midriff.

The popping kept coming, and the cracking sounds from the skinny one's gun.

Then from his left came a roar of thunder. He had forgotten that this was a check-cashing joint in Overtown, one of the most heavily armed enterprises this side of Fort Knox. The ones behind the counter were shooting back!

The gunfire was like an invisible wave that swept the staggering one away. His gun flew into the air, and a faint pink halo of blood seemed to surround his head. His face changed as he fell, from alive to dead. Stiller knew *that* one was dead meat from the wet thudding sound as his body hit the floor.

That left the one with the rifle, who had fallen back straight through the door. He was out of the line of fire of the black cashiers who had drawn the guns that had killed the robber with the revolver.

But he was dead in line with the one who had first opened fire ... dead in line with Eddie Stiller of the Shotgun Gang.

And Stiller saw it clear. As the man raised the .22-caliber semiautomatic rifle, Stiller saw one of the bloodied kids that was mewling by the fallen body of the fat woman. He scooped her up, grabbed her as a shield, hugged her to him. He snapped off three fast shots at the man in the doorway, who ducked back, unscathed.

"Stay back," Stiller shrieked. "You don't want to be hurtin' this little sister!"

"Fuck you both," screamed the gaunt black man behind the door. He swung his rifle out blindly and fired five fast shots.

Stiller hugged the child close to him to protect himself. He heard sounds like hornets going past his head. He was aware of a thumping sound on the body of the child, and of the child making a high-pitched sound that ended in a wet gurgle, followed by silence. The child went limp.

Stiller was in terror now. He turned, ran blindly, diving out of the door of the check-cashing place.

He heard someone scream "Police!"

He pivoted toward the sound, his gun coming up, pulling the trigger of the Cobra even as he moved.

He was aware of two blond white people, a man and a woman, aiming blue-steel guns at him. He was aware of his own gun only going click, click, and then of white-orange flames at the muzzles of their guns, and breathtaking impacts that threw him on his back.

Suddenly there was blood in his mouth. Eddie couldn't breathe. There wasn't a gun in his hand anymore, and all he could feel was the agonizing cramping pain in his belly and the unspeakably cruel fire in the right side of his chest.

"No mo'," Eddie "Noble" Stiller cried, aware that his voice was bubbling with the blood in his mouth and chest. He sounded to himself like a man talking under water. "Don't shoot me no mo'! I give! *I give!*"

J. D. LANG WAS BLIND with panic. Last night he'd gone over to Max Rogers's place with Lamar Johnson. Drank a little. Drank a lot, actually. Smoked some, too. Talked about how all three of them had been screwed by the powers that be. Talked about getting even. Talked about that Shotgun Gang getting a hundred *grand,* dressing up like women to do it, knocking over that check-cash place. The Shotgun Gang didn't even *live* in Overtown, didn't have no claim at all like they did on them check-cashing places that vampired God knows how much percent from brothers like him, just for cashing a welfare check! It made your blood boil.

They'd decided it right there. Max's bitch got all high an' mighty on 'em, but Max put her in her place righteous. Then they was on they way, Max with his .32, and Lamar with his big shotgun out of his car trunk, and J.D. with that .22 with all those many bullets that he got from Lamar.

And they were in there, takin' the money, when some false brother started shooting, man, and Lamar be down, Max be down, but J.D. cool, man, J.D. shoot him right out from behind that little sister he took hostage, and now J.D. running out the back, J.D. gonna make it like always, J.D. a survivor, man. J.D. almost out the back door when the back door open and there, about arm's length away, there a gray bastard, hair all gray, face all gray, gun all gray, saying "Po-lice! Don't move!"

But you don't say that to J.D. when J.D. got a gun in his hands.

MIKE COHEN HAD BEEN inside the check-cashing joint a few blocks away when the police radio announced the alert on the intended hit by the Shotgun Gang on Official Check Cashing on Twenty-first.

His first thought was, Phony! Diversion! Setup! But he knew he couldn't take the risk of ignoring it, with him and his team sitting somewhere else when it went down.

Real? Diversion? There was only one compromise. He put Baranck in charge of the inside stakeout and told him and the rest of the team that Carmody and Hoffritz in the Team Two rover car were moving on it and so was he. Then he was outside and behind the wheel of his own unmarked Chevy, and flooring it toward Offical Check Cashing.

Coming up Twenty-first, he saw two blocks ahead the rover car pulling up to the curb, Hoffritz and Carmody getting out, slamming the doors behind them. A popping sound came to his ears. He realized it was gunfire.

His partners were already gone around the corner when he pulled up and double-parked behind their car. He jerked out the car keys and locked the door behind him, though later he wouldn't remember doing either.

Mike Cohen's first thought was to follow them, and his second thought was the realization that this would be stupid and redundant. They were the first stakeout response to arrive, and they were going to the front.

That meant someone had to go to the back. Miami was a more thinly policed city than anyone other than a Miami cop realized, all the more in the ghetto. Mike Cohen had monitored the instructions that had gone out over the air: "Silent response, invisible deployment." He hadn't seen a marked car all the way over here.

It didn't surprise him. Overtown was heavily patrolled. But Overtown also had fifty thousand calls a year for police services.

He was the second. That was it.

He scanned around, saw where the back of Official Check Cashing was and ran toward the back door. As he ran, he drew his Glock .45 pistol. The gun he hated suddenly felt very comforting in his hand.

He reached the back door, breathing hard. Cohen paused. He reached down with his left hand, gently opened it.

A face appeared in the doorway. Cohen almost fired before he realized that it was a black woman in a state of terror, one of the victims from inside.

He touched his fingers to his lips. He gestured for her to go. She ran.

Cohen stepped inside the door.

And suddenly he was face-to-face with J. D. Lang, who was holding a .22 rifle and looking like a skeleton from hell covered with black leather and ready to do some recruitment to the place from which he'd come.

J. D. LANG SAW a specter of death in front of him, a little white guy with close-cropped iron gray hair and a gun the same iron gray, pointed right at Lang's chest. "Police," yelled the little white guy. "Don't move!"

Lang believed it. There was a badge clipped to the guy's belt. There was a gun in his hand. Yeah, he was the *po*-lice.

But there was something in his voice. Something in his stance. J. D. Lang knew well who was strong and who was weak, and this one, he realized, didn't want to kill him.

Lang looked at the guy with the iron gray hair. He didn't realize that he was involuntarily beginning to grin, his lips peeling back from his rotting teeth. He only realized that the man didn't have the balls to pull the trigger... and that he, J.D., still had a loaded rifle in his hands. It was going to be victory after all.

The gray dude was saying something like "It'll be all right. Put down the gun. No one wants to shoot you. No one needs to get hurt. I'll get you some help. Put down the gun. It'll be all right."

Was this guy from outer *space?* He's gonna help J.D.? He's gonna help J.D. by dyin' in fuckin' *place* and clearin' a *path,* is how he gone *help* J.D.!

The gray dude's eyes looked like they was gonna cry. Like he was saying, please, please. J.D. knew weakness when he saw it. He heard the man say "Put down the gun. Please, put down the gun."

I got no time for this bullshit, J.D. thought.

Lang began to swing up the gun, his finger already closing on the trigger.

The gray man with the gray gun in front of him dissolved into orange-white fire. Brutal impacts drove into Lang's chest like red-hot pokers, and then something tore savagely at his throat and made him choke. And then there was a sensation of impact in his head, and there was a bright white flare and then—

And then there was nothing at all, but the darkness. J. D. Lang was dead before he could even feel his body hit the floor.

THE THREE AMBULANCES got to Official Check Cashing at almost the same time. The cops were yelling, "The kids! Take the kids first!"

The fat woman Eddie Stiller had used as a human sandbag was dead. One of Lang's .22-caliber bullets had pierced her heart. The paramedics left her there for the death-scene pictures.

Maximilian Rogers was dead, his chest and head savaged by the pistol bullets fired from the vengeful guns of the cashiers.

J. D. Lang was dead. Dr. Joseph Davis, chief medical examiner of Dade County, supervised the autopsy and said in his report that any of the four large-caliber bullets that hit him—the one in the neck that broke the cervical spine and severed the spinal cord, the one that exploded the cerebrum or either of the two that pierced the heart—would have been instantly, or almost instantly, fatal.

Lamar Johnson was dead. He had sustained three .38-caliber gunshot wounds. Two had been survivable. The third had severed the aorta just before it bisected the spinal cord.

Shalonda Pearson, age nine, was still in surgery with multiple .22-caliber gunshot wounds. She had already gone into cardiac arrest once on the operating table. The surgeons at Jackson Memorial Hospital were fighting to keep her alive.

Kateena Duvernay, age eight, Shalonda's cousin, would survive. With her own body her grandmother had shielded her and Shalonda from the hail of J. D. Lang's rifle fire. The bullets that had entered Kateena's buttocks and shoulder, causing only minor wounds, had spent themselves first in the body of her grandmother. The grandmother had also stopped two bullets that otherwise would have killed Shalonda. Shalonda, the evidence technicians determined later, was hit only when suspect Edward Stiller had used her as a human shield to ward off the gunfire of suspect J. D. Lang, deceased.

13

John Kearn peered into the darkness of his bedroom. He couldn't sleep.

At his side, snuggled next to him despite the expanse of the king-size bed, his wife's shoulders rose and fell in the rhythmic breathing of sleep. He didn't want to wake her.

He didn't want to wake the kids, either. He slid slowly, carefully out of bed and managed not to disturb her. He threw on a robe and padded toward the living room.

Kearn turned on the dim light beside the wet bar and grabbed a tumbler. He pressed the button on the side of the minirefrigerator and filled half the glass with ice and then selected a bottle of Canadian blended whiskey to pour in to finish the drink.

He screwed the cap back on the bottle and brought the glass up to his lips. The hot brown liquid that streamed across his tongue and down his throat seemed to wake him up.

It was time to think about the Stakeout Squad.

Okay, okay, he had pissed off the mayor. It was time to be philosophical about it. The mayor was going to get pissed off anyway as soon as he found out Kearn wasn't going to be his political toady. It had been only a matter of time, a matter of sooner or later.

It had just been sooner rather than later—that was all.

Things were getting better, in a way. There had been the dead kid in the bank, and there had been the dead Thelma-and-Louise women in the bank robbery. Now there was the thing at the check-cash place.

Dead innocents there? Sure there were. But at least Stakeout had gotten there. At least Stakeout had done something.

At least, to be frank, Stakeout had left some *bad* guys bleeding on the ground for a change.

No, wait. That wasn't fair. He sipped at the whiskey again.

As far as any logical person should be concerned, two bad guys were on the ground dead when West and Baranck shot the two women. They had been dressed as men, after all. They had opened fire on the cops first. The cops had done what they'd had to do.

Of course, the Stakeout cops had done the same with the kids in the bank on that first run. But that didn't seem to matter to the media.

At least they were gaining some ground. They'd get another crack at the Shotgun Gang. Kearn was certain of it. The way these scumbags were playing up to the media, trying to tease the cops . . . no, they weren't going to quit, and they weren't going to get out of Dodge. They were going to stay here until the final showdown. Crazy sons of bitches.

His drink was gone. He poured himself another. He wished he had a cigar, but he knew his wife hated him to smoke them in the house, and he didn't even have any at home. Sitting on the bar was a pack of Marlboro Lights that one of his wife's girlfriends had inadvertently left. There was a book of matches next to it.

He shook a cigarette out of the pack, lit it and took a deep drag. The whiskey didn't make him dizzy, but the cigarette did, just a little. It had been a while since he'd quit smoking cigarettes.

Back when he was a New York cop. Back when he carried a gun every day at work, and every time he left his house off duty. Off-duty carry was mandatory then.

Kearn took another lungful of the thin gray smoke and smiled into the darkness at the irony of it all. He had quit smoking as a young city cop, and here he was, a city chief of police, smoking a purloined cigarette like a little kid behind the barn, hoping Mom wouldn't catch the scent.

As a young New York cop, he was an activist in the African-American patrolmen's group—it was politically correct to call it the Afro-American group then—and he was shocked at the fact that the Stakeout Unit had blown away black guys, black guys, and more black guys. And now here he was, a black chief of police, inaugurating a Stakeout Unit of his own.

And amazingly, almost everybody they'd shot so far was white. Wonders would never cease.

The .38-caliber revolver had been his constant companion then, the two-inch snubby off duty and the four-inch with the big square butt when he was "in the bag," that is, wearing the uniform. Now the first thing he did when he got to work was put his gun in his desk drawer.

Hell, he had fought for 9 mm automatics for the patrol force, and in New York they still didn't have them yet. Irony of ironies, they already had the 9 mm Glock when he got here, they *issued* him one for God's sake, and he carried it in that ultimate holster of the bureaucrat cop, his desk drawer.

The ironies compounded. He still got his copies of the *Finest,* the New York City patrolman's union magazine, and *Spring 3100,* the journal the city police department itself published, named after the old phone number that everyone in the city had once known would bring the cops post haste. He couldn't help but notice that the past three New York City police commissioners had made a point of mentioning in their interviews that they carried guns.

He chuckled. Never mind that in New York City the commander of cops, the police commissioner, wasn't actually a cop himself but an appointed official not per se authorized to carry a firearm. Even the ones who had been promoted from the ranks of the police department's superchiefs had lost their police status as soon as they swore the oath of commissioner. To carry a weapon, they had to be issued a civilian concealed-carry permit.

Of course, he thought wryly, as soon as they were commander in chief of the NYPD, which issued such permits, they could order one issued to themselves. Was this a night to think of ironies or what?

He shook his head sadly. His drink and his cigarette were almost gone. He decided that he would stop putting his gun in the drawer when he came into work, and would wear it conspicuously throughout the day. The same with the badge clipped to his belt. The badge and the gun were the marks of the job. Let his people know he still considered himself one of them.

He took one last drag of the cigarette—it was almost down to the filter—and exhaled. It had been satisfying. So, in every way, had every other whiff of the past he had inhaled this night.

He looked for a place to stub out the cigarette butt and couldn't find an ashtray. He had been dumping the ashes down the sink of the wet bar, but it wouldn't swallow a cellulose cigarette filter.

He sighed, drank down the dregs of his whiskey and pushed the glowing ember of the Marlboro butt down into the ice cubes. It hissed and died.

Satisfied that it was cold and dead, he dumped the whole mess into the discreet little trash can beside the bar, rinsed out the glass and left it in the bottom of the little sink.

Kearn hoped there was an allegory there. He wanted to see the life hiss out of the Shotgun Gang, wanted to pour the dregs of their dead threat into a trash can and call in somebody to clean up whatever stains had been left.

And it would happen, he swore to himself. *It would happen.*

He turned out the light over the bar and walked purposefully back to the bedroom to go to sleep.

14

The whooping sound of the siren filled the cubicle of the ambulance as it raced toward Jackson Memorial. Eddie Stiller writhed in pain, twisting his body as much as he could with his wrists handcuffed to the sides of the steel gurney.

Dan Harrington wiped the sweat from his balding forehead with the back of his left hand as his right thumb pressed the dual buttons on the tape machine that made it record. Harrington read in the date and the time.

"Sir," he continued, addressing Stiller, "you have been shot multiple times. It is my considered and reasoned belief that you may die of your wounds. If there is anything you wish to tell us, it will have the legal status of a dying statement. It will be almost irrefutable. If you should survive your wounds, nothing you say at this time can ever be held against you. Do you understand what I have told you?"

Cops learn to memorize the *Miranda* statement and even so, carry cards with the full wording to read to the suspect just to be sure. Dying declarations happen so seldom that not only do cops never get cards to read the proper wording from, but also they seldom get to give one in their career.

Dan Harrington had memorized his, for better or for worse, and he had delivered it better than most.

And Eddie Stiller believed every word, every syllable. The agonizing pain of his bullet wounds had convinced him that he was in fact going to die.

Stiller had been shot once in the abdomen, once in the right shoulder, and twice in the right chest. The Stakeout cops who shot him had been taught to aim for the center of mass. His right side had been toward them and his gun was coming up, his finger pulling the trigger, when they had each pulled the trigger twice.

That was why each of their first shots had hit him in the right side of the chest, tearing out his lung, but missing the pleural and pulmonary arteries. Melinda Hoffritz's second shot had been jerked low, entering the stomach and missing the vena cava and stopping, fully mushroomed, two inches below his lower left floating rib, having also missed the spleen. Carmody's second shot of the double tap had gone high and to his left, shattering the knob of the humerus, or upper arm bone, as it entered the joint. Later the X ray would look like a two-toned snowstorm with the fuzzy white outlines of the smashed bone chips and the starker white outlines of the lead bullet fragments.

But when they read him his dying declaration, Eddie Stiller didn't believe he was going to live. Frankly neither did Detective Dan Harrington, who held the recorder to the wounded man's lips, nor Officer Shirley Montague, who knelt on the other side of the man whose hemorrhage was so violent the paramedics were working valiantly to stop it.

"I know," cried Eddie Stiller into the tape machine. "I know I'm gonna die! Never shoulda messed with them white mothers!"

"Tell me about it," said Harrington in a soft and seductive tone of voice, a strange way to talk to a dying man. "Tell us about the white mothers."

His tone of voice had been chosen well. It struck a responsive chord. "Win," Stiller gurlged from inside his ruptured lung. "Win! Shotgun Gang! We're the Shotgun Gang! I was casing the Official, these mothers started shooting—" His words were choked off in a bloody gurgle.

"Come on, guy, tell us about it! There isn't much time! *Kids* got shot today!"

"Not my fault," gurgled Stiller. "Didn't mean . . . hurt kids—" He broke off into another fit of wet coughing.

"I don't think you're any 'Shotgun Gang,'" Harrington broke in. "If you're really the Shotgun Gang, tell us where you're headquartered."

"None a your biz," Stiller burbled angrily through the blood that foamed in his face.

"Tell us," Montague said. "You're gonna *die*, man. Don't die with these dead kids on your conscience! Tell us about Win! Tell us where he is."

"Back off, bitch," Stiller burbled back.

"You aren't a member of the Shotgun Gang, *are* you, punk," Harrington asked suddenly.

"I am, too! I *am*," said Eddie Stiller, bits of bloody foam flying in the air as he spit out the words.

"You saying you *are* a member of the Shotgun Gang?" Shirley's question came through crystal clear on the tape recorder.

"Fuckin' right I am," Stiller said back defiantly. He still sounded like a man talking underwater because of the blood in his lungs.

"Yeah," the female cop challenged, "then where's your next hit?"

"Dunno...gonna be Official's...not now...no more..."

There was a wet and gurgly wheeze.

"Get away from him," one of the paramedics shouted. "I think we're gonna lose him."

"No great loss at all," muttered Miami Officer Shirley Montague, who had just shut off the detective's tape recorder.

RONALD PEARSON SAT alone in his tiny apartment in Overtown. He crushed out a used-up cigarette in an ashtray that was full of the cork-colored butts.

It had come to this.

His daughter was in the hospital. The hospital where he worked. Where he had told his little girl he went, every day, to do his part to save the hurt and the sick.

His daughter was dying there. They as much as told him. "We're doing everything we can, Mr. Pearson."

He knew *exactly* what that meant. He'd heard it so many times at the hospital. *We're doing everything we can.*

What they meant was that she was going to die, and there wasn't anything they could do about it except try to make him feel good for a few minutes.

Shalonda. *Shalonda!* He dropped his head in his hands.

Ron Pearson was fifteen when he got Marsha pregnant. Sixteen when they had their baby, Shalonda.

They decided on the name together. What they didn't agree on was Ron dropping out of high school along with Marsha, the one to take care of the baby and the other to get a job to make the money to feed her.

It didn't matter. They were a family, Ron and Marsha and Shalonda.

Then the day came when Shalonda was six, and Marsha was walking her across the street, carrying a bag of groceries in her left arm and holding Shalonda's hand with her free hand. There was the howling sound of the motorcycle, the crack addict running from the police car behind him.

They were too close. It was too late. Marsha swung her arm with all her might—they said that was the only thing that would account for the dislocated shoulder that was found at the autopsy, everything else was a crushing injury—and his wife threw their baby girl out of the way just before the collision. Just before the crackhead on the six-hundred-pound bike hit her full force at ninety miles per hour and crushed the life out of his Marsha, and left their baby girl without a mother.

Ron Pearson was father and mother both after that. He still had to work at the hospital. One thing you had to say about medical people: they didn't care where you got your degree—they cared how well you did your job. Before too long Ron Pearson was a senior maintenance superintendent at Jackson Memorial Hospital. He had to work a lot of overtime—to get the promotions, to get the money for him and Shalonda—and while he was gone, Marsha's momma, Gramma Hayes, took care of Shalonda, just as she took care of Kateena, her grandchild by her useless son

Tyray, who got himself and her daughter-in-law both sent to prison for dealing crack cocaine.

Kateena and Shalonda were both with Gramma Hayes when she went into Official Check Cashing in Overtown to cash Gramma Hayes's Social Security check. When Gramma Hayes put her body up as security to keep her granddaughters alive, stopped the bullets these scumbags had pumped in her direction.

It looked as if Kateena was okay. She was going to live. It looked as if Shalonda was going to die. What the hell was it all for?

Ron Pearson didn't know anymore. He didn't care anymore. He reached down to the drawer in his night table and opened it.

He took the ugly blue-black metal thing out in his hand. It was an RG model 14, .22 caiber. It held six hyper-velocity Stinger hollowpoint bullets.

Ron Pearson looked down at the gun and smiled without mirth. This, he knew, was what they called a Saturday night special. He had read about it in an article in *Tropic,* the paper magazine folded inside the Sunday edition of each *Miami Crier.*

But he also knew that you couldn't believe everything you read in the *Crier.* He also read other papers. He spent his lunch hours reading what they had in the hospital library. In the *Wall Street Journal* he had read about the history of gun-control laws. He had learned that the phrase *Saturday night special* had come from down-South cops during the segregation years, and had meant "niggertown Saturday night." The history had become clear to him: a gun a black man could afford to have to protect his wife and his children was bad, but an expensive target-grade Magnum a white rich bastard could have—to protect *his* family from niggers—was good.

The RG, which he'd bought from a friend down on his luck for twenty dollars in a bar one payday night, had become a symbol for him. A symbol of "niggertown Saturday night." A symbol that, while he might have to eat peanut butter sandwiches for lunch during his working day so he'd have more money to take care of his wife and daughter, he would sure as hell also have something to protect his wife and daughter.

But he hadn't been there to protect Marsha when she was run down by a cocaine monster on a speeding motorcycle. And he hadn't been there to protect his Shalonda, or his mother-in-law who took care of her, who died trying to take care of her.

But it was better late than never. The gun was in his hand now. Alive, almost, and assuredly deadly. And there was only one thing left to do with it.

Gramma Hayes, dead. Shalonda, he knew, dying. *And the mother who shot her was alive, going to recover, right there in the post-op wing of his very own hospital.*

Ron Pearson crushed the cylinder closed on the six Stinger bullets. He was still wearing his hospital uniform, the one he'd been wearing when he'd gotten the message that Shalonda had been shot.

He shoved the gun into his pocket. He clipped to his breast pocket the plastic ID card that let him go anywhere he wanted, any time, in Jackson Memorial Hospital.

I'm coming to punish you, he said silently. Don't matter if it's Saturday or not. Niggertown Saturday night is comin' for you, and it's comin' for you now.

THE THIRD FLOOR EAST, the post-op wing of Jackson Memorial Hospital, was always full. The guy in 304E was by no means unusual. A lung blown out by gunfire? A shoulder shattered? Half a stomach removed from the damage a bullet did? He was one of the lucky ones. The less fortunate wound up one block down and one block over, on a stainless-steel table at one of the busiest medical examiner's offices in the world.

Eddie Stiller had just woken up. It took him a long time to realize he was alive.

It didn't take him a whole lot longer to feel the pain. Or to find out that both his hands were handcuffed to the stainless-steel horizontal bars that were part and parcel of a hospital bed in a Miami trauma ward.

And just when he was waking up, just when he was starting to worry about where was Win and all the lawyers that Win had promised, there was the black guy that came through the door and shoved the barrel of an ugly little gun in Stiller's mouth.

RON PEARSON HAD no problem at all to get up to the third floor and into the secured area. The Jackson Memorial tag on his scrub greens indicated that he was authorized to be there as a senior maintenance man, if anyone had failed to recognize his face.

There were two stumbling blocks, both easily overcome. The guy outside the door in the crisp blue Miami Police uniform with the yellow circle on the shoulder said, "Sorry, sir, this is a protective-custody area."

"Yeah," Pearson answered with faked weariness, "and you got a guy in protective custody with a malfunctioning bed, an' he's gotta have his bed fixed so it can elevate right and not fool around with his blood pressure and kill him, all right? You got a question, call the chief of staff, I ain't got time for this bullshit, oh-*kay?*''

The cop was a young one, and he backed off. Pearson was clean into the room so far.

Then the guy in plainclothes stood up. "Be cool," Pearson said with the weary voice he had down pat now. "Doc said his bed wasn't workin' right for lift, to keep his circulation goin'." He moved to the right side of Stiller's bed by now, and he knew that they couldn't stop him from here.

The young uniformed Miami patrolman was starting to say "Sir, I'm not sure you can do that yet," when Pearson made his move.

The gun came out of the waistband of his scrub greens. He shoved the muzzle of the gun into the open mouth of Eddie Stiller.

"Don't move," Pearson yelled. "Don't anybody move! This bastard put my little girl downstairs dyin', and this bastard is gonna pay!"

LESS THAN FIVE MINUTES after Ron Pearson stuck his gun in Eddie Stiller's mouth, the phone rang in Chief Kearn's office.

"I think you better take it, sir," Charlene said, and Kearn punched the button.

He listened for a moment. Then he said, "Okay. Keep it cool, you understand? Keep it copacetic. What I'm saying is, however much he's got the right, don't let this guy shoot that bastard, at least, hold him off till I get there. And I want Bartlett there, too, and I want SWAT up and running and ready to go, and the same for all three Stakeout teams.''

EDDIE STILLER WAS wide awake now. His mouth was wrapped around the barrel of an RG revolver. The index finger of Ron Pearson was wrapped around the trigger of the same gun.

"How's it feel?" Pearson asked in a purring voice. "How's it feel to know you gonna die like my little girl's gonna die? Like she's gonna die, 'cause you used her for a human shield against another scumbag like you?"

For emphasis, Pearson twisted the gun barrel inside Stiller's mouth. He felt the blood spill out over his hand. He could also feel his captive shaking, convulsing with sobs.

"Ron!"

The voice came from outside the room. It was commanding. Pearson was sure it sounded like a black man's voice.

"Yeah? What? Who are you, anyway?"

"My name is John Kearn," the voice came back, smooth and steady. "I'm the chief of police for Miami. Ron, I need to talk to you."

"What the hell you want to talk about," Pearson yelled back. "My girl gonna die. They as much as told me. And he's gonna die with her, Kearn! He's gonna be dead before she's cold. He got her shot, got her grandma shot, too!"

"I know that, Ron," Kearn's voice said back. "I know something else. Shalonda's not dead. She's got a damn good chance of surviving. Folks here in the hospital, they told me what happened with your wife.

Dammit, Ron, your daughter's probably gonna live! What good are you gonna do her if your ass is in Raiford State Penitentiary for killing the scumbag who shot her? Let *his* ass go to Raiford, Ron!''

Ron Pearson looked down at his gun in the mouth of the man whose eyes were pleading for survival. "Not enough, Chief," he yelled back. "I gotta *know* my little girl is gonna live! I gotta *know* he's gonna pay!"

John Kearn gritted his teeth. "Hey, Ron," he said, "we don't have to measure dicks with each other here, all right? They told me when you stuck the gun in his mouth, my cop pulled his Glock and said drop it or he'd waste you. They told me, you cocked the hammer and said, you had the trigger already pulled and if they shot you, the hammer would fall out from under your finger and kill this bastard even if you were already dead. That true?"

"Damn straight," Pearson yelled back, "an' I gotta tell ya, Chief, my thumb's gettin' some kinda tired!"

"Don't call me 'Chief.' My name is John. You're Ron, I'm John, and we're both letting this bastard control us."

"Shit, John, everybody in this city knows the Shotgun Gang's been screwing around with your people, messing up your head! Why should I listen to you when I got the guy you can't take, got him here by the balls?"

It was then that Kearn would make the statement he would spend the rest of his career explaining. Both detectives and reporters were in the hall with their recorders running.

"Listen, Ron," he said, "you got something in there I'd kill for. You got a member of the Shotgun Gang. They've terrorized this city for months. My city! One good reason for you not to kill him is that he's got information we need."

There was a long silence. Then from inside the post-op room where Ron Pearson was now alone with Eddie Stiller there came the suddenly calm and deadly quiet voice of Ron Pearson. "You think he's got something you want to hear. Okay, Chief, I guess you think he knows what you need to hear?"

"Of course he does," Kearn said impatiently.

"Fine, then," said the suddenly and unnaturally calm Ron Pearson. "Tell you what. I know you got your SWAT team with their telescope rifles trained on me through the window. But you know I've already pulled the trigger and my thumb holdin' the hammer back is gettin' real tired. You know that also means when I get a bullet through the head and my body like, relaxes, this hammer is gonna slip out from under my thumb, and this gun gonna go off, right?"

"Yeah," sighed John Kearn. "That's understood."

"Okay, then," said Ron Pearson. "Tell your people to hold their fire on their sniper rifles there. See, I got this gun here, but I also got a pair of pliers in my pocket. They out now in my other hand. Can your sniper through the window see that?"

There was a flurry of communication on Kearn's end, and then he said, "Yes, Ron. I can see that."

"Okay, then," said Pearson. "You break in on us, he dies. I'm gonna put my pliers down on his balls now, and I figure he knows better than you what it is you need to know about the Shotgun Gang."

The tapes from the intelligence microphones were running the whole time. They recorded Pearson saying "Last chance," and Eddie saying "Fuck you, nigger," and then there was a scream.

And then there was the long stream of statements by Edward Stiller that would soon give the City of Miami Police Department sufficient cause to allow a judge of Dade County to authorize a no-knock warrant for a certain condominium at a certain address in Coral Gables, Florida.

"Don't kill him," Chief Kearn said when the statement was over. "Ron, your daughter's going to live. Your daughter's going to need you."

"Yeah, right. She's gonna need me, need to grow up knowing her father pulls guns in hospitals, got killed by the SWAT team."

"That won't happen, Ron. Dammit, I won't let it happen. Take the gun out of his mouth. Put it down. Come out of there."

"They'll kill me if I do. You know that, John."

"Like hell. Put it down, Ron, and you and I will come out of there together. Hand in hand, bro."

"You know," said a very tired Ron Pearson with a sigh, "I think I believe you. Can I go up, see my daughter in ICU before I go to jail?"

"You and me together, we'll do it, Ron."

Ron Pearson took the gun out of Stiller's mouth. He carefully lowered the hammer. He set the gun down and then he opened the door to the sequestered hospital room, waiting to be shot.

Instead, Chief of Police John Kearn was there. He reached out his arms. They hugged each other. SWAT cops rushed in from behind them, and Chief Kearn raised a hand that made them stop in their tracks.

"It's okay, Ron," the chief said softly. "It's okay."

Cops were rushing into the hostage room to see if the suspect was still alive. He was, but fresh blood was dribbling out of the corner of his mouth.

Kearn looked at his cops. "Did you get what that bastard said?"

They nodded.

"Then get over there. Bring me a portable phone to call the chief of police in Coral Gables. If this 'Win' that he talked about is there, we'll hit him and we'll hit him hard."

Chief of Police John Kearn put his arm around Ron Pearson's shoulder. "Later," he said softly, "my guys are gonna have to take you in. You knew that up front. But it's gonna be okay. For now you and I have to go upstairs. I want you to see your daughter."

15

John Blaisdell tossed fitfully, then awoke. He was lying in bed in his suite at the Intercontinental Hotel on the bay. He glanced at his Rolex—3:12 a.m. Hell! He had slept less than an hour!

He rolled over and sat upright, glancing absently at the black .380 pistol on the night table by the high-tech phone. He was uncomfortable about the way he felt, and the reason he couldn't sleep. It wasn't guilt. It was annoyance he was feeling. That, and righteous anger.

What a bitch that stupid Kimberley was for making him kick the crap out of her like that.

She had no right to make him feel small. It wasn't *his* fault that the *Crier* hadn't gotten it.

He reached over his pistol and picked up the crumpled newspaper clipping from where he'd thrown it on the other side of the phone. He sensed that he had already read the damn thing too many times, but the anger in him insisted that he read it once more.

Miami Justice
Death Orgy in Overtown
by Oliver Teasdale

Yesterday's tragic massacre in Overtown was all the more tragic because it could have been avoided. It would have been avoided if Miami wasn't an armed camp. And at least part of it would have been avoided if Miami Police Department's vaunted Stakeout Squad had for once been where they were supposed to be: in place to protect citizens against such criminal elements as the Shotgun Gang.

The guns of the cashiers gave them fool's courage that was as false as fool's gold, but deadlier. The same modern urban myth—that having a gun makes you a hero who can prevail—cost the lives of three ArmorDade security guards in another recent tragedy, also believed to be the work of the Shotgun Gang.

Our mayor, to his great credit, agrees that guns have no place in this society, except in the hands of police and soldiers. Lately, seeing the way the Stakeout Squad has been using their guns—two children dead, one holding a toy pistol, and two helpless women "suspects" dead—one wonders if His Honor may be too optimistic about cops and guns. Perhaps Miami would be a safer place if the Stakeout Squad, and perhaps the rest of the cops, hung up their guns and carried only whistles and truncheons, like British bobbies.

Then, the only violence we'd have to worry about would be the kind offered by such as the Shotgun Gang, who in their latest lethal robbery became transvestites. Criminals insecure of their gender identity, who dress as women and use guns as surrogate phalluses, are a danger to us all.

A danger as great as—though not necessarily greater than—the Miami Police Department death squad that calls itself the Stakeout unit.

Blaisdell flung the worn clipping away. *Criminals insecure of their own gender identity, who used guns as surrogate phalluses.* Lying bastards! That idiot Teasdale! And the guy had been so right before!

Blaisdell had slept in till noon the previous day. Kimberley brought him his paper with the lunch she'd carefully prepared. He turned first to the "Miami Justice" column, which had become his favorite, and when he read what Oliver Teasdale had written, Blaisdell threw the paper across the room.

Kimberley said, "What's the matter, honey?"

He had just blurted out an obscenity.

Kimberley had tried to hug him and said, "Don't worry, hon. Want me to dress up some more guys like foxes, make 'em up, go out and do a—"

She never finished the sentence. He hit her first.

And kept hitting her. He couldn't stop himself. She had become the very embodiment of the stupid idea that had made him and his Shotgun Gang a laughing-stock.

He didn't cease hitting her until he stopped for breath. By that time, she was unconscious. He stood over her, breathing raggedly.

Her face was a bloody mask. Her breath was raspy, bubbly. Her blood was all over him. Messy and disgusting.

He wasn't hungry anymore. He stepped over her, walked into the fancy bathroom off his master bedroom in the Coral Gables condo, dumped his bloody bathrobe in the hamper and took a long hot shower. When he was done, and shaved and moussed, he dressed carefully.

A fashionable, wealthy-looking professional man in a tailored Armani suit looked back at him from the full-length mirror. He clipped the SIG .380 in its soft holster into the back of his waistband under the side-vented suit coat and walked back into the dining room.

Kimberley was still there. Not quite where he left her. She had crawled a few feet. In the half hour he'd taken to shower and dress, her face had puffed up like an ugly Cabbage Patch doll.

She looked up at him through her swollen eyelids with an expression of terror. "Don't hit me, John," she mumbled.

He drew back his leg to kick her in the face and then realized that he'd get blood all over his Gucci shoes. Instead, he just spit on her. She cringed away from the glob of phlegm that caught her just above the eye.

He turned on his heel and walked out, locking the door behind him.

The rest of the day was a bit of a blur. Drive around, case this; drive around, check out that; go to a movie... A little after seven he decided he didn't want to look at that stupid ugly bitch or have to slap her around anymore, either, so he checked into the Intercontinental.

He cruised the lounges there for hours, the regular one and the expensive one, and came up empty all night. At one he went to bed, but tossed and turned.

He glanced at his watch again. Almost three-thirty in the morning.

He was still pissed at Kimberley. It was time to set some things straight with that bitch. He dialed the private number of his condo.

It rang half a dozen times before it was picked up. Blaisdell heard a vaguely familiar voice say "Yeah? Who's this?"

Blaisdell roared, "Who the hell is this?"

"Win? That you?"

"Chen? Is this Chen?"

"Yeah! Win, where *are* you, man?"

"Never mind that! What are you doin' there?"

"Hey, Win, be cool, man, okay? Kimberley called me. She's been hurt, man, all beat to shit!"

"*Who* beat her to shit?"

There was a long pause on the line. "She said you done it, man," Chen answered.

"I just slapped the bitch around, that's all," Blaisdell snapped back. "She needed some discipline. What do you mean, beat to shit?"

"Her eyes are all swole shut, John," Chen answered nervously. "Face is a mess... teeth all loose. John, she's real bad. Like half the time she's sleepin', half the time she's awake, half the time she's in between." Chen paused. "She was mine, I'd take her to the hospital, Win."

"Yeah, well, she *ain't* yours! She said I beat her to shit?"

"Well... yeah."

"Screw it. Ignore her. Stupid bitch. What are you doing, stayin' with her?"

"Well, yeah, Win, she asked me to. Said she was scared to be alone. Look, Win, she's hurtin'."

"Like I said. She's okay. I just slapped her around. She's okay."

There was another long silence on the other end. Finally Win said, "Hey, what's new?"

"That thing in Overtown, guess you know about that. Wasn't any of our guys, was it?"

"Hell, no," Win snapped almost too quickly. He had been worried about it since he'd heard it over the car radio, but he knew it couldn't have been any of his people working without him. Noble? Noble would have found a way to get in touch if it was him. Besides, Noble would have been too smart to get involved in a holdup in progress.

"That shit ain't got nothin' to do with us," Blaisdell said. "Look, where's Kimberley now?"

"She's out of it, man. Sleepin' on the sofa. I'm tellin' ya, Win, she's messed up. What you want me to do?"

Blaisdell shook his head. He was a long-term planner. Short-term impediments were something he only knew how to deal with by pulling the trigger on a shotgun.

"I dunno," he almost said, but he stopped himself. The guys in prison had taught him to never tell your underlings that you don't know. You stall them somehow until you do know.

"Make sure she's okay," said Blaisdell. "Then get the fuck out. Look, Chen, you don't take your orders from that stupid bitch. You take them from me. Understand?"

"Sure, Win, sure! I understand," Chen said eagerly. "It's just . . . she's *yours,* you know? You're my man, Win, you're my main man, somethin' of yours is in trouble, I'm here for you, you know?"

Chen couldn't see Blaisdell sneering on the other end of the line. "Yeah, right. I know. Look, just get the hell out, all right? I'll call you when I need you. That'll be soon," he added placatingly.

"Right. Got ya, Win. I'm outa here. I'll lock up behind me. But look, man, I think she's in tough shape, ya know? Ya might want to—"

Blaisdell cut him off. "*I'll* figure out what I want to do, goddammit! Now, get out of there!"

"Uh, yeah. Right. Gotcha, Win, gotcha. I'm outa here, man!"

"Fuckin' better be," snarled Win as he slammed the phone down in its cradle.

John "Win" Blaisdell was on his feet now. What the hell was Chen doing in *his* place? It was Kimberley. *Kimberley!*

Stupid bitch, he fumed to himself. Calling Chen. Making out like I was some abusive bastard that beat his women. Well, she's ready to call my friends to make me look like a bastard, she's ready to call the pigs and do the same.

He couldn't sleep anyway, so he began reaching for his clothes. Something in the back of his mind nagged at him. Could that maybe have been Noble in the check-cashing joint? Noble hadn't returned his calls after he'd heard on the news about the shooting. But he'd been so pissed off by the Teasdale column, he hadn't tried again to get hold of him. Hell, he knew it couldn't have been him in there.

He threw on his clothes. And his gun. It was time to get out of this damn hotel. Time to go home.

Time to kill this stupid bitch that was making him look bad.

IT WAS a little after 3:20 a.m. The police task force began to assemble around the huge condominium complex in Coral Gables, Florida.

Coral Gables Police Department's SWAT team would hit the condo. Twelve officers were assembled for the team. Another eight supervisors and senior officers were on the scene. A dozen more patrolmen from that department had been assigned to block off traffic—even in the early-morning hours, that could be a problem—and another sixteen Coral Gables patrol officers had been called in to help evacuate adjacent condo apartments and to seal off strategic areas like the parking garage.

Three members of the FBI Armed Robbery Team attached to the Miami office were present. They had been assigned to follow the depredations of the Shotgun Gang.

Four members of the robbery and homicide unit of the Metro Dade Police Department were there, too. Because some of the early hits by the Shotgun Gang had gone down outside the Miami city limits in unincorporated Dade County, part of the case was theirs.

Also present were the commanding officer of the Miami Police Department Stakeout Squad and the supervisor of Stakeout Team Two.

Riding up to the sixth floor, Ken Bartlett said to Mike Cohen, "Can you believe it took this long?"

Cohen answered flatly, "Sure, Lieutenant. How long did *you* think it'd take to convince a Dade County judge to give us a no-knock warrant based on what a guy told us, with somebody's gun in his mouth. With the guy holding the gun in his mouth also being the father of the kid that got shot in a holdup? *And* to roll a full SWAT team and get enough blues to cover the area?"

"I hear you," said Bartlett, "But, goddammit, this is the Shotgun Gang. You'd think for something like this they could move a little faster."

Cohen looked at him with anger. "Hitler acted faster for Jews than he did for Gypsies. We don't have that here, Ken. It's due process. Remember that, 'due process'? I haven't worked out the due process on Jonathan David Lang yet, and he's been cold a while now. At least we took some time on this one."

"Oh, man," said Bartlett softly, "don't talk that garbage to me now. Not *now*. You shot J. D. Lang because he *had* to be shot. I'd much rather go to his funeral than go to yours, and that's the choice he gave you when he made you smoke him."

"No choice at all, Ken," Cohen said bitterly. "You'd have had to go to *my* funeral. I know for certain you're not going to his. You can decide that all you want. I've *got* to go to his funeral. I don't have any choice in the matter."

"You should have a choice," Bartlett snapped back. "Or, rather, you shouldn't have a choice. It doesn't say in our rules you can't go to the funeral of somebody you had to shoot, but it sure as hell doesn't say you need to. He was coming up on you with an automatic rifle, Mike!"

The slow elevator had reached the sixth floor, the floor that the intelligence from the hospital had told them held the apartment of the leader of the Shotgun Gang. The doors of the elevator began to open.

Ken Bartlett's dark hand reached to the control panel and hit the Door Close button and held it there. The doors closed again.

"Tell me, Mike," Bartlett said urgently. "Tell me if you can't handle this. Because, Mike, whatever happens tonight, you and me and Stakeout have all got a lot to do yet. I have to know you can take it, Mike. If you can't, *say* you can't, and I'll get you covered. I'll cover you myself. But dammit, Mike, I must know!"

"I can handle it," said Mike Cohen in a voice that had a choking sound. "I can handle it. Open this door. Let's get it done."

Bartlett stared into Cohen's dark eyes for a long moment. Then he took his hand back away from the control panel. The elevator door opened onto the sixth floor. They stepped into the hallway.

The place resembled an atrium. There was a square hollow that ran from the floor with its colored fountain all the way to the twelfth storey. On all four sides were condominium apartments. All in front of one apartment were Coral Gables cops, dressed in their ninjalike black SWAT suits. A few held shotguns. Most were grasping Heckler & Koch MP-5 9 mm submachine guns. Clustered on either side of the door were men holding either submachine guns or pistols, and one held a shotgun that seemed to be aimed at the door itself.

It was about to go down.

CHEN HO LEE had just hung up the phone. He felt relieved in a way. Chen, since childhood, had learned to do what he was told by the authority figure. The authority figure, Win, had just told him what to do. He was back in his element.

The phone receiver lay in the cradle where he'd just set it down. He glanced over toward the sofa. Kimberley was still lying there, her face dark with the caked blood she wouldn't let him help to remove. She seemed to be asleep. Chen looked down at her anxiously. Her breathing didn't seem regular, but at least she was breathing. Well, that was all he could hope for. He had done his job, a job he hadn't even had to do. He resented Kimberley for this. He understood that she had put him in bad with Win. He remembered Win's tone of voice on the phone. Angry. Win was the one man Chen did not want to get angry.

He'd been here for what seemed like all day and all night with this spaced-out, beaten woman. She had been saying things like, "I know what he does! Goddamn him! I can hurt him! He's got no right to do this to me...."

Chen shuddered at the thought. If he had been a good lieutenant for Win, he would have slit her throat. But how do you slit the throat of the boss's mistress without permission?

Decisions...decisions...but thankfully that was over now. Win had spoken. Chen was out of here.

All he had to do first was take a piss. His bladder was bursting. He glanced over at the sofa. Kimberley was twitching, moving around. Well, at least she wasn't dead or anything. She wasn't his problem anymore.

Chen stepped into the huge bathroom and closed the door behind him. It was the habit of life in America. Never mind that there's no one to watch—close the door behind you when you go potty.

He unzipped, pointed himself into the toilet, and sighed as his bladder unleashed itself. As the spray streamed into the toilet, he looked around and sighed again: fancy bathroom, fancy condo, that was what Win's money had bought for him.

Chen's money, his share of the robberies, had bought something different.

He only vaguely remembered his family's departure from Korea. But he remembered vividly the lessons his parents had taught him: ignore the racial slurs, ignore the prejudice, ignore everything except working hard for your family. His brothers had fit their ideal. Chen had not.

Chen had learned quickly that crime was the fastest way to money. He had learned also that his parents held crime and criminals in contempt. He had convinced them that he made his money, the money he sent them, working honorably as a bodyguard.

The ones who had died before his gun . . . well, they didn't count. They were part of the job. That was all. All that counted was your family and what your family thought of you. They were proud that he sent them so much money. They didn't care that he lived in a furnished room. And they would never know what he did to get the money he sent them, because he would rather be dead than have his own family ashamed of him.

Chen was shaking his penis dry when he heard the crash of the door coming down and the explosive sound that followed. He instinctively ducked and felt his penis cut itself on the edge of the zipper.

Win had told them about this. SWAT cops. Concussion grenades. Followed by hordes of black-clad men in ninja suits who would kill you as soon as look at you, or maybe sooner.

Chen didn't remember reaching to his ankle for the gun that was strapped there. He just suddenly had the gun in his right hand. With his left hand he struggled to put his penis back in his pants, a reflex of the Western propriety he had absorbed.

Outside the bathroom the noises were coming fast and loud. The trampling feet that he knew belonged to the SWAT cops. The baritone voice that roared, "Police! Get down! *Get down!*"

They were coming toward him, toward the bathroom.

The Taurus .38 Special stainless-steel revolver was in Chen's hand. He had always thought that Win made them carry guns on their own time the same way police departments made cops carry guns off duty, so they'd be armed and ready if they had to do their job. Chen himself had always thought of the .38 on his ankle in a different way: as a final exit for when anything happened that would make his family more ashamed of him alive than they would be ashamed of him dead.

Chen put the muzzle of the gun in his mouth. He tasted a sick-sweet flavor on the back of his tongue.

There were more noises outside. He heard someone yell in a booming voice, "Police! Don't move!"

What a stupid thing to say, Chen thought to himself, with the barrel of his .38 revolver in his mouth. They can't see me. They don't know if I'm moving or not, obeying them or not.

Then there was another explosive sound, and the door of the bathroom came crashing inward toward him. On the other side he could see men dressed in black, with stubby machine guns pointed at him. Their faces were swathed with black nylon. He saw eyes and gun muzzles and blackness behind them.

They were shouting something. Chen wasn't sure what. He was only aware of the bitter tang of the steel in his mouth, and he could see in his mind's eye the image of his mother, bailing him out in court or watching him sentenced for murder.

It was an image he had to shut out.

The men with the machine guns were still yelling, but he couldn't hear them anymore.

Chen Ho Lee closed his eyes and pulled the trigger as hard as he could. For the briefest instant there was redness and a splash of stars, and then the black nothingness enveloped him totally.

IT TOOK BLAISDELL less than half an hour to get his leased gray Volvo out of the hotel parking garage and make it to the Gables. Traffic was almost nonexistent at that hour of the morning.

He was still blocks away from the condo when he saw the police lights flashing in the darkness. My God, there had to be an army of them. He knew instinctively where they were clustered and why.

He swerved down a side street before he ever reached the protective roadblocks of the Coral Gables Police Department's outside perimeter that guarded the scene. The bitch, his mind raced. The bitch and the gook! If they've ratted me out, I'll kill them both!

He steered back toward the city of Miami, wondering how much time he had to ditch the car. He would head for Krome Avenue, he thought. It was there that he had rented one of the private storage areas that abounded through the city. They were his safe-deposit boxes, scattered all around. Some held the disguises. Some held the weapons. This one held money, fake ID and stolen credit cards.

Soon the glow of the police lights were long gone in the distance behind him.

16

They met at the unpretentious quarters of the Miami FBI office, in North Miami. John Kearn and Ken Bartlett were there. So was Bob Litton, the Miami chief of detectives. So were two men each from the Metro Dade homicide and armed robbery squads, and two from FBI's own major crimes team. So was the SAC—Special Agent in Charge—of the Miami FBI office, along with the assistant special agent in charge.

And there was a twelfth man. Fiftyish, pale and be-spectacled, Dr. Louis Wiggins normally worked out of VICAP—the Violent Criminal Apprehension Program—located at the FBI headquarters in Quantico, Virginia. A clinical psychologist named Wiggins would inevitably come to be nicknamed ''Wiggy,'' but no one called him that to his face.

''The first thing I have to tell you, gentlemen,'' he was saying to the others, ''is that one of the few things Dirty Harry ever had right was that a man has got to know his limitations. My own work is primarily in the field of tracking and profiling serial killers. The serial killer murders one victim at a time, with that murder and subsequent mutilation and sexual activity being his primary goal. Whatever your Shotgun Gang leader is, he is not a serial killer. His goals are different.

"He is not a mass murderer, either. A mass murderer kills a number of people at once, and usually once only. Again the deaths themselves are the sole goal of his actions. This also does not describe your man.

"This individual, whom you tell me now is tentatively identified as a John Blaisdell, does not kill just for the sake of killing. He and his gang members kill instantly, and without compunction, only to stifle resistance to their achieving their primary goal, which is the theft of large amounts of cash." Wiggins paused.

"Doctor," asked Kearn, "how would you diagnose him?"

"He's a sociopath—that much is certain," the psychologist answered without hesitation. "He exists solely to serve his own personal and psychological needs. He will lavish attention on others for as long as he needs them to do his bidding. He will make it very clear that he is the alpha male, utterly dominant. He cares for no one but himself, and is a user of others. However, he will appear to be generous and will have a charismatic personality that draws others to him."

Chief of Detectives Litton said, "I understand you spoke with both the suspect who was wounded in the robbery, and the woman, at the hospital this morning, Doctor. Did that flesh out anything?"

"Not much," Dr. Wiggins sighed. "The woman's in a bad state, half-delirious. If she dies, though I don't think she will, nothing she said in that state will be admissible as evidence. Basically a very dependent young woman, low normal intelligence before the head injury, would be my guess. A classic and typical case of the battered woman. She was as devoted to this Blaisdell as a whipped puppy.

"The wounded suspect? Eddie Stiller is not in the best of shape, either. Your people shot him four times with .45s. It's a miracle he's alive. The gentleman who terrorized him with the gun barrel didn't help much. The front sight tore up the inside of his mouth, by the way. *Beaucoup* stitches. It was all I could do to understand him. Basically he recants everything he admitted. His statements in the ambulance, such as they were, constitute a dying declaration and can't be used at trial, since he lived. He says he went into Official Check Cashing to cash a money order, which the evidence shows he did in fact do. And, as we all know, nothing he blurted under duress with a gun in his mouth can ever be used against him as evidence."

The SAC stood impatiently and glanced out the window at the traffic on Northwest Second Street, below. He craved a cigarette, but for some time now FBI field offices had been officially smoke free.

"That's correct, Doctor," he said. "I've checked with our best legal people in Washington. Miami PD and Coral Gables PD are covered on their use of his statements under duress to gain access to the condo. Exigent circumstances and all of that. The fact that the woman was in a life-threatening state after the beating greatly strengthens those actions. But as far as what was learned from Eddie, most of that intelligence was limited to Blaisdell's description and how many gang people there were and where the condo was. What else can you draw from what you've seen to predict what this Blaisdell will do from here?"

"Well," Dr. Wiggins began, "I can tell you that he's not nuts, at least not in the sense of not being able to tell right from wrong. Certainly there are significant indications that he's not normal, either. For instance, I would postulate from what I've seen that he suffers from narcissistic personality disorder."

The doctor saw some eyebrows go up. He explained, "Narcissistic personality disorder is common among sociopaths. They preen themselves, consider themselves superior, almost godlike. They will reward handsomely those who reinforce that feeling in them and will punish brutally those who do not. They will generally be intelligent, or at least very cunning, but will seldom be as intelligent as they think they are. They will be good at master plans but will often overlook critical details. They will project their own bad habits onto others. For instance, they will accuse others of betraying them when they themselves are inclined to betray the other person, or accuse others of lying or having false intent when in fact it is they who are guilty of that."

"Hell," said one of the Metro Dade detectives, "you just described ninety percent of the chiefs of police in this country."

John Kearn laughed good-naturedly along with the rest. Then he said, "Doctor, you hit on something important there. The planning, and possible flaws in the planning. Can you expand on that?"

"Certainly. The study materials I've been furnished indicate that when the shooting went down during the mall robbery, the one with the armored car, this Blaisdell was apparently the leader who yelled 'Go to Plan B' or something like that. His people apparently did so, like clockwork. That tells me that he had trained and drilled his team, had thought everything out into the third dimension and had contingency plans in place. Very bright, very thorough, very... professional, if you will.

"You see the same with the layoff men, the backup criminals seeded among the bystanders or the victims. They emerged to kill in the first Overtown check-cashing robbery. They emerged to kill at the Coconut Grove bank robbery. Again, planning and virtual choreography of the movement of multiple participants. One man at that scene picking up spent shotgun shells so they couldn't be traced to his weapon. It's in the details that you see the professionalism."

"But you implied that he wasn't as smart as he thought he was," said one of the FBI agents, probing.

"I was getting to that," said the doctor. "Apparently he invited some gang members to his own home. Not the one in the hospital, who felt slighted by that, angry, according to what he blurted when the gun was in his mouth. Yet he'd been told the location of that place by another gang member—that means the iron discipline this man seems to wield over his people isn't as iron hard as he'd like to think.

"Moreover," he continued, "the whole 'robbery in drag' thing was out of character for a professional armed-robbery gang. The transvestite clothing and makeup tie in with the mocking letter he left for the Miami Stakeout Squad. It was as if he had taken their formation personally and wanted to strike back personally.

"In that incident, for the first time I believe you witnessed killing out of rage instead of killing out of expedience. The Asian had already shot down the two armed citizens. The primary robbery team was out of danger, but the white male transvestite robber came back and put a gun in their mouth or to their head and pulled the trigger.

"That is a particular type of signature killing, we've found," the doctor went on. "A shotgun wound like that, either contact distance to the head or intraoral, tends to explode the head and virtually destroy the face. It is a particularly vindictive sort of wound, and particularly when associated with a coup de grace shot, indicative of great personal anger and malice. These, as I say, are out of character for a man who sets stock in being a cool professional, who has ego investment, as it were, in being unruffled and imperturbable.

"Now, if we combine that with the accelerated pace of the robberies of late, *and* the accelerating degree of violence—not only the violence of the robberies themselves, but personal violence, such as the gun-to-the-head killings and the nearly fatal beating he gave his mistress, poor little Kimberley Miner—you have the profile of a man going out of control. A man whose ego is taking over his native intelligence. A man, in short, who is beginning to make mistakes, and who seems to make more mistakes the more the pressure builds on him. The pressure is certainly building on him now more than ever. He's like a vampire whose castle has been discovered, whose coffin has been burned. He'll be in a state of rage against those he perceives to have thwarted him."

Chief of Detectives Litton asked, "Doctor, you're familiar with his pattern of selecting targets. Anything you can predict from there?"

Wiggins shrugged. "I would expect one of three things. He's been trying to be unpredictable, hitting a couple of banks, a couple of armored cars, a couple more banks, now the check-cashing thing. If he followed the previous pattern, he'd go back to hitting the money trucks or the banks.

"But I don't think that's what he'll do. Remember, that was his pattern before things started going badly for him. I think, given what I've seen so far, he's far more likely to pursue one of two other courses.

"One, he has an obsession with not being thwarted and with punishing those who do thwart him. There is an excellent chance that he'll do another hit of the check-cashing place, this time more successfully.

"The other, equally real, possibility is this—the recent events may have jolted him back to reality, may have reminded him that it's time to return to being a cold professional. If that is in fact what happens, I would look for him to hit something new, do something completely different from what he's done before."

The FBI ASAC spoke for the first time. "Doctor, what do you think are his chances of surrendering?"

Wiggins smiled ruefully. "Blaisdell himself? If he thinks he has no choice but to surrender or die, he'll probably surrender. Remember, we're talking about a sociopath with narcissistic personality disorder. His own survival will be paramount to him, beyond anything else.

"His gang members, however, are another story. They're slavishly loyal to him and desperately afraid of him. Witness the suspect that wouldn't talk until there was a gun barrel in his mouth. Witness the poor little girl who stayed with him through all the beatings. Those, the accomplices, I would expect to die rather than surrender. The man who killed himself in Blaisdell's condo is a good example. It would have been very easy for him to outer-direct the killing impulse that instead, he inner-directed, in this case. I would be expecting most of them to outer-direct."

Kearn asked, "Any final suggestions, Doctor? Any prescriptions?"

Wiggins laughed mirthlessly. "MD psychiatrists write prescriptions, Chief Kearn, not clinical psychologists such as myself. However, in this case, I think I can make an exception." He looked at Bartlett. "Lieutenant, what sort of bullets do you issue to your Stakeout officers?"

Bartlett looked puzzled. "They carry .45s, Doctor. The ammo is Winchester Silvertip hollowpoints, 185-grain. We selected that load because it was the most likely to mushroom and stay inside a felon's body instead of exiting and perhaps striking a bystander."

Dr. Wiggins nodded. He drew a Cross ballpoint pen from his pocket and reached for one of the memo pads on the conference desk. He wrote:

R_x for Shotgun Gang:

185 gr. pB
IC
PRN

Dr. Louis Wiggins

He ripped the note off the pad and handed it to Kearn, whose eyebrows knitted as he read it. "I don't get it, Doctor—pB? IC?"

Wiggins was no longer smiling. He answered, "A hundred eighty-five grains of lead. Inject intracardiac. Repeat as necessary."

He looked around the table. "That," the psychologist concluded, "is the best prescription I can give you for the kind of people you're dealing with."

DRIVING BACK to Miami PD headquarters, with Bartlett at the wheel of the unmarked Chevy, Chief of Detectives Litton was in the right front seat and Chief of Police Kearn in the right rear, his legs stretched across the back seat as he leaned against the door.

"God, I'm tired," groaned Kearn. "It's almost noon. Did any of you guys get any sleep last night?"

"Not me," said Litton.

"Same here," said Bartlett.

Kearn asked, "Bob, where are we on this? What've we got for ID so far?"

"We're working on computer comparisons of the facial shape and bone structure of the one who killed himself in Blaisdell's apartment, Chen Ho Lee. Looks like it's going to fit exactly the Asian in woman's makeup who did the killings in the first check-cash hit, in comparison with the pictures taken on the hidden security camera. He fits the descriptions of the witnesses at the bank, too. The one in the hospital with the sore mouth doesn't fit any of the security-camera pictures, but it's almost certain he was involved in at least one of the early hits. He fits the Identikit description of the black guy in the first Shotgun Gang hit, before you came on, in the northwest district.

"The prints lifted from the condo match those of John Blaisdell, 33, long juvenile record and one stint at Pendleton Reformatory in Indiana. The feebs have got their Indiana agents at Pendleton now, trying to find someone who can give us anything we can use on him.

"Nothing yet on Kimberley Miner. It's like she came out of nowhere. It may not be her real name, given his tendency to use disguises and code names for his people. Probably picked the kid up someplace like a stray cat. Stiller, now that he knows he's gonna live, is telling us to get lost. I think he told us everything he had when that hospital guy had the gun in his mouth. Like the feebs said, all we can use it for now is intelligence.

"We got the license number of his car from the register at the parking garage at the condo. It was leased from a Miami firm under a fake name. Paid up to date and all. We put out the BOLO this morning. They found it a little after 9:00 a.m. in the long-term parking lot at Miami International. Metro Dade ran a sketch of Blaisdell by all the ticket agents and the people in the airport rent-a-car places, but he hadn't rented anything from there. Ticket in the car shows it went into the parking lot around 6:00 a.m. He probably took a cab from the airport and got wheels someplace else. Judging by the number of stolen cars the Shotgun Gang's been using regularly, that wouldn't have been a problem for him."

"Hell," muttered the exhausted Kearn. "Ken, what do you think Stakeout ought to be looking at?"

Bartlett shrugged helplessly. "The doc said the least likely thing would be doubling back to armored cars and banks. There's too damn many of both to stake them all out, anyway. He said one of the likely things would be something new. What the hell is that, something new? We're chasing smoke. My feeling is, go for the third alternative. If this guy's really got a bug about Stakeout and has an obsession with doing everything right, the single most likely thing is that he'll hit another check-cash joint, either Overtown or Liberty City. I figure that if we extend those monitor alarm systems, we can have three two-man rover cars in each district."

"Two men won't do much against the Shotgun Gang," Litton said glumly.

"True," answered Bartlett, "but I won't send two men in on the bastards. They'll deploy silently outside, give a discreet tail to the getaway and coordinate on point while the other units and the sector patrol cars zone in."

Litton shrugged. "Sounds like a plan to me. Chief?"

"I can't think of anything better. Go ahead with it, Ken. Look, on to something else—how are your teams holding up?"

"Different as night and day and twilight," Bartlett answered. "Team Three is cool. They haven't been involved in any real action yet. They've all been reconsidering. They're all watching what happened to Team One with the kids and Team Two with everything else. They're like, 'What the hell have we gotten ourselves into here?' But they're cool, Chief. There isn't a one of them won't stand up.

"Team One is down a man. Pavlicek is gone. Shooting that kid tore him apart. The three who did the Maloney kid are okay. They saw him fire the shot, they know he could have killed them or somebody else and they're using Teasdale's columns in the *Crier* to wipe their asses, if you know what I mean."

Litton grunted. "Tell them to be careful. They could get a disease, wiping their ass with the *Crier.*"

Bartlett smiled in spite of himself and went on. "I don't know about Pavlicek. He was a good detective. Maybe there's someplace for him teaching other guys investigations or something. I know he's done for the street. Says he doesn't want to carry a gun, even see one as long as he lives. I haven't got a replacement for him yet, so we're running one light in Team One.

"Team Two? A lot more complicated. Just between us, it was the weakest of the three teams on the squad to begin with."

Bartlett began ticking them off on his fingers. One, Frank Cross. I just don't trust him. I think he's a weak link, medal or no medal.

"Two, Dan Harrington. Glory grabber. Every bust he runs in and has to be the one to put the bracelets on. I reamed him out over the thing in the bank, when he and Cross came in on that situation where Melinda Hoffritz had disarmed the punk. He handed his shotgun to Cross so his hands would be free for the cuffing. Great, *his* hands are tied up on the cuffs, Cross's hands are tied up, each holding a two-handed weapon so he couldn't have fired either one of them if he'd had to, if for instance there was a layoff man in there. One of the inside guys with just a pistol they could stick in a holster should have been doing that. Harrington's out for Harrington, not for the squad.

"Three, Mike Cohen. Mike's a good man, but he's 'new breed,' if you know what I mean. I had an instructor at the academy years ago, used to dump hard on the new-breed types. Said they were social workers with guns they didn't want to carry. There's a little of that in Mike. A lot of it, maybe. At first that was one reason I wanted him on the Stakeout Squad. I was afraid there'd be a lot of Rambo mentality among the people who volunteered for a unit like this. I thought he'd be a good influence, you know. Brakes for something that could start going so fast it went out of control. Now, after the shooting at Official, I don't know. It hit him real hard."

Kearn asked, "As bad as Pavlicek?"

"No. Pavlicek is broken, man. Mike ain't broke, but there's some real deep cracks in the foundation, you know? He's been saying that he wants to go to the funeral of the guy he killed. Shee-it, he doesn't realize Lang's family, if he's got one, is gonna dance on his grave, they'll be so grateful a scumbag like him is dead. I told him not to, but I can't forbid him."

Litton asked, "He seen the department shrink?"

"Yeah." Bartlett sighed. "But they didn't accomplish a thing. Wouldn't open up to him. I told Mike, he's that worked up about killing that scumbag, go see his rabbi."

Litton perked up. "Yeah? Who's his rabbi?"

"Damn," Bartlett muttered. "I think he told me the name. Shulman? Shuller? Something like that."

Litton's head rocked back against the seat. "Oh, no. Don't tell me it was Schiller. Say it wasn't Rabbi Schiller!"

"Yeah, that's it, Schiller! What's the problem with him?"

"Only," groaned Litton, "that he's on this coalition to ban handguns with our beloved mayor. Goes on TV and stuff, the talk shows, talking about why we should ban guns and all love our fellow man.

"You just lost another man, Ken. Rabbi Schiller gets done with Mike Cohen, Mike's gonna be ready to go start a chicken farm with Pavlicek and melt down his gun to make a chicken-shit pooper scooper!"

17

Mike Cohen parked his private car, a Subaru, in the lot of the Temple Beth Jacob synagogue on the Edge of Coconut Grove. Night was falling. He paused while getting out of the car and took his Glock .45 out of the plastic holster on his belt. He put it into the console and locked it there, as if he were locking the cage door on a serpent.

A tool of death, he thought, had no place in the sanctum of God.

He walked to the back door of the ultramodern structure and pressed the buzzer. In a moment he was face-to-face with a short, slender, gray-bearded man who wore a yarmulke.

"Come in, Michael," the rabbi said warmly. "You're right on time."

Cohen just smiled sheepishly. "Good evening Rabbi Schiller. I'm sorry to have to come by so late. Work, you know..." His voice trailed off.

"Fe," said the ebullient rabbi. "I have seen many pictures of shepherds. It is an image you cannot escape if your calling is theology. And you know, Michael, I never once saw a picture of a shepherd looking at his watch. Every spiritual adviser is a shepherd. I don't look at my watch very often, either. Here. My private office. Come, sit.''

Cohen settled himself into a comfortable easy chair next to the mahogany desk and saw the rabbi distribute his weight into the swivel chair on the other side. "I'm sorry to take your time, Rabbi," he apologized again. "It's . . . I guess you'd call it a crisis of faith."

"What waste? Crises of faith are what I'm here for, Michael. Tell me of this crisis."

"It happened a couple of days ago," Cohen began hesitantly, and then the words poured out in a torrent. How he had been a Miami cop for eighteen years and had never fired his gun. How he never carried it off duty like most of the others, and when he got home went first to the locked steel box in the closet to unload the weapon and secure it away, even after the children were grown. How he volunteered for this thing—this *thing,* he said, in a tone of disgust—that was called the Stakeout Squad. It seemed a good career move. There was the affirmative-action thing, and a man who was not the politically correct color had to stand out far and above the others to get promoted, to earn more money for his family, and commanding a team on a special squad seemed a good way to do this.

And then came the awful realization of just what the Stakeout Squad would do. They were ambushers, pure and simple. Cohen thought at first they would be in a position of such dominance over the armed suspects that there would be a harsh command, followed by instant surrender, no bloodshed, no heartache, no death, no grieving. . . .

But it didn't work out that way. The first confrontation with Pavlicek and Team One—the shooting of the young boy robbers—was the first terrible harbinger. Then the two women shot down outside the bank by his own men, Michael's own subordinates, on the Tamiami Trail.

And then, God forgive him, the third one at Official Check Cashing. He told Rabbi Schiller how he ran around the back door, the pistol in his hand. How he came face-to-face with the gaunt specter of death that was J. D. Lang.

"I told him not to move," said Mike Cohen to the rabbi, barely able to keep the tremors from his voice. "I begged him! I'm a cop, and I begged! I begged him not to make me shoot him."

There was a long pause, and Mike Cohen took a deep breath that seemed to rattle in his throat and he continued. "I saw the gun coming up in his hands. I saw his finger on the trigger. He was going to kill me.

"I know what this is going to sound like. It's going to sound like every guilty man I ever arrested trying to alibi himself. They'd always say, 'The gun went off.' They never once said, 'I shot him.' It was like they were saying, 'I didn't do it. The gun did it. Don't blame me. Blame the gun.'

"It was like that with me, Rabbi. I honestly don't remember thinking, I must now squeeze the trigger. I was looking over the gun, the white dot on the front sight was on his chest, and he came up with the rifle and I saw the gun go off. And again. And again. And again . . ."

Cohen's voice choked off. He took a moment to compose himself and then he continued. "He was on his back then. The blood was all over him. I had shot him four times. The medical examiner said any one of those bullets would have killed him. I killed him four times over.'' The voice was dull now. Michael Cohen stopped talking.

At length Rabbi Aaron Schiller asked, ''And what did you do then, Michael?''

Michael looked at him quizzically. ''What was there to do? He was dead. I knew no power on Earth could help him.

''The pistol was still in my hand. I took my finger off the trigger. I went through the door.

''There were people on the floor. Some had blood on them. Some of them didn't. But the blood was everywhere. I saw the old woman and the two children this man had shot. I looked out the door onto the street. I saw two of my people, Bob and Melinda, standing over another black man, holding their guns on him. I found out later they, too, had shot him four times. Theirs lived. Mine didn't. I never heard their shots. They never heard mine. It turns out that both shootings went down at the same time.

''I did what I had to do. I took over. I took my radio out of my pocket and called for the appropriate assistance. We call it 'controlling the scene,' Rabbi. I 'controlled the scene.'''

Cohen stopped talking. He was leaning forward in his chair, his hands clasped. Rabbi Schiller was leaning back in his own chair.

After a while the rabbi said, ''So this is your crisis of faith? That you killed a man? That this made you unclean, no longer a righteous Jew?''

Cohen hung his head. ''Yes, Rabbi. I have become the thing I existed to prevent. I have violated the commandment 'thou shalt not kill.'''

The rabbi's chair rocked forward suddenly, and the palm of his hand came down on his desktop like a thunderclap. Just as explosively, he blurted one word.

"Bullshit!"

Mike Cohen looked up at him in shock.

The soft brown eyes were as hard and dark as coals now above the gray beard. "The commandment never said 'thou shalt not kill,' Michael," the rabbi boomed. "In the original script, it said, 'thou shalt not commit murder'! 'Thou shalt not kill with evil intent'!"

Cohen looked at him, stunned.

"Fe," barked the rabbi angrily. "Did the *machers* at your police academy never tell you this? Did they send you out into the streets with a gun at your hip, knowing you were a devout Jew, and never see that this had to be explained to you? It is a miracle you did as you did inside that place, Michael! It is a miracle that you survived, as you should have survived!"

The rabbi stretched out his arm, pointing his finger at the leather-bound books on the shelves that covered all four walls of his office. "Have you not studied the Torah and the Talmud, Michael? Obviously you have read them, but just as obviously you have not studied them!"

The rabbi's voice softened, and he continued. "You have read the Talmud, Michael, but you missed things. When you speak of Jewish law in these things, you must look to Sanhedrin. 'He who comes to kill you, arise and kill him.' It is a principle of our Jewish law that a righteous man's life must be preserved that he may continue to do righteous things, and that the evil must not be allowed to snuff out the lives of the righteous, not even if the price of preserving that righteous life is the snuffing out of an evil one in turn.

"You told me what this person—no, this *thing*—had done before you shot him Michael. True, at the moment when you pulled the trigger you didn't know he had shot the old woman, had shot the two children, but that didn't change the fact that he had done these evil things.

"And because God gave us minds to think and reason, we know that there was nothing to stop him from murdering or attempting to murder helpless women and children again. Nothing to stop him, that is, but you."

The rabbi paused for a breath. Cohen was staring at him raptly.

"The Bible says the same thing, Michael," the rabbi said gently. "It is in Leviticus, 19:16, I believe. 'Thou shalt not stand idly by the blood of thy brother.' You fulfilled this injunction, Michael. The man you slew was wicked. By every law of God and of man—by every word of the Talmud and the Torah, by every sacred word known to every faith I have ever studied—what you did was righteous. What you did was right. What you did was sanctified by the word of the Almighty."

"Sanctified," Cohen said numbly.

"Of course," said the rabbi. "Do you remember none of your learning as a young man in the synagogue? Did not God himself order the Jews to kill the wicked Amalekites, and Midianites and even some of the tribes of Canaan? When the wicked prey upon the righteous, it becomes righteous to slay the wicked.

"This thing—I hesitate to call him a man, this *thing* that you killed—had ceased to be a righteous man and had become instead a shooter of children, a murderer of old women, and was about to become a murderer of policemen at the time you stopped him in the only way you could."

"And what of him, Rabbi?" asked Cohen. "Perhaps he had become a 'thing' but he was still a man, and I ended his life!"

The rabbi reached out and gently placed his hand on the policeman's. "You speak of the soul, don't you, Michael? It is difficult to speak of religion without speaking of the soul. Very well, then. Let us discuss the soul. What is more important, Michael, a man's corporeal body or that distilled human essence that we theologians call the soul?"

"The soul, of course, Rabbi!"

"Exactly so, Michael. And is it worse, therefore, to destroy a man's physical, fleshly body, or to ruin forever with polluting wickedness, his immortal soul?"

"To destroy the soul would be worse, of course."

"Correct again, Michael. Murder was already on this man's soul when you shot him and stopped him from murdering you, stopped him from murdering who knows how many righteous men and women and children. You prevented him from polluting his soul further. In ending his physical life, you took upon your own soul the tremendous burden of showing yourself righteous to have done it, the burden of spending the rest of your life on this Earth doing good for others and proving that there was a reason that you lived that terrible day and he did not."

The rabbi paused and looked Sergeant Cohen straight in the eyes. "There is no doubt in my mind that you can prove that, Michael, no doubt in my mind that you are worthy of that survival. You don't have to be a rabbi or a priest or a minister to know that the man you shot deserved to die, that he had to be stopped from preying on the innocent any further, and that a man like you should live, should live to continue protecting others.

"Remember earlier, Michael, when I spoke of that universal image of theology, the shepherd and his flock? And I said that I never saw a shepherd with a timepiece? Well, I also never saw a shepherd without his staff. The staff is a weapon, Michael, and there is a reason shepherds carry them.

"And I very seldom saw one of those pictures where there wasn't a sheepdog in the background. What is a sheepdog for, Michael? He exists to keep the lambs together in the fold, that's true, but he is there also to ward off the predators. Usually he does that just with his menacing presence, or perhaps with a growl, as you did for your eighteen years as a sheepdog protecting your flock of innocents in Miami.

"But the day comes, inevitably, when a wolf comes too close to the flock and is too foolish to fear the sheepdog. When that happens, Michael, the sheepdog must use his fangs for more than something to growl through. The sheepdog must close his fangs upon the throat of the wolf, for if he does not, the wolf will claim the innocent lamb.

"You came to me because your fangs had to close on the throat of a particularly rabid wolf, Michael. Do not fear that the rabies is contagious. In this case it is not. All you did was avenge innocent lambs and save countless more lambs from the jaws of that rabid wolf. And the wolf itself can lie in its grave knowing at least that it had contact with *one* decent and righteous creature—the sheepdog that ended the evils of the wolf's soul."

The tears were beginning to flow down Sergeant Michael Cohen's cheeks. But, Rabbi Aaron Schiller saw, they were the good tears not the bad ones, and the rabbi had seen enough of both to know.

He stood up, stepped forward, reached out his arms. He and the sobbing police officer embraced each other.

At length Cohen sniffed and said, "You amaze me, Rabbi."

The older man chuckled. "And why is that?"

"I saw you on TV," said Michael, "when you debated the guy from the National Rifle Association. You spoke of the evils of guns and of killing. I never thought I would hear you tell me it was all right to do what I did. What I had to do."

"What you had to do. That's good. You do understand. But Michael, let me show you something. Something no other man but I has ever seen in this place. Something no other man before you, and except for me, has ever needed to see."

The rabbi took a couple of steps to his desk. From his pocket he fished out a key ring and instantly separated one key from the others. He inserted it into the lock on the top right desk drawer and pulled the drawer open. Reaching under a sheaf of papers, he withdrew something Sergeant Cohen instantly recognized.

The cop's jaw dropped. "A gun? You—"

The rabbi smiled. "Go ahead, already, finish saying it, 'You of all people.'"

He looked down at the ugly pistol that was now in his hand. "Yes," Schiller mused almost inaudibly. "I, of all people."

The rabbi reached deftly to the butt of the gun, pressed a latch and withdrew a magazine full of live cartridges. He set the cartridge clip on the desk and, with his right hand still holding the gun, grasped the slide with his left and snapped it back. A gleaming copper-jacketed bullet arced out of the gun, landing with a soft bump on the desktop.

"It's a Nazi gun," the rabbi said, handing the pistol to the sergeant. "A Czechoslovakian CZ-38. One of my people gave it to me before he died. He had taken it off the body of one of the few Nazis who resisted when the Allies took control of the death camps in 1945. He looked up the serial number later. It was made with Jewish slave labor. They had made our people manufacture the guns that threatened them, just as they made them dig their own graves at Dachau and Auschwitz and Bergen-Belsen."

Cohen examined the gun, holding it gingerly, like a defanged snake. "Why do you keep this, Rabbi?" he asked in a tone of wonder.

The rabbi chuckled. "Do you remember a popular ballad, many years ago, about a soldier caught playing cards in church? And he explains how the number of the cards reminds him of the number of the weeks in a year and all of that, and ultimately his defense is that his deck of cards serves him as a Bible, an almanac and a prayer book? That gun is like that for me, Michael.

"Some Nazi official carried that gun when he sent some of our six million to their deaths in the camps. Some Jew who was subjugated by an oppressor society, or perhaps more than one, manufactured that gun like a slave forging his own leg irons. Yet a Jewish soldier shot and killed the wicked man who had been issued that pistol as a tool for the subjugation of the innocent, and took it home. He took it as a souvenir—no, as a war trophy, he told me—until he realized what it really stood for, before he gave it to me.

"That gun is in my desk to remind me of many things, Michael. It reminds me of the power of man to harm his fellow man. It reminds me of the helplessness of the innocent before the might of the ruthless who go unresisted and unchecked.

"It reminds me of those who had the courage to rise up against evil and smite it down, as the Canaanites were smitten, and as you yourself, Michael, smote down the wicked and soulless golem who had shot down the innocent.

"It reminds me of the death camp at Sobibor. I see your eyebrows rise in surprise, Michael. Most people's do. They have not heard of Sobibor unless they are students of the Holocaust, as I am.

"It was at Sobibor that one of the few rebellions took place, where some of the very few inmates overpowered their guards and took their guns, guns like this one. Only a few escaped and survived, but when it was over, the Nazis shut down the death chambers of Sobibor. It was as if they no longer had the courage to face the innocents who had turned upon their tormentors and fed them back their own righteously deserved deaths."

The rabbi sighed as he reached out and took the gun back from the policeman. "That is what this gun means to me, Michael," he said as he reloaded it carefully. "The same forces that destroy can protect. The fire that burns can warm. I do not like guns, Michael, and that is why I speak against them. Sheep should not have guns. But shepherds need them, and sheepdogs need their fangs. This is why I have this gun."

He slammed the drawer shut after he put the pistol inside, and twisted the lock closed. "And that is why you have yours. That is why you fired it that day. That is why you are here."

Mike Cohen stood silently, breathing deeply.

"Is anything different now, Michael?"

"Yes, Rabbi. Yes. A great deal."

"Do you think you'll go back?"

"Yes. Yes, I think I will."

"The shul is always open for you. Would you like to pray?"

"I think I would," the policeman said softly.

"I think you should," the rabbi answered gently.

18

Night was falling on Miami. John Blaisdell—though he was registered at the desk downstairs as William Barton, Jr., courtesy of his false ID—stood alone in his executive suite at the Miami Hotel Mart Plaza. Overhead he could hear the roar of the jets taking off from Miami International, even through the sound-proofing of the ultramodern building.

He no longer looked like John Blaisdell. The mousse was gone from his hair, and so was most of the black. Now he had a "dry" look, and Silvertone hair coloring had tinted his temples gray. A silvery British-cut mustache was spirit-gummed to his upper lip, completing the face. Augmenting the look itself was a conservative blue European-cut suit.

Parked downstairs in the lot was a new Oldsmobile coupe, leased yesterday in his new name with his new look. No one would ever make him for the John Blaisdell whose pictures and sketches were all over the TV news and the front page of the *Crier*.

Locked in his Vuitton suitcase was a sawed-off Winchester Model 1200 shotgun. It was the last of the three Winchesters that had been taken in the Ta-miami pawnbroker hit so long ago. The first was gone, chopped up with torches and dumped into the ocean after he had lost his composure just a little bit during the ill-fated "transvestite" hit.

Another gun was out of his control now, though. A Marlin pump gun. The man code-named "Marlin" was out of his control, too, and that was what was so infuriating. A second-string gang member, Joey "Marlin" Trueter was whiter than white, stupider than stupid and more loyal than loyal until things had broken in the media.

John Blaisdell had memorized all their phone numbers. Earlier that day he had tried to contact his underlings to arrange their next hit. It took forever to get an answer at Joey's. The old broad Win knew to be Joey's mother had finally answered and said, "Joey's gone. Gone to California. He said to tell anybody who called he didn't leave anything behind, and he couldn't take it anymore, whatever that means." The old woman's voice seemed tired, empty.

Win politely thanked her and hung up. Only then did he vent his rage. Win growled to himself, out loud but soft enough that no one in another room of the hotel could hear him. He can't tie me to anything with his guns—little prick never shot anybody—but he betrayed me, and now he has to die!

Win knew there wasn't time to bother with it now. Things were getting too heavy here in Miami. But he marked Marlin's death down in his mental calendar as an eventual certainty, a fait accompli. It was just a matter of waiting until he had time to get it done right.

Next was Juan Ocampo—"Brown," in code, for the Browning BPS pump shotgun Blaisdell had issued him. Ocampo at least had the balls to talk to him, on the phone if not face-to-face.

"You're too hot, my man," Ocampo said. They got your name in today's paper. John Blaisdell. Now, you never trusted *me* to know your real name, never trusted *me* to know where your crib was. But you apparently trusted that to some of your other people, or they never woulda crashed in there with Coral Gables SWAT, never woulda bagged your bitch an' made your man stick his .38 in his mouth. If he really did that, an' they didn't do it for him. An', let me get this straight, you want me to come and do another gig with *you?*"

Blaisdell burned with shame as the memory hit him, the memory of his own mouth saying, pleadingly, "Come *on,* Brown, we're gonna be like before. The Shotgun Gang's ridin' high! Diamonds this time, man, diamonds to make you rich, like I made you fat before, what do you say?"

And Juan "Brown" Ocampo sneered at him over the phone—sneered at him! Blaisdell could visualize his face!

"You ain't winnin' no more, Win!" Brown said. "You too hot to mess with. That Browning gun is gone, man, in the Miami River, an' so's that pistol you gave me. I got my own pistol and my own shotgun, dig it? My ass gonna be gone, too, outa here by tonight, Win, an' if you've got a brain left in your head, you're gonna be gone, too! The heat's comin' down, an' I'm a pro, and I'm outa here!"

Win raged at him for a moment before the line went dead. Then he tried to get himself together, calm his voice and call the other members of the Shotgun Gang.

Moss was still with him, of course. And Fox. And Savage. And Ruger, the Mediterranean guy. And Berg, the other white guy with one of the Mossbergs, from Homestead. The Shotgun Gang was the best deal Berg ever got, even working second string.

The new guy Win had recruited a couple of months ago, the Nicaraguan, was ready and eager. Win would give him a slightly rusty 12-gauge pump gun that had been sold through the Montgomery Ward catalogs back when the guy who had pawned it had bought it. He'd code-name the new guy "Ward." The Nicaraguan was eager. The talk in the papers about all the money the Shotgun Gang was making with its continued string of hits was making this fool salivate. Fine with Win—get him excited, get him on the hook, and he'll give his life for you. Give his life for Win. For Win and the money Win gave them.

Like the others.

Like Chen. Damn, he was going to miss Chen. Little gook knew how to take orders. Died silent, too, with the gun Win gave him right in his mouth. Beautiful.

Some others were not that beautiful. John Blaisdell frowned at the thought of Eddie Stiller. Not near as loyal, not near as good as Moss! When this blew over, he was gonna hunt that damn Eddie Stiller down and put a shotgun in his mouth and pull the trigger, like he did on that other coon in the ghetto check-cash robbery!

And Kimberley. Oh, God, Kimberley! What had possessed him to bring that weak-minded slut into his home, make her privy to the innermost workings of the Shotgun Gang? But she was probably dead already. That was good. The thought made Blaisdell feel warm. He had instinctively kicked her to death, beat her to death, whatever, even when he hadn't meant to. Didn't they say in the papers that she was "hovering near death" at Jackson Memorial? Served her right, he thought viciously. If she lives, I'll finish her, he thought. If she doesn't, she doesn't. She was too damn stupid to live, anyway.

But what was done was done. John Blaisdell—now William Barton, Jr.—had more-important things on his mind.

Things like making a hit that would leave the Stakeout Squad and its chief of police screaming. Things that would make him and the ones wise enough to follow him all rich.

Things like the kind of hit that had never been done before in Miami. Hadn't been done because those with the balls hadn't thought of it, and those who'd thought of it hadn't had the balls.

But John Blaisdell had thought of it, and he had the balls, and it would be the crowning triumph of the Shotgun Gang.

He'd learned it from one of the other cons he'd met in prison in Indiana. Joel "the Icemonger" Farrell. The one time when ice—diamonds—were flowing free, along with the cash that bought them, and weren't surrounded by armed guards.

The new jewelry-sales schtick of dumping diamonds in volume at near wholesale prices. Dumping them at the superupscale flea markets that people in the jewelry trade had resorted to after the recession of the early nineties. The so-called trade mart sales of precious stones.

Blaisdell smiled involuntarily at the brilliance of his plan. The Miami Hotel Mart Plaza had the Miami

Hotel on one side, and on the other, the Mart Plaza. Part of the plaza included upscale shopping boutiques and styling salons. But part of it also featured, each weekend, the open-bazaar-like booths of the people who had their seminars and their conferences.

And their flea markets.

The Jewelry Extravaganza at the Mart was coming up tomorrow. The extravaganza would have millions upon millions of dollars there, in a mix of precious stones and cold hard cash.

Millions of dollars there for the taking.

The taking by the Shotgun Gang.

For the taking of John Blaisdell.

JOHN KEARN WAS ALONE in the sumptuous office suite that was the legacy of any current Miami chief of police. He stood behind his desk, rubbing himself above the eyes. His head ached badly from lack of sleep.

He looked down. He saw his own gray necktie against the pink cotton of his Hathaway shirt, blending with the gray of his all-wool suit pants. A black dress belt held a black leather DeSantis holster tight to his hip. The holster held a compact Glock 19 9 mm semiautomatic pistol.

The sight of the gun, as he looked down, amused Kearn. He remembered being a young patrolman on the New York City Police Department and being restricted to carrying a .38-caliber revolver. He had joined both the PBA, the Patrolmen's Benevolent Association, and the Guardians, the black cops' fraternal and bargaining society. He remembered how abruptly he had been cut out of the patrolmen's association once he had made sergeant. He was "one of them now, not one of us." Jesus, wasn't that just the story of his life as a black cop? Always "one of *them,* not one of *us.*"

It was apparent that, having been a union man, he wasn't going to advance any further than sergeant at NYPD. It seemed suspiciously frequent that the most articulate spokesmen for the rank-and-file street cops got promoted to supervisory level and away from the union. The rank and file never seemed to see that, though; all they seemed to see was that you were a sergeant now: "One of *them,* not one of us."

John Kearn saw the handwriting on the wall. He took a position with lateral transfer to another East Coast city, one that needed good black supervisors to keep ahead of the court cases that were finding in favor of affirmative action and against the "good old boy" network. Kearn was promoted almost instantly to lieutenant, and within the year to captain.

At that time the guns in that department were still .38s. As a patrolman in New York, he fought for 9 mm automatics or at least, hot hollowpoint hand-loads for the duty .38 revolvers. That campaign was unsuccessful.

But by the time he left his new department—at the rank of deputy chief—he had overseen the adoption of 14-shot 9 mm automatics by the entire patrol force. Shortly after that changeover, the chief of a good-size midwestern department was fired for "lack of sensitivity to minorities," and the ad for the chief's position appeared in *Police Chief* magazine.

Kearn applied. He was one of perhaps half a thousand cops who did. He was one of thirty invited to take the written exam, one of fifteen invited back for the oral boards and one of seven finalists. He won the position.

He served there for a couple of years, with distinction. Formerly a dirty department, it was clean by the time Kearn applied for the position of chief in a major southwestern city on the border. That city was twice the size of the one he worked in in the Midwest, with twice as many cops.

Kearn won the position easily. When he retired from the midwestern city, he left as his legacy a hand-picked deputy commander who had come up through the ranks—indeed, who had broken Kearn in when he was a rookie chief there. The new Smith & Wesson automatics that had just been issued to the patrol force were one of his two last legacies: the other was a salary rate that was nearly double what it had been before Kearn became chief.

In the new, southwestern department, Kearn put in a series of new programs—neighborhood policing, Operation Crimewatch and so on—that in two years reduced the death tolls of both violent crime and citizen carelessness. He was like Scarlett O'Hara: "steel under velvet."

The community appreciated it.

Then, after the upset victory of the new mayor, the opening in Miami beckoned. The southwestern city wept to see him go—their newspaper had editorialized, "Our Loss Miami's Much-Needed Gain"—and he became the chief of police of Miami, Florida.

It was his twenty-sixth year in law enforcement. John Kearn was in his late forties now.

And what did he have to show for it? Here he was, sitting over his desk looking down at his own uncomfortable belly that was burning itself from the inside out with stomach acid. He had a controversial special squad he had put in the field with the honest hope that it would ameliorate some of the crimes of violence in his newly adopted city.

And he had the realization that he couldn't remember the last time he had spent a few minutes in peace with his daughters, Elizabeth and Lauren, nor even shared a few precious moments alone with his wife, Ann.

It had to break soon. It *had* to.

19

Frank Cross lay back against his Soloflex, spent. The workout had been exhausting.

He took just a couple of moments to get his wind back, then stood up from the exercise machine and padded across the carpeted floor of his bachelor apartment. He tugged on a pair of jeans. The DeSantis hip holster for his Smith & Wesson .45 was still threaded onto his belt.

He checked the weapon with extra caution: empty magazine, empty chamber. He on-safed the gun and thrust it into the holster.

He felt he had been humiliated once. Blowing a hole through his apartment wall would be the final step to making a mockery of him. Cross set a Micronta timer for one second. His finger paused on the Start button. Then he jabbed the button with his right index finger and sent the hand flashing to the holster.

He grasped and drew, his thumb running forward along the slide to pop the safety catch into the fire position even as the gun came into line with the dark police silhouette target he had taped to the living room wall. He stroked the trigger, and the sights were dead on the target when the hammer clicked and the timer beeped at the same moment.

Not good enough. He wanted a faster draw to a shot than one second. He wanted half a second. He thought he might have it in him to do a quarter second one day.

He set the timer, drew again. As the big Smith & Wesson came up, he flashed back to that terrible night in the projects.

He had been in uniform then. It was a routine service of a bench warrant. A precinct detective whose partner was home sick was working alone that night, and he asked the shift sergeant if he could have a couple of uniforms to go along for the ride. The sergeant assigned Cross and his partner, Tim Reed.

So routine, so routine...

After they had flanked the sides of the door, the detective knocked sharply. A man's voice inside snapped, "Yeah?"

"Police," the detective snapped back. "We need to see William Brown."

They were poised for the sounds of running feet toward a back window. Cross was a good sprinter. He was the one who'd have darted outside and begun the foot pursuit. But instead, footsteps shambled toward the door. Cooperation. No problem....

And then the door swung open, and all Cross could see was the revolver. Examining it later, it seemed tiny, a little .38-caliber 5-shot Chief's Special. But at that moment it seemed huge.

And Cross, inches from the gun, ducked to the side. Ducked behind Tim Reed. It was then that the unearthly cacaphony of the shots began.

Reed blurted, "Oh my God" before the bullet hit him. Even the roar of the gunfire couldn't drown out the sickening thump of the bullet taking flesh. Reed sagged back against him, dead weight. Cross tried to grab him, hold him up. From the corner of his eyes, he saw the detective fall.

Then the man was back inside his apartment, running for the back door, and Cross, still holding his partner, ripped his Glock from his duty holster and reached it around the door. He opened fire wildly, blindly.

Crime-scene technicians later recovered eighteen spent Federal brand 9 mm shell cases in the hallway, all from Cross's gun. They recovered almost that many bullets. Two had gone out an apartment window. The rest had smashed into the TV, the furniture, the wall, the floor, the clock and a house cat. None had touched the fleeing perpetrator.

At least, the others said sympathetically, he had fought back. When they gave him his medal, a police administrator described Frank Cross fearlessly holding his wounded comrade with one arm, shielding him with his own body, as he unleashed the barrage of deadly fire that drove the cop-killer back.

Only Frank Cross knew the truth.

That he was holding his partner desperately as a human shield. That his eyes were shut tight as he fired and fired again until his 9 mm pistol ran out of bullets.

The detective couldn't contradict him. He had died instantly with a bullet in his brain.

Officer Tim Reed couldn't contradict him, either. The bullet that smashed into his chest and severed his spinal cord had rendered him unconscious at almost the moment of impact.

William Brown, the cop-killer, wouldn't contradict him, either. Run off the road by state troopers in the Everglades half an hour later, he tried to shoot it out and died in a hail of return fire from the Florida Highway Patrolmen.

Only Frank Cross knew.

But his chance to make it right, to prove that he wasn't a coward, was coming. It had to be coming. It had to be proved!

He reset the timer. The dry-fire exercise was becoming more difficult. It was hard to line up the sights with tears in his eyes.

DAN HARRINGTON'S HAND slipped as he reached for the glass, and he spilled the whiskey. "Hell," he muttered, slapping the glass away. He grabbed the open bottle of Seagram's and tilted it to his lips. The whiskey went down his throat like liquid fire.

This was the way to drink, he knew. At home. Not in a public bar, and never in a cop bar, with a bunch of drunk cops with guns.

How many cops did he know who'd gotten into trouble that way? Hell, he'd lost count. Drinking, Harrington knew, was like screwing. It should be done in private, where it can be controlled and enjoyed and can stay no one else's damn business.

He didn't miss going to the bar with the others. What a bunch of idiots. All gung-ho like young kids. Some of them *were* young kids. And not a one of them had yet discovered Harrington's first rule.

The rule was simple. People were resources. You used them for what you wanted and then got rid of them. It didn't mean you had to hang around with them and listen to their bullshit.

You just had to select the right people. He'd learned that early on. Partner up with a family-type guy who wanted to get home to wifey and the kids. Fine. All the more courtroom overtime for you. Take his arrests for your own, give him a little kickback . . . he was happy, you were happy, and more important, the paperwork all showed you as one of the most productive cops on your squad.

There was also, of course, Harrington's second rule. That rule was, let the other guy take the risks. He had been through, what, four shootings? Twice he'd just ducked behind cover. Once the guy got away, which was fine with Harrington, since the SOB wasn't shooting at him anymore. Another time the other cops returned fire, wounding the perpetrator and making him drop his gun. Also fine with Harrington. Hell, he'd been in a shooting, hadn't he? That was all that mattered. Shootings were rich coin in the world of the cops. The public only knew the job from TV, and they figured that all cops were heroes who were always in shootings. The more shootings you were in, the bigger a hero you were. Hell, it was even that way with some of the other cops.

In two other cases he *had* fired. A guy he wanted for questioning pulled a little pocketknife and started to open it. Harrington drew his 5-shot .38 snubnose, the gun most Miami detectives carried then, and emptied it as fast as he could pull the trigger. One of the bullets struck the man in the calf—the other four went wide—and so surprised him that he dropped his knife and surrendered. The other time, he emptied his gun at a fleeing car thief, and missed not only the man but the car.

After that Dan Harrington started taking marksmanship seriously. After all, being in a shooting was heady stuff, but being in a shooting and having shot someone was a whole lot better from his point of view. He started taking to heart this stuff about hold the gun firmly, watch the front sight and squeeze the trigger through instead of jerking on it. Next time . . . yeah!

And there would be a next time, yes oh yes, he thought smugly as he swigged from the bottle again. Everybody thought Stakeout Squad was dangerous. That was only if you didn't know what you were doing.

Like the broad. Melinda Hoffritz. Jumping a guy with a loaded gun. Gee-zus! You're standing right there behind him, so all you've gotta do is stick your gun behind his ear and pull the trigger. Tell the papers it was a "hostage rescue" thing, what with the gun pointed into the teller's cage already and everything. And if the guy's gun goes off when you shoot him, so what? Tom West had had a vest on, hadn't he? If he'd shot the little broad, what the hell, Dan would have been a bigger hero still for shooting a murderer dead.

That was his idea of Stakeout duty. An ambush, pure and simple, solidly controlled. Never give them a chance. If he had his way, he'd only take places where you could be in above the action, an eye-in-the-sky kind of thing like in a gambling casino, behind a bulletproof wall and with one of those sniper rifles. Blow their brains out before they even knew where you were.

Running in trying to rescue the suckers, like Cohen did? Bullshit! The little kike was out of his mind, Harrington told himself. Lucky he didn't get killed.

Not Dan. Anybody needed to go in on point, he had the ideal partner, just like always. It was a gift. Muscular young Frank Cross. You could see the self-doubt in his eyes, the need to show that he was a man. Fine. Let him go in and draw the fire. Harrington would sit back and shoot. Or maybe just sit back. The kid did good, Harrington would go in and slap on the bracelets and become the arresting officer. Kid didn't make out good, he would stay safely behind cover and blast the shit out of whoever hurt him. Be the hero cop who smoked the cop-killer and avenged the fallen young officer.

Dan Harrington burped as he reached for the whiskey bottle. Life was good. You just had to know how to manage it.

TINA WEST SAW that her dad was sitting in his favorite chair in the living room, not reading the paper in his lap, just staring at the wall. She bounced in, leaned over the back of the chair and gave him a hug.

"Hi, Dad!"

"Hi, princess."

"You look sad," the pretty twelve-year-old said. "What's on your mind?"

He smiled reassuringly. "Nothing, really."

"Okay, then," she answered brightly, "what's on your mind, *not* really?"

He laughed and shook his head.

His daughter's tone changed to concern. "It's the shooting, huh?"

He shrugged.

"You had to do it, right?"

"No choice at all," he sighed. "Hey, they're not giving you trouble on that in school, are they?"

"I don't think they even know at school, Dad. Your name wasn't in the paper."

Tom West could thank God for that. They'd made it policy not to release the names of Stakeout Squad officers involved in shootings. It was one thing they'd learned from the LAPD and NYPD experiences. It insulated the member cops and their families from revenge.

"Bothers you, though," West said softly.

"Not me," she said. "If I've got a choice of some low-life junkie or my dad, I want it to be my dad. I want you to come home."

He suddenly felt an impulse to hug his daughter tighter.

"I will, princess. Always! I promise you that. I'll always come home."

STAN BARANCK WALKED into the family room and saw Stan Jr. with the kid next door. Junior was behind a sofa and Anthony, also seven, had ducked behind a chair. They were snapping toy clicker guns at each other.

Baranck clapped his hands together. "Hey, kids. C'mere."

Junior looked worried. "We weren't that loud, were we, Daddy?"

"Naw," said Baranck, taking a seat at the middle of the sofa. "Come sit down, you two. I wanna talk about some stuff." The kids sat next to him obediently.

"You know, I played with toy guns myself when I was your age," he began. "Cowboys and Indians, soldiers, cops and robbers. But I want to tell you what I found out when I grew up.

"I found out guns aren't toys. I look at you two now, and you know what I see? Two good buddies, playing at killing each other. You think that's right?" He looked from one boy to the other.

"We was only playin', Mr. Baranck," Anthony said defensively.

"Sure you were," Stan Baranck said softly. "That's the point. Where's the fun in pretending to kill people? When you play like that, you pretend to get shot, but then you get back up again. The actors on TV and in the videos are the same. They only pretend to get shot, and then they get up and they're okay. But it's not like that in real life.

"Now, Anthony, I don't know about your house, but we've got real guns in this one. We have to, because I'm a policeman. Now, if there are real guns in a house, maybe loaded guns, you see why it's not a good idea to get in the habit of pointing guns at each other and pulling the trigger. You guys follow me so far?"

"Yeah, Daddy," said Stan Jr., "but we can tell real guns from play guns."

"Not everybody can," said his father. "Some of those toy guns are awful real. Some good friends of mine on the police force were in a shooting this month where a young boy not much older than you two pointed a toy gun at them. It was so real looking they couldn't tell it was a toy and they shot him. He's dead, kids. He's not going to get back up.

"Now, Anthony, every family has their own rules about guns. I don't know what the rules are in your house, and they're none of my business, but—"

The little boy interrupted him eagerly. "My dad's got a .38! I'm not supposed to know about it, but it's right in his night table drawer. He says it's for protection."

Great, thought Stan Baranck, making a mental note to warn his next-door neighbor that his kid knew where the hidden gun was. He remembered his own childhood. There wasn't much his parents could hide from him, either.

"Well, that's okay," he told the boy diplomatically. "A lot of people have guns for protection. But kids shouldn't touch them at all, should they?"

"Not unless a burglar broke in," the boy replied solemnly. "If a burglar broke in, I'd get my dad's gun and blow him away!"

Baranck decided he was talking to this kid's dad tonight.

"Guns aren't for kids, Anthony," he said firmly. "If you ever want to shoot a gun, and your parents give you permission, I'll take you and Stan Jr. out to the range.

"Stan, you know that offer's good for you, anytime. But it's like this. When there are real guns around, you can't be getting into the habit of pointing any guns, even toy ones, at people. You're my son. I carry a gun to keep people from killing people. I don't want my son playing at shooting people.

"I don't know about your friends' houses. But that's going to be the rule in *this* house. Understood?"

BOB CARMODY and Melinda Hoffritz were side by side at the range. Hoffritz was trying his holster. "You're right," she said. "It's better. Much better. The gun comes out a lot smoother, and it goes back in a whole lot smoother."

"Bruce Nelson makes them custom out in California," said Carmody. "He was a narc before he retired and went into leather. I've got the catalog at home. That little suede thing you've got with the belt clip, it's gonna come out with your gun one day."

"What I like is that the leather's stiff, the gun goes right back in," she answered. "In the bank the other day, when I jumped that guy for the gun, my hand had already been on my Colt. If I'd drawn it, there was no way to get it back in the holster and leave my hands free for the disarm. The thing I've got now just collapses inside the belt after you draw. You practically need a shoehorn to reholster. I worry about that more than the quick draw."

He grinned. "I've got to admit, you got it out pretty quick the other day."

She frowned. "Bummer. I can't believe we hit him as bad as we did. Two shots each, and nothing really dead center."

"Hey, we did all right. National average for cops is only one shot out of four fired even hits the bad guy at all. Under the circumstances, I'm not disappointed. But I guess after your other shooting, you've got higher standards. Oh, heck, wait a minute...I didn't mean that the way it sounded, Melinda."

"No problem. I came to terms with the other thing a long time ago. Besides, the circumstances were different. I had the car door to brace the gun on."

She changed the subject. Looking down at his pistol on the range table, she said, "Can I try your Colt? It looks different from mine."

"Sure," he said. "It's custom made, built on the Colt, with a street compensator. The recoil compensator is built in to where the front of the slide used to be. You have to look twice to see it's not a regular Government Model."

She slid in a magazine and released the slide. When she fired the first shot, she seemed to do a double take. The recoil had been so soft she thought she'd had a misfire. Then she brought the gun back up to line of sight. She squeezed off one more shot and then triggered a rapid fire burst of five more. The slide locked back, empty.

"Unbelievable," she said. "What kind of a scumbag did they get something like this from? Being top shot on the department has its perks, huh, Bob? You get first pick of the confiscated .45s?"

He smiled sheepishly. "No, that's mine. I bought it before they ever thought of stakeout squads here. I think I'm the only one on the unit carrying his own gun. You know, the SWAT team used to be armed with confiscated .45s taken out of the property room and gone over by the armorers. They took the .45s away after the department went to the 9 mm Glocks. I guess they wanted to have everyone carrying the same gun. When the Stakeout Project said we should have .45s,

I guess they went back to the old method. That Gold Cup you've got is a good piece, though, as good as anything they had in the property room.''

"Yeah, but I love the way yours shoots. What did it cost?''

"Couple grand.''

She pretended to choke. "Still, there's almost no recoil. The way it shoots, I guess it's worth it. What did that gal say in the old shampoo commercial? 'It's more expensive, but I'm worth it.'''

"Amen,'' her partner agreed. "I figured it was cheap for life insurance that keeps you alive.''

THE PHONE RANG on the Stakeout lieutenant's desk. He picked it up and said, "Stakeout, Bartlett.''

"'Morning, Ken,'' said the voice on the other end. "This is Bob Litton.''

"Hey, Chief, what's new?''

"That's why I called. The feeler we and the Feds sent out to Indiana paid off. The folks at Pendleton remember Blaisdell hanging out with an old dude whose specialty was GTA. And Grand Theft Auto ties right in with how smoothly the Shotgun Gang has been grabbing the cars they use in the robberies. Another one of his special buddies was an old Baltimore native like himself. Seemed the guy belonged to an outfit up there called the Shotgun Gang. We talking role models or what?

"He was tight with a former mercenary out of Rhodesia—I don't see the connection there yet—but one of his other prison pals was into jewelry heists. The guy's out of there now, jumped parole a couple of years ago. Now, I got to thinking—if Blaisdell is due to make another switch in M.O., what about a gem heist?

"I had my guys check around, sniff the air. They've got a big retail jewelry show at the Miami Hotel Mart Plaza this weekend. A few million in stones, between all the dealers. It's almost an upscale-flea-market thing. I thought you might be interested."

Bartlett groaned. "Flea market, huh? That means, like, acres of tables. Sounds grim for a stakeout."

"No shit," agreed the chief of detectives. "My robbery detectives are talking with the organizers now. You'd have to coordinate with the show's security people, too. But, what the hell. I thought you might want to kick it around. I'd clear it with Chief Kearn before you do anything, though. Something does go down in there with all those bystanders, the way the Shotgun Gang works, it could turn into a slaughter-house."

"All those jewelers," Bartlett agreed, "probably carrying their own guns, it'd turn into a slaughter-house whether we were in there or not, Chief. Damned if we do, damned if we don't."

"Exactly," Litton answered dryly. "Welcome to the wonderful world of protecting the public."

HOMESTEAD IS an unincorporated suburb of Dade County that stretches from the Miami city limit to rural swampland that resembles Dogpatch, USA. It contains both slums and farms, both mainline hotels and tiny vacation cottages. At such a remote vacation cabin, rented by John Blaisdell, the remainder of the Shotgun Gang had convened for the first time.

"It'll be our last hit for a while," Blaisdell told his assembled troops. "That's why we'll all do it together. It's a big job. I see us pulling between two and three million worth of stones. They ought to fence to a clear mil, mil and a quarter. Plenty for all of us. We take a few months off, let the heat cool down, give the Stakeout Squad time to get enough rope to hang itself."

"Must be big, you need all of us at once," said Tony Alonzo.

"It is, Savage, it is. The biggest yet. The jewelry fair at the Miami Mart."

Some of them whistled. Some muttered things like "Holy shit!"

"That's bitin' off a lot, Win," said John Swift.

Blaisdell grinned broadly. He was back to his old charming self. "Damn right, Fox. It's a big bite. But we've got big teeth."

Dewey Edmonds looked doubtful. "Ain't that like acres an' acres of booths an' tables an' shit, Win? They gonna have their own security all over, and jewelers carry their own guns."

Blaisdell waved his hand dismissively. "They had their own guns in the check-cash joints, too. Trouble for the amateurs, but it didn't hurt us any! Show starts tomorrow, Moss, Saturday morning at 9:00 a.m. prompt. I've been there casing for a couple of days, in the hotel that's attached right to it.

"They're not all that spread out. The tables and booths are already set up. Remember, they're worried about covering a big area, too. Gems are small, they don't need a lot of layout space. Costume jewelry, the flashy designer shit with no real intrinsic value, is all on one end. The fakes, the zircons and stuff, are all at the other end. The good stuff is right in the middle."

Blaisdell opened his Vuitton case and pulled out a pile of leaflets. "Ruger, pass these around. Everybody comes into the show will get one. It's a map showing which booths have what, where. We want the ones I've circled on your leaflets. We're going after the diamonds, the rubies, the emeralds, the sapphires. Figure they'll be half loose stones, half in settings. Take 'em all. Gold rings carry light, and they'll melt down to a good chunk of change. All of these places will have these little attaché cases under the tables and in behind the salesmen. We grab them, too. That's where they've got the really good shit.

"That little section I've marked out is one strip in the big Mart walkway, less than thirty paces long. We roll in a big electric cart—not a little golf cart, but one of those big ones, like they use for cripples at the airports—and roll it right out the door and into a semi. The Miami is right off the highway. We'll be steering for the open sea less than sixty seconds out from the hit. One exit up, we dump everything into the escape cars and we're home free. You still got your commercial license to drive a semi, Berg?"

Harry Hamilton nodded his pale head in the affirmative.

Moss said suddenly, "Any word on Noble?"

The false cheer was suddenly gone from Blaisdell's face. "Just what's in the papers."

"Yeah," Moss persisted, "but I mean, you got him a lawyer yet? You always told us, we get nailed, you'd cover us with a lawyer."

Blaisdell's face reddened with anger. "Yeah, and I also told you if you ratted the rest of us out, you were dead! That bastard ratted us out, Moss! How do you think the pigs found their way to my place? Why do you think Chen's dead? The cops murdered Chen and beat the shit out of my lady 'cause of that bastard! Get him a lawyer? Bullshit! Time comes, they stop surrounding him with four or five pigs every day, and he's gonna pay the price!"

The members of the Shotgun Gang looked at one another nervously. They knew a closed subject when they saw one.

20

Mike Cohen paid for his coffee, took a few steps away from the roller cart and leaned against the wall to survey the inside of the Miami Hotel Mart Plaza.

It was not good.

Bartlett and Kearn had decided that the chance of a change in the Shotgun Gang's pattern was too remote to dedicate the entire Stakeout Squad to the Mart. After all, there was no solid tip, just speculation. Team Two was in place there. Team One was in Overtown and Team Three in Liberty City, both covering check-cash joints.

Cohen scanned the swarms of people and the tables. The terrifying thing was, you couldn't tell who was carrying guns. It looked like a convention of off-duty cops. Everyone behind the tables, the vendors, seemed to be wearing a Banana Republic vest or a nylon jacket or a black fanny pack worn in the front. All the marks of pistol packers.

He hadn't thought about it before, but of course, gem dealers would be licensed to carry guns. At least he didn't see anything baggy enough to be covering a sawed-off shotgun, and he knew that both the private security guards and the jewelers had been briefed by Ken Bartlett at the vendors' meeting last night. If guns were pulled, if shots were fired, they had been told in no uncertain terms that they were not to reach for their own guns, but instead to dive prone under their tables and stay there.

He hoped they took it seriously.

The rest of Team Two was in place. Carmody and Hoffritz, blond and fit—a striking couple, really—appeared to be well-dressed customers wandering among the tables. They looked like classic yuppies from the Gables. Chip and Buffy.

The tables with the heavy goodies seemed to be clusterd in the middle of the Mart Plaza, in a strip perhaps eighty feet long. Frank Cross was at one end, Dan Harrington at the other. Both were wearing business suits, and the distinctive Vendor name tags Cohen had finessed for them from the nervous organizers of the retail jewelry festival. They fitted in well. They looked like professional buyers wandering around.

Tom West and Stan Baranck weren't in sight, but Cohen knew they were around somewhere. The hotel had provided them with custodian's jumpsuits. No one would look at them twice, and it gave them a good excuse to have portable radios on their belts. The loose-fitting coveralls hid their .45s and their Second Chance vests, well. As maintenance people, they had good reason to be in the parking lot or the main Mart area, and they were functioning as rovers.

Cohen pushed up the sleeve of his nylon Windbreaker and checked his watch. It was a little after 10:00 a.m.

He fought the urge to cross his fingers for luck.

JUAN DIAZ AND JOHN SWIFT hunched over their coffee in the first-floor restaurant of the Miami Hotel. They wore ties and sport coats. In the attaché cases at their feet were their sawed-off double-barreled shotguns. Win had thought that they wouldn't be able to walk the long distances from the parking lot into the Mart area with big guns slung under their coats, hence the attaché cases. Each of them, of course, also had a handgun under his jacket.

"I don't like it," Diaz muttered. "Too big an area, too many people. Too much chance for a fuckup."

"Yeah," agreed Swift, "but what ya gonna do? You heard him yesterday. If a one of us had stood up and walked out, we never woulda' made it to the door."

Diaz shook his head. "All I know is, you and I ain't on none of them bank cameras with nothin' serious. We were out of line of sight. They can't tie us to those guards except for the witnesses, and it's their word against ours."

Swift looked him in the eye. "What're you sayin'?"

"I'm sayin', this thing goes bad today, I ain't dyin' for Win or nobody else. Most they can nail either one of us for is the hit an' the sawed-offs. Four years, five tops, we're back out the door. Maybe just the min-man."

"Not me, bro," Swift muttered grimly. "I'll fight. I gotta be free. I ain't doin' a day inside, never mind no three years min-man." He paused, looking grim at the thought of serving minimum mandatory time, the three years' guaranteed prison time for any felony committed with a firearm in Florida.

"Do what you gotta do," Diaz sighed. "Just remember, bro, it's a business, that's all."

He looked at his watch. It was nearly a quarter past ten. A little more than fifteen minutes to the start time.

NOTHING SEEMED UNUSUAL about the Arab and the tall Caucasian who strolled down the center of the display area. They wore ties and jackets and carried attaché cases, but so did many of the other shoppers at the jewelry expo.

Abdul Mohammad, known to the Shotgun Gang as "Ruger," glanced casually up and down the tables. He was mentally rehearsing his role. When the signal came, the sawed-off Ruger Red Label with its over-and-under double barrels would snake out of the case. The case could be dumped; he wouldn't need it anymore. Once they knew there wasn't going to be any resistance, he'd hold the gun in his left hand and scoop trays of diamonds into the open burlap sacks that would be in the golf cart. Piece of cake. It would be his biggest job yet with the Shotgun Gang.

His partner, tall pale Chester, would be backing him all the way with his cut-down Winchester pump gun. He didn't know that his partner's name was George Hamlin. He only knew that Chester had done more jobs than he had, and that was a confidence builder.

He glanced down at his fake Rolex—10:28. Two minutes to show time.

WARD AND SAVAGE rolled the big electric cart down the ramp from the semitrailer that was parked at the rear entrance of the Mart, the loading area. They wore loose white coveralls, like workmen. At their feet were the attaché cases that held Hector Gutierez's Montgomery Ward 12-gauge pump gun and Tony Alonzo's Savage Model 775 12-gauge automatic. Harry Hamilton stayed at the wheel of the semi, his cut-down Mossberg pump gun on the seat beside him under a carefully spread denim jacket.

The wide automatic doors to the delivery entrance hissed open to admit the golf cart, then closed softly behind it.

Perhaps fifteen yards away, around the corner of the building, Tom West said to Stan Baranck, "What do you think of that?"

Baranck frowned. "Doesn't compute. There's nothing to deliver—the tables and stuff are all set up. Why a big golf cart?"

"Worth a look," said West.

They moved forward, separating. Baranck went around the right while West approached the driver's door from the rear of the tractor trailer.

Hamilton swore under his breath. The hotel puppet was coming to tell him to move the truck. Automatically his hand went under the denim jacket and closed on the cut-off stock of the Mossberg. The finger rested on the trigger, the thumb on the safety catch on top.

"Excuse me, sir," said the black man in the Miami Hotel coveralls that Hamilton had seen approaching in the side-view mirror. "Are you making a pickup?"

"Uh, yeah, right," Hamilton answered nervously. "Display stuff."

There was a pause. The black man looked at him suspiciously. "Sir, I wonder if you could step out of the truck please."

"What the fuck for? You think you're a cop or something?"

"Just step out of the truck, please."

Hamilton snapped open the door with his left hand, bringing up the shotgun in his right.

To Tom West, it seemed like slow motion. The door coming open, the muzzle of the sawed-off pump gun coming into view, arcing toward him. He clawed his hand inside the coveralls, groping for his .45, and knew he wasn't going to make it. A vision flashed in his mind of himself hugging his daughter, saying, "I'll always come home." And now he looked into the deadly black eye of the shotgun's muzzle.

The shot was loud, but he saw no flash at all.

EDMONDS AND BLAISDELL pulled into the wide circular drive that served as a dual entranceway to the Miami Hotel on the left and the Mart Plaza on the right. Each picked up his attaché case as he stepped out of the car. Dewey "Moss" Edmonds tossed the keys to the stolen Honda Accord to the valet who came to meet them. They wouldn't need the car anymore. They'd be leaving with the others in the semi.

They walked in through the main entrance. Up ahead was the mall strip and the milling crowd.

On their left, coming in from the big hallway that connected the hotel with the Mart Plaza, were Fox and Stevens. Blaisdell wished he could have left them in the background as layoff men the way he had with the hit at the mall in the Grove, but the job was too big. He needed all the hands possible to shovel the jewels into the burlap bags on the electric cart.

What backup would they need, anyway? These weren't hard guys, like cashiers in a ghetto check-cash joint. Guns under their coats or not, these lightweights would crap in their pants as soon as someone racked a shotgun, he knew. And the cops, especially the Stakeout Squad, would never dream that the Shotgun Gang would be so bold as to hit this many people at once. Besides, the gang had always gone for cash before. They wouldn't know that Win knew what to do with jewelry until after the big heist was over.

Down at the opposite end of the main mall, he could see the electric cart rolling toward him and Moss. Fox and Stevens had already moved out ahead of them, homing for the center of the tables where the diamonds were.

John Blaisdell couldn't keep from smiling. It was going like clockwork. And in thirty seocnds the biggest and best hit of his life was going to come down.

TOM WEST'S HAND CLOSED on the .45 inside his coveralls when the muzzle of the shotgun had leveled on his eyes and the sound of the shot had come. He flinched involuntarily.

And suddenly the big white guy and the shotgun were both pitching out the door, slamming heavily into him, driving him back. He felt his head crack painfully on the concrete.

But he was alive. *Alive!*

Fighting the weight of the man on top of him, he struggled to clear his pistol. It came free. He thrust the gun muzzle into the man's throat, forcing his head back. He looked into his antagonist's face.

It was the face of death.

The mouth hung open slack, blood pouring freely out of it and onto West's coveralls. The eyes, half-open, were blank. He suddenly realized that the bulk on top of him was all dead weight.

No vitality. No life.

The voice seemed to come to him from a distance. "Tom! Tom!"

West pushed the dead weight away from him. The corpse rolled heavily onto its side, on top of the still-unfired shotgun that had fallen harmlessly to the pavement.

He realized what had happened. Baranck had shot the gunman in the head from the other side of the truck.

His partner emerged now, above him, in the driver's door. He had dived across the front seat, his SIG ahead of him in his fist, tendrils of gun smoke still wafting from the black muzzle.

"Tom," he cried again. "You okay?"

"Yeah," grunted West. "Get on the radio quick!"

"Team Two Rover, Team Two Leader," gasped Baranck into the portable. "Suspect down, shots fired, truck outside, back entrance! Shotgun Gang! Two perps, white coveralls, big golf cart! It's going down!"

WHEN HE RECEIVED Baranck's excited message, Mike Cohen was strangely calm. There was no time to panic, time only to do.

They had worked it out the night before. There had been no way to have every Stakeout person inside wearing a microphone in their ear, or they'd be as obvious as Secret Service men. The Mart managers had given Cohen a pager that reached directly into the main office. No one else would use the pager that day.

The pager tone would mean only one thing, and an innocuous code phrase would be broadcast immediately over the loudspeaker, throughout the Mart.

Cohen pressed the button on the pager urgently. It seemed an eternity to him, but only three seconds passed before a woman's voice, electronically amplified for all to hear, announced, "There will be a happy hour at the Miami Hotel lounge beginning at 5:00 p.m."

Cohen wondered if he was the only one who could pick up on the tension that seemed to throb in the woman's voice. Looking around, he saw his Stakeout people seem to stiffen, their heads slowly turning around as they came to full alert, making sure their hands were free to go to their guns.

If he had thought to look at the big clock on the wall, Cohen would have seen that in ten seconds it would be exactly ten-thirty.

BLAISDELL GLANCED AROUND. Stevens and Fox were on his left, north, alongside the tables there. Ruger and Chester were south on the right, standing near a couple of well-dressed blond yuppies. He and Moss blocked the aisle to the west, and from the east end of the hall, the big electric cart with Ward and Savage had come to a stop at the point where the most expensive jewelry displays began. The box was closed.

Show time!

John Blaisdell knelt down and set his attaché case on the floor. Beside him Moss did the same. He reached in and grabbed the Winchester, pumping it sharply and loudly as he came to his feet. People spun and stared at him when they heard the sound. The terror in their faces gratified him.

He opened his mouth. He was about to yell "Shotgun Gang! Nobody move!"

But before he could speak, everything around him seemed to erupt into thunder.

IT ALL HAPPENED at once.

Mike Cohen heard the sound of a shotgun being pumped. He reached instinctively under his jacket for his Glock .45. Two men a few feet away, their backs to him, dark-skinned men in sport coats, were pulling double-barreled shotguns out of attaché cases.

Team Two had discussed it at the briefing. There would be no time for a shouted warning to drop weapons. If guns were drawn, sawed-off shotguns amid crowds of the innocent, there was only one course of action to take.

The smaller man was directly in front of him, ten feet away. Mike Cohen did as Carmody had taught them on the range. He dropped to his knee to angle the shot upward in case it missed or overpenetrated, put the white dot of the front sight at the base of the first man's skull and squeezed the trigger.

The man pitched forward. The man to his right, Hispanic looking, seemed to freeze, his gun still pointed to the floor. Only his head turned, staring in horror at Cohen.

There were shots elsewhere, loud and rapid. People were screaming. But in that instant it seemed to Cohen that there were only two people, he and the man with the shotgun, locked alone in their own corner of time and space.

"Drop it," Cohen snapped.

He saw the Hispanic man slowly open his hands and let the shotgun fall, then bring the hands slowly up. In the din of the gunfire and the screaming around them, he couldn't hear what the man was saying, but he could read the movements of his lips.

"Don't shoot," the suspect seemed to be pleading silently. "Don't shoot!"

THE ARAB and the tall white man were only a few feet in front of Hoffritz and Carmody when the shotgun's unmistakable shucking sound came from the center of the floor. Both men reached into their attaché cases, and the cops could see the blue steel of their shotguns.

The blond cops' guns came out simultaneously, rising, locking on target. They followed their training: cop on left shoots suspect on left, cop on right takes one on right, then swing across and cover for one another.

Their two Colt .45s exploded as one.

Abdul Mohammad pitched forward as the two heavy impacts from Hoffritz's pistol caught him high in the back.

The first Silvertip from Carmody's gun slammed into the back of George Hamlin's bulletproof vest. He spun toward the shot, bringing up his gun. He felt another brutal impact. The vest stopped this one, too, this time in the chest, but the force drove him backward. He tried to bring the gun up toward the blond man who was aiming at him, and toward the blond woman beside him. She had a gun, too, and was swinging on Hamlin now.

He saw muzzle-flashes, and agony streaked through his brain. He was no longer aware of the Winchester sawed-off that was falling now from his fingers. He was no longer aware of anything at all.

Mohammad was on the floor, gasping for breath from the blows of the heavy bullets that had smashed into the back of his Spectrashield vest. He looked over his shoulder, oblivious to the screams and the roar of the gunfire that surged around him, focusing only on the threat of the thing that had almost killed him.

He saw the blond woman and the man, both firing at Chester. He saw his partner's head snap back in a spray of blood and saw him begin to fall. Their eyes were off *him* now, though, and that was what mattered.

Pulling himself to his knees, Mohammad threw himself into a roll toward the cover of the display tables a few feet away. He fired the shotgun wildly toward the man and the woman as he spun, two blasts. Then he was behind the cover of the tables, knowing both barrels of the Ruger over-and-under were empty. He broke the weapon open, ejecting the smoking green shells onto the floor, fumbling in his pocket for fresh ammo.

AT THE FIRST SHOT, Dan Harrington had ducked down behind a display table. The jewelers were all hitting the floor around him. He jerked his Glock out of his holster and held it in front of him defensively. Deafening thunderclaps of gunfire were exploding all around him. He knew he would stay down here where it was safe. He was already formulating his explanation. He would say he had ducked down to protect the merchants who were already on the floor where he was, behind the display tables.

Suddenly, up ahead, he saw a man in a torn blue sport coat roll into cover between the tables. He looked like a Hindu or a Pakistani to Harrington.

The man held a double-barreled sawed-off shotgun with one barrel over the other. Cold fear gripped Harrington. There was no cover between them.

But then he saw the man open the shotgun, saw the smoking shells drop out, saw the man clawing in his pocket for more. The gun was empty now, no threat at all. And the man hadn't seen Harrington yet, only fifteen feet away.

Perfect, Dan Harrington thought.

Already on his belly, Harrington brought his Glock .45 into a two-handed prone position, the bottom of his fist braced solidly on the floor. The white square outline of the rear sight bracketed the front sight dot perfectly, and both settled on the man's ear. Harrington slowly squeezed the trigger.

The gun bucked. The man collapsed instantly, slumping forward in a fetal position over the open shotgun, and didn't move. There was blood on the side of his head.

Harrington didn't take any chances. He aimed at the dead man's head and squeezed off one more shot just for good measure.

JOHN BLAISDELL was stunned by the gunfire that had surrounded him. He ducked, turning wildly, trying to find a target for his Winchester.

He saw the yuppie blond couple, the man and the woman, firing, saw Ruger and Chester go down. He pivoted toward them, coming up with the shotgun, when something that felt like a sledgehammer smashed into his right arm. The room spun and suddenly he was on the floor, doubled up, clutching the wounded right arm to his belly, choking with the agony.

He made no sound. Blaisdell's terror held him silent. It was only in his mind that he screamed, Moss! Help me! Get me out of here!

WHEN HE HAD HEARD that first sound of a shotgun being pumped, Frank Cross drew his 4506 faster than he had ever done in practice. It was in his hand, off-safe, and he was crouching. He cringed inwardly as the first shots went off.

The terror was cold inside him, strong, gripping.

Not again. Not again! *No!*

Everyone was ducking, shooting, screaming.

He saw an expensively dressed white guy and a black guy, standing together, both holding shotguns. Shotguns they were raising to kill people with.

No!

Frank Cross willed the weapon up in both his hands. He lined up the three white dots of the gun sights on the white guy whose side was to him and rolled the trigger back.

The blast of his shot seemed lost in the deafening roar around him, but he saw the nimbus of flame at the front of his weapon, saw the man in the suit spin and fall, dropping the shotgun.

And in that instant, he knew. He knew he could do it. He knew that this time wouldn't be like before.

His surroundings slid into an eerie slow motion. The cacophony of the screams and the shots around him seemed to recede. He focused on the black man who seemed to be turning slowly toward him, raising a sawed-off Mossberg shotgun.

''No,'' screamed Frank Cross as he fired.

The black man seemed to jerk at the shot. A tongue of orange flame spit upward from his shotgun toward the ceiling.

Cross fired again. ''Not this time,'' he cried hoarsely, unaware that he was moving forward, still firing. ''Not this time!''

The gun bucked in his hand as he advanced, the black man jerking backward at each shot until a red blossom bloomed at his throat and he fell. The slide had locked back empty, all nine bullets gone, and Frank Cross stood over the man now and looked down at him and knew that he was dead, saw that the other man he had shot was doubled over on the floor facedown and still, too...

And suddenly the fear was gone. Frank Cross was on autopilot. His right thumb punched the magazine-release button, dumping out the spent clip, as his left hand scooped a fresh magazine and jammed it into the butt of the gun. He thumbed the latch that slammed the slide closed, and turned, turned toward the rear entrance to the hall.

TONY ALONZO DUCKED down instinctively inside the golf cart when the shooting had started, almost dropping his Savage automatic that he'd just taken out of its case. Suddenly the whole place was up for grabs.

He saw Ruger and Chester go down. He glanced through the crowd and saw Stevens at the far end, his hands high in the air. In the swirling mass of screaming humanity, he saw Win spun around by a bullet and going down, Moss grunting and jerking and firing as bullets plucked at his body.

"Fuck, get us out of here," he screeched at Ward, beside him.

Hector Gutierez needed no further urging. He threw the electric cart in Reverse, the motor humming urgently as it propelled them backward, away from the shooting, toward the back door they had entered through.

Alonzo swiveled his head back and forth. The battleground was receding behind them. He turned toward the door. People were ducking out of the way. They'd be out of there soon and—

Two guys dressed like maintenance workers were coming through the door they were heading for. One black, one white, both were holding pistols. The black guy was covered with blood, and they both looked like grim death to Alonzo.

"Watch it," he exclaimed to Gutierez, trying to swing his shotgun toward the door at the same time. Gutierez flinched, his hand jerking on the tiller, and suddenly the cart jerked sideways, fishtailing out of control. The momentum threw Alonzo off-balance, and he felt himself falling. He reflexively let go of the shotgun as he clutched at the handrail of the cart. Then the other end of the cart slammed into the wall, and the world seemed to spin.

Tony Alonzo went flying, trying to land on his shoulder and roll as he hit the floor. Everything was topsy-turvy. Suddenly he saw the blood-covered black guy with the silvery pistol in his hand. Tony knew his shotgun was gone. He thought about reaching under his white coveralls for his pistol.

And the black guy's boot came out of nowhere, smashing him in the jaw, sending dazzling sheets of pain through his head. He saw stars. As his head lolled to the side, he could see Hector Gutierez in the stalled electric cart, his hands raised in surrender. Alonzo felt something hard and cold against the side of his head and knew it was a gun muzzle.

"Do it," came the black cop's angry, grating whisper. "Just do it! Give me an excuse!"

"I give up," Alonzo said, slurring the words through his broken jaw.

He couldn't hear the gunfire anymore.

THE SHOTS HAD STOPPED. Mike Cohen stood behind Juan Diaz, who was on his knees with his fingers interlaced behind his head. Cohen's left hand held the entwined fingers in a crushing grip; his right hand still held the Glock .45 in tight to his hip, the finger stiff outside the trigger guard.

At the far end, Cohen saw, Baranck and West had two suspects in custody. Harrington was rising from behind a table, his eyes darting around, his gun in his hand. Cohen's other three cops were standing, too.

From the moment Blaisdell had pumped the shotgun, to the dying echo of the last shot, no more than fifteen seconds had elapsed.

Mike Cohen wasn't thinking in terms of time. All that went through his mind was an awareness that said, It's over.

And then came the voice, shrill with hysteria and thwarted rage. The voice shrieked, "Freeze! Drop your guns or this kid dies!"

21

John Blaisdell had lain frozen in horror for a few moments, clutching his ruined arm to his belly, as motionless as a rabbit in the terrifying presence of a wolf. There was a hollow thudding sound near him, and turning his eyes, he saw the corpse of his main man, Moss, the blood gushing from his throat and mouth, the eyes fixed wide open, staring at nothing. There was a clinking sound as an empty pistol magazine hit the ground, followed by the sound of a big automatic being reloaded.

Soon the shooting stopped.

It was finished, Blaisdell knew. The Shotgun Gang was done.

The Shotgun Gang. But not John Blaisdell!

His eyes darted around furtively. Everyone around him was on the floor, huddling. The nearest was a young woman on top of a little boy—her own kid obviously—shielding him with her body. She was looking the other way anxiously.

Blaisdell's right hand didn't want to move. He glanced down. The bullet seemed to have gone in a third of the way down the forearm and come out by his thumb. He didn't know where the hell the shotgun was.

But he still had his pistol. He snaked his left hand under the back of his coat, grasped the .380 automatic and slipped it free. The woman and the kid were only inches away.

He knew she'd try to protect her child, and he didn't have time to tussle with her. He brought the gun up to shoot her in the head, then realized that the shot would alert the pigs sooner than he could afford. Instead, he slashed the gun down brutally against her temple. She made no sound, but her eyes rolled up as she passed out from the blow.

There was no time to waste. Blaisdell reached with his right hand, ignoring the pain, and grabbed the child cruelly by the throat. A few of his fingers felt numb, and he realized the bullet must have hit a nerve. But the boy was only three or four, and two adult fingers were enough to shut off his wind and keep him silent. He jerked the child to him.

Now he had his shield.

He brought the gun up to the side of the boy's head, holding him tight and close, and carefully cocked the hammer with his thumb. Then he screamed, "Freeze! Drop your guns or this kid dies!"

He liked the sound of his voice. It was strong, he told himself. Win was back! Win would prevail!

Suddenly there was silence around him.

The only ones standing seemed to be cops. A big bald guy. A big young guy. A man and a woman, light-colored hair. They pointed their guns at him.

"Drop 'em," Blaisdell screamed. "Drop 'em, or I'll kill him, I swear it!"

The guns were still pointed at him. But they weren't firing, either.

It was happening too fast. He was hurting too much. No time to think things out. Blaisdell felt the pain shoot up his arm as he pulled the squirming child tight, bringing the kid's head up in front of his own. He dug the gun muzzle cruelly into the child's temple.

"You can't shoot me! This gun's *cocked!* My finger's on the trigger! You shoot me, he's dead!"

HE'S RIGHT, thought Melinda Hoffritz. None of us but Bob is good enough a shot to snipe him out from behind the kid, and even Bob can't try with the cocked gun to his head. We've got to get the gun muzzle away from the boy.

Then she remembered the profile. If this was Blaisdell, he was a woman beater, a woman hater.

She had the answer.

She took a breath to make sure her voice was calm and, with her gun still aimed at the man behind the little boy, she began to speak.

CARMODY'S HEART was pounding. His finger was just off the trigger of the Custom Colt automatic. He knew how well the weapon smith had tuned that trigger. It would release with about as much pressure as a key on an electric typewriter.

He forced himself to breathe slowly, to steady down. The killer's bloody right hand was holding the kid in front of the bastard's face, the boy's head right in Carmody's line of fire. One eye peeked out from behind him, one wild and hate-crazed eye. They were perhaps a dozen feet apart.

Enough for a brain shot, Carmody knew, but even a brain shot wouldn't be enough. To shut off this bastard's nervous system without the trigger finger even twitching, the bullet would have to enter midway down the head or lower and penetrate the deep brain, the medulla. Carmody had to wait until the muzzle of the cocked automatic strayed away from the child's skull.

Then Hoffritz began talking. It was confusing, terrifying at first. Carmody wanted to tell her to shut up. But then it came to him, as if by telepathy, and he understood, and made himself ready.

"You're Blaisdell, aren't you?" Hoffritz began, softly but clearly.

"Fuckin' right!" Blaisdell snarled.

"Stakeout Squad," she said firmly. "Why not just put the gun down, Blaisdell? You might have the guts to hurt the kid, but I know you haven't got the balls to hurt *me*."

"You bitch," Blaisdell growled in reply.

"Go ahead," she said tauntingly. "Look at me, Blaisdell. I'm putting my gun on safe, see? My finger's off the trigger, see? I'm pointing it at the goddamn floor, *see*? You think you got the balls to shoot me *now*?"

Carmody saw the facial muscles working madly, focused on the one eye he could see as it narrowed in a murderous rage.

Blaisdell shrieked and swung the gun away from the boy, toward Hoffritz, his finger tightening on the trigger.

Bob Carmody fired.

HOFFRITZ KNEW it would happen now. She sensed it. She heard the killer scream in rage, saw the black pistol swing toward her.

Even as Carmody's gun exploded, even as the halo of pink burst around the killer's head, she was lunging forward, reaching for the wild-eyed little boy. And then she had him, pulling him free, rolling to the floor, rolling on top of him, shielding him from a bullet.

But it was over.

CARMODY DIDN'T MOVE from where he was in the moment after the shot. The kick of the recoil-compensated gun had been so mild that he had seen the bullet strike, seen the glaring eye turn into a hollow red socket, seen the pink haze of blood and brain matter surround the head even as the hostage taker began to collapse, even as Hoffritz came from nowhere and pulled the child away into a protective roll.

Only then did he step forward, the gun still level. He saw the cocked .380 lying on the floor, unfired. Saw John Blaisdell's body twitch convulsively once, and then no more.

Bob Carmody's thumb flipped the safety catch into the locked position as he lowered the Colt .45.

"It's over, you bastard," he breathed. "It's over."

But the words were wasted, because, of course, the corpse could not hear.

22

The following Monday evening, John Kearn and Ken Bartlett and their wives went to dinner at the Chart House. It was something of a celebration. The restaurant was only a few hundred yards from the mall where the ArmorDade robbery had gone down a few weeks ago.

When the after-dinner coffee came, Kearn said, "Ladies, if you don't mind, Ken and I are going to take a little walk. We've got some office things to discuss."

The breeze was cool and crisp off the bay, but they left their raincoats unbuttoned. The misty rain had been falling on and off through the evening.

They left the restaurant through the side door and strolled down the cobblestoned path to the bay.

Kearn asked, "How's Team Two doing?"

"Okay, by and large," Bartlett answered. "West damn near bought it, and he knows it. He and Baranck are cool, though, as steady as I've got. Bob and Melinda came through like champs. Harrington considers himself the hero of the whole thing. Cross seems almost relieved, like he's finally proven himself to the rest of us."

"Or maybe just to himself," said Kearn. "What about Cohen?"

"Holding steady, doing better than I thought. It took a lot out of him, the guy at the check-cashing place. The one he shot in the Mart was like an anticlimax. We brought the shrink in Saturday night, ran them all through, and he said it didn't look like we had anything to worry about. How's it going on your end?"

"Better than I could have hoped," the chief replied. "I suspect the mayor's first reaction sent him through the roof—six dead in one shooting. What saved us was that it went down in the morning, and the TV people got to the story before the damn *Crier* could. Their big angle, as you know, was no bystanders hit, Shotgun Gang wiped out, little kid saved from the jaws of death, all that."

"I loved it," said Bartlett, chuckling. "By the time I got there, my heart all in my mouth, you know, more ambulances than a plane crash on the scene already, and all those Minicams were there ahead of me. Folks just lining up to get their fifteen seconds of fame. Every one of them talking about how Melinda risked her life to make Blaisdell aim the gun at her, and how Carmody just plinked him right out from behind the kid. My favorite was that old retired police chief from up north that was there when it went down. Kept talking about the 'surgical precision' our guys used so none of the bystanders got shot, and the 'great restraint' they used in taking three of them alive. The kid's mom that Blaisdell hit was up and around by then, hugging the little guy, not too bad of a cut on her head, thanking God for the Stakeout Squad. No wonder, by the time their Sunday issue came around, there was nothing the *Crier* could take for an angle but how we wiped out the Shotgun Gang and—what did they say?—'ended the reign of terror.'"

Kearn nodded. "It could have turned out a lot worse. Word from the hospital is, both the little girls that were shot in the check-cash robbery will be just fine. That one had been touch-and-go for a while."

"What's the outlook for that one's father, the guy that stuck the gun in Stiller's mouth?"

"Without him, the Shotgun Gang might still be out and running. I've already sat down with the state attorney. They're political animals in there. I reminded them that it might not be too cool to prosecute a black single parent for taking a pistol to the man that got his little girl shot. They suddenly saw the sense in letting the whole thing go away. He's lost his job at the hospital, of course, but I've made a few useful friends in this community in the last few months. He'll have a better-paying job by the time his daughter is ready to come home."

Bartlett shook his head. "That Stiller is one lucky dirtbag. If you hadn't been there, his head would have been blown all over his hospital bed. Maybe it should've been. They were saying that since he could show he'd just cashed a money order in there and had pulled his gun on the 'real' robbers, he might get off."

"Not hardly," answered Kearn with grim satisfaction. "Litton and I brought that up with the state attorney's office, too. There's the little matter of the gun he had with him. They traced it to a guy who sold it to a pawnshop on the Tamiami Trail a couple years ago. The place was cleaned out of all the guns, and the pawnbroker murdered. Looks like we'll be able to trace most of the other Shotgun Gang weapons to that hit, too. It's circumstantial, of course, but we've got more. Litton tells me the three that gave up in the Mart have been running a race to see who can snitch out the rest fastest. We've got Stiller dead to rights on one of the earlier robberies, and at least two more for murder one at the hit up the road here, and all three in the Mart for felony murder. The perps in custody make it sound like there might be a couple of minor players still out there, but the Shotgun Gang itself is history."

"Yeah," sighed Bartlett with pleasure. "Sometimes the system does work, huh? Nobody gets killed but their scumbag accomplices, but people died while they were committing a felony—ergo, felony murder. Justice is sweet."

They were silent for a moment, looking out over the water. The rain had stopped, and the moon came out from behind a cloud, casting a bright sword of light on the bay. It was the kind of moment that made for Miami postcards.

"The heat is off me to disband the Stakeout Squad," Chief Kearn said softly. "What do you think?"

Bartlett shook his head. "If you'd asked me that a couple of weeks ago, I'd have told you to drop it like a rock. Now? It's funny. I feel bonded to these people. I hated the whole concept at first, but you know, we've been able to do some good. Do some justice. Tell you what, if you're ready to keep it, I'm ready to stay on. I know my people are."

"I'm inclined that way," the chief said. "The Shotgun Gang is finished, but it's still Miami. There'll still be armed robberies that need to be interdicted. There'll still be a need for a squad like this.''

"That's no lie," the lieutenant answered. "Sometimes it seems like the only thing that's ever going to change is the faces behind the guns."

**Gold Eagle presents a special
three-book in-line continuity**

THE
ARMS
TRILOGY

★   ★

In THE ARMS TRILOGY, the men of Stony Man Farm target
Hayden Thone, powerful head of an illicit weapons empire.
Thone, CEO of Fortress Arms, is orchestrating illegal arms
deals and secretly directing the worldwide activities of
terrorist groups for his own purposes.

Begin in March 1995 with the ever-popular
THE EXECUTIONER #195—SELECT FIRE,
continue in April with
THE EXECUTIONER #196—TRIBURST
and finish in May with
THE EXECUTIONER #197—ARMED FORCE.

Don't miss out on this new trilogy!

Available at your favorite retail outlets starting in March.

GOLD
EAGLE ®

AT95-1

Cold-war agents rise to threaten the free world

DON PENDLETON's

MACK BOLAN.

KILLPOINT

Violent global chaos has erupted, and Bolan is fighting it
head-on. Sudden death is rocking the free world as old-
guard KGB moles are reactivated to carry out assassinations.
Among those targeted are the Joint Chiefs of Staff.

**When all is lost, there is
always the future**

JAMES AXLER
DEATH
LANDS®

Genesis Echo

The warrior survivalists are guests in a reactivated twentieth-
century medical institute in Maine, where mad scientists pursue
their abstract theories, oblivious to the realities of the world. When
they take an unhealthy interest in Krysty Wroth, the pressure is on
to find a way out of this guarded enclave.

In the Deathlands, the war for domination is over, but the struggle
for survival continues.

Remo and Chiun stay in the dark
to deflect an evil spectrum in

THE

Destroyer

The Color of Fear
Created by
WARREN MURPHY
and RICHARD SAPIR

When a diabolical superscientist turned supercrook
creates a laser that uses color to control emotion, he puts
the world in a kaleidoscope of destruction. CURE goes on
red alert. And the DESTROYER is determined to catch the
enemy blindfolded!

Look for it in April, wherever Gold Eagle books are sold.

**Don't miss out on the action in these titles featuring
THE EXECUTIONER®, ABLE TEAM® and PHOENIX FORCE®!**

SuperBolan

#61436	**HELLGROUND** In this business, you get what you pay for. Iberra's tab is running high—and the Executioner has come to collect.	$4.99 ☐
#61438	**AMBUSH** Bolan delivers his scorched-earth remedy—the only answer for those who deal in blood and terror.	$4.99 U.S. ☐ $5.50 CAN. ☐

Stony Man™

#61894	**STONY MAN #10 SECRET ARSENAL** A biochemical weapons conspiracy puts America in the hot seat.	$4.99 ☐
#61895	**STONY MAN #11 TARGET AMERICA** A terrorist strike calls America's top commandos to the firing line.	$4.99 ☐

(limited quantities available on certain titles)

TOTAL AMOUNT	$
POSTAGE & HANDLING	$
($1.00 for one book, 50¢ for each additional)	
APPLICABLE TAXES*	$_____
TOTAL PAYABLE	$_____
(check or money order—please do not send cash)	

To order, complete this form and send it, along with a check or money order for
the total above, payable to Gold Eagle Books, to: **In the U.S.:** 3010 Walden Avenue,
P.O. Box 9077, Buffalo, NY 14269-9077; **In Canada:** P.O. Box 636, Fort Erie, Ontario,
L2A 5X3.

Name:_____

Address:_____ City:_____

State/Prov.:_____ Zip/Postal Code: _____

*New York residents remit applicable sales taxes.
 Canadian residents remit applicable GST and provincial taxes.

GEBACK9A